CW00747002

SHA
OVER THE
FENS

A gripping crime thriller with a huge twist

JOY ELLIS

Detective Nikki Galena Book 2

JOFFE
BOOKS

Revised edition 2024
Joffe Books, London
www.joffebooks.com

Previously published as *Shadowbreaker* by Robert Hale
in 2011

First published by Joffe Books in 2016

This paperback edition was first published
in Great Britain in 2024

Cover art by Nick Castle

ISBN: 978-1-83526-603-8

For Rosemary Keywood and Rachel Appleby

CHAPTER ONE

As Detective Inspector Nikki Galena locked the door of her Fenland home, a shiver of anticipation coursed through her. She gazed across the wide expanse of remote marsh, took a deep savouring breath of the fresh salty air and smiled. It felt good to be back where she belonged.

Across Cloud Fen she could see the mist clearing, and a green gold morning slowly waking up the salt marsh with its bright clear light. She stepped into the garden and wondered what this new dawn would bring with it, apart from the arrival of her new sergeant. Her smile widened. She had been waiting for this moment for a while and it was something she both welcomed and dreaded.

Detective Sergeant Joseph Easter was joining her CID team. It was also his first day back after being injured on duty. She had no illusions that his new position would be a breeze, because it wouldn't be. It would be a testing time for both of them.

She just hoped that he was as match fit as he claimed to be.

Nikki crunched her way across the gravel drive to her car and muttered a small prayer of thanks that for once the nick was unusually quiet. At least she wouldn't be throwing the poor sod straight in at the deep end.

'At last! Nikki! I was beginning to think I'd never see you again!'

A tall, craggy faced man, wearing tracksuit bottoms, a bright red rugby shirt and a black rucksack, brought his bike to a halt, hurriedly climbed off and grinned warmly at her.

'Martin! How have you been?' Nikki welcomed the friendly hug, then pushed him back and stared at him. 'Hey, you look good!' She had known him for more years than she cared to remember. He was her closest neighbour, even though he lived some quarter of a mile away down a narrow track that led onto the marsh.

The man beamed at her. 'I'm fine, but all the better for hearing your news. I've seen the workmen out here for a few weeks now. They told me that you were planning on moving back.'

'It was time to come home, Martin.' As Nikki spoke those words, she knew it was true. She'd been gone too long. Stuck in the town; spending every waking hour hunting down drug dealers. She had driven herself on until she could barely remember what life was like before her drug-crushing crusade had eaten into every part of her existence.

'Glad to hear it.' Martin Durham brushed a swathe of wavy iron-grey hair from his eyes and looked up appreciatively at her old farmhouse. Fresh paint glistened in the morning sunlight. 'Nice job! The weather out here takes no prisoners. I was beginning to wonder if the east wind was going to claim it before you!'

'It was in a bit of a state, wasn't it?' She suddenly felt horribly guilty for neglecting her old family home for so long. 'But this winter, I promise you'll see smoke rising from the chimney again.' She glanced at her watch. 'Oh Lord! I'm sorry to dash off, but the Fenland Constabulary calls. Why don't you come round for a coffee at the weekend? We can catch up.'

'Thanks, I'll do that. Actually I've got a little bit of interesting news for you, but it can wait until then. Oh, and . . .'

he looked at her weather-beaten front gate, '. . . I see your workmen didn't get as far as this. I was going to give my fences a coat of wood preserver tomorrow, I'll do this at the same time, if it helps?'

'Great. If it's no trouble?' Nikki clicked the central locking on her car. 'But be sure to let me know what I owe you, that stuff costs a fortune.'

'I don't think one gate will break the bank! Consider it a welcome home present.' With a wave, he climbed back on his bike, hauled his rucksack up over his shoulder, and pedalled off in the direction of his cottage.

Nikki slid into her car, leaned back, and allowed herself a long sigh of relief.

It had not been an easy decision to return home, but then her last case had changed a lot of things in her life. Now, having had some time to reflect, she knew it had thrown her a life-line. Her vigilante-style, one-woman mission to clean Greenborough of drugs had nearly cost her her career, and was beginning to turn her into the most blinkered and disliked officer in the area. And that was not the kind of woman she wanted to be. Just meeting Martin again made her realise just how thoughtful people could be. Maybe the whole world was not populated by evil shits after all.

As the tall figure in the scarlet shirt slowly disappeared from view, she felt a kind of peace wash over her. It was really good to be back. She belonged here in this strange and remote water-world, with its great stretches of marshland, teeming with wild life, and with a big, big sky hanging over everything.

With one final glance up at the old house, she turned the key in the ignition and pulled out onto the lane. At last, she was ready and willing to take on whatever Greenborough nick decided to chuck at her. It was going to be a good day.

* * *

As Nikki began her drive from Cloud Fen, Joseph Easter touched his fingertips on the turquoise tiled wall of the pool and burst through the surface of the sparkling water.

Fifty lengths. Nowhere near the distance he used to do, but he was getting there. He stood for a moment getting his breath back. Every day showed improvement. He could now do a pretty impressive ten miles on the hardest programme on the exercise bike without too much pain. He lay on his back and floated for a while. And it wasn't even pain any more, well nothing like what he had suffered just after the operation.

He glanced at the clock. He didn't want to be late on his first day at his new station. He swam easily back to the steps and pulled himself reluctantly from the warm pool. Until today he had spent almost two hours every morning in the club gym and the small pool, doing all he could to get strong enough to pass the medical that would let him return to work.

Joseph padded into the changing room, collected his towel and toilet bag from his locker, and went for a shower. The FMO had grudgingly allowed him back, with a few reservations about what duties he should avoid for a while, but all in all it had been a pretty good outcome. His only worry was that although his body was recovering, he had no way of knowing how his mind would react to an unexpected situation. And he wouldn't know that until the next time the shit hit the fan. He could test his muscles and his physical endurance, but as far as he knew, there was no simple test for his mental state. Which meant there was little point in worrying about it. He was finally free to join DI Galena's team, so he'd better just get on with it. He grinned to himself as the soapy water cascaded down his back. Into the lion's den.

As he rubbed shampoo into his mop of light brown hair, he remembered his first meeting with his new boss. Instead of welcoming him to his temporary assignment, she had been acid-tongued, short-tempered and bloody rude. Joseph laughed aloud, then stuck his head under the stream of hot water. Because despite all of that, he had liked her. Well, maybe 'like' was not quite the right word, but he *had* recognised a dedicated, honest copper beneath the hard-as-nails exterior. He could not have been more delighted when she asked him to leave his old nick and work with her permanently at Greenborough.

He towelled himself down and dressed. Somewhere during that last case that they had worked together, they had forged some sort of unspoken bond. He had felt it, and he was pretty sure that she had too. Why else would she have requested that he transfer from Fenchester?

Joseph dried his hair and stared at himself in the mirror. He didn't look different, but he knew that deep down he had changed. He looked at his reflection. In his eyes he saw the same old intensity, although maybe there was something else there now? He forced a grin to banish the gloomy mood that was threatening to wash over him. Maybe it was just that the locker-room mirror needed cleaning.

Joseph gathered up his kit, pushed it in his gym bag and walked down the corridor to the foyer, thinking as he went about his new position. He wasn't daft enough to believe that working with DI Galena would be easy. As individuals, they were complete opposites, but somehow their varied approaches brought them, by different avenues, to the same conclusions. And *that* would catch them villains.

As the automatic doors sighed back, he smiled to himself. They had all the right ingredients to make a damned good team. His expression darkened. Just as long as they both allowed the past to stay where it belonged and not creep into the present.

Sunshine warmed Joseph's face as he stepped outside, and his smile returned. This was not the time for raking up old garbage. Today was all about fresh starts, and if he didn't get a wriggle on, his first words from his new guv'nor would be a rollicking for being late.

He loped across the car park, unlocked his boot and threw his bag inside. As he closed it again, he noticed someone give him a friendly wave. He lifted his hand automatically, then walked around and got into the driver's seat.

The other early morning swimmer was a dark-haired woman who he had seen briefly a few times before. She was thin, but not in a skinny way. She looked lean and core fit like an athlete. He paused and watched her make her way towards the club entrance. Her stride was confident, and her limbs moved with a graceful fluidity. Joseph found himself staring unashamedly through the windscreen at her, and for a man who had always believed that looks were not the only thing that mattered, it came as something of a shock. There was definitely something very attractive about the woman's appearance.

Joseph shook himself. He'd never been late for work in his entire life, and he didn't intend to start today. With an annoyed snort, he started the engine, released the handbrake and sped noisily from the car park, but not before one last glance in his mirror to watch the dark-haired woman disappear into the building.

* * *

He had not been sure what to expect from the team, but Joseph's entrance into the CID room was accompanied by a rowdy chorus of cheers and an assortment of handshakes and back-slapping.

'Great to see you again, Sarge!' DC Cat Cullen's grin almost sliced her face in two.

'Love the hair!' Joseph stared wide-eyed at the short blond spikes and the emerald green Mohican-style strip that ran from her forehead to the nape of her neck.

'Yeah, cool, isn't it? The guv'nor's had me getting down and dirty with some of Greenborough's youth. On a covert surveillance case, you understand.'

'I'm never quite sure with you, Cat. Your disguises suit you a bit too well!'

'Sarge! How are you?' The big form of Dave Harris muscled in and grasped his hand, pumping it up and down with ferocious delight.

'Doing well, my friend. And happy to be here, I can tell you. There are only so many old movies you want to watch!'

'So, you really have decided to join us at last, Detective Sergeant.' Nikki Galena's voice instantly quelled the chit-chat.

Joseph had not even noticed her come in. 'Yes, ma'am. But only on the condition that our next case is considerably less injurious than the last one.'

A pained look passed swiftly across her face, then the Inspector shrugged her shoulders. 'There are no guarantees in this line of work, Joseph. Let's just hope that lightning doesn't strike twice, shall we?' She threw him a rare smile and held out her hand. 'Welcome to the team. We are glad to have you on board.'

The room rippled with comments of agreement, and as Joseph gripped her hand in his, he felt a lump form in his throat. He'd worked with this small group of people for such a short time on his assignment, but they were already his trusted comrades. That was what that kind of case did to you, brought you close together and tied you with the tightest bonds.

With difficulty, he tried to formulate a reply, but the words would not come.

'Okay, you lot!' The guv'nor saved him. 'Fun and games over! Bugger off and catch me some criminals!' She studied him carefully and he wondered what she was thinking. 'Coffee and a chat in my office sounds good to me. You're buying.'

DI Galena turned and marched out of the CID room, and Joseph smiled to himself. He'd heard that she had mellowed, and wondered how such a metamorphosis could have been achieved. Now he knew. It was subtle. She still yelled at everyone, but there was just the hint of a twinkle in her eye now. The Ice Maiden was still very much in charge, but there was the slightest melting, a softening around the edges, and it suited her.

As he scurried obediently off to the coffee machine, the smile remained on his face.

* * *

Behind the closed doors of her office, Nikki allowed the facade to fall away. 'Good to have you back, Joseph. There were a few moments back there, when I wondered . . .' The rest went unsaid.

'You and me both, ma'am.' Joseph took a deep breath and held it for a while. Then he slowly exhaled and said, 'But here we are again.'

'And this time as a fully paid up member of the team.' Nikki sipped her coffee. 'Are you going to move into the town?'

'Not sure yet, ma'am. I want to get it right, not just grab the first thing that comes along.' He pushed his hand through his hair and leaned back in his chair. 'I feel kind of different since I came out of hospital. I think I'll stick it out at the B & B for a while. My room's not too bad, and I'm actually getting sort of attached to Mrs Blakely's 1960s retro-style of decoration.'

Nikki nodded. 'Probably a wise move not to rush things.'

'Yes. I think I'll get my flat in Fenchester on the market, then when it sells, sit on the money until I'm ready to make a move.'

'Well, if you get stuck, you can store whatever you want out at Cloud Cottage Farm. Apart from the house itself, I've got some pretty useful outbuildings, and they're all dry and secure.'

'Thanks, ma'am. I may take you up on that.' He looked at her hopefully, 'So, anything interesting going down in CID?'

'Before I fill you in on our work status, I need to say one thing.' She leant forward. 'I'll bring this subject up only once, then it's going to be business as usual, okay?' She didn't give him chance to reply, but hurried on. 'If anything bothers you, or if anything is too strenuous, I want you to be perfectly honest with me, and we'll find a way around it. I want no big hero stuff, and no being a martyr either, got it?'

Joseph nodded reluctantly. 'Loud and clear, guv. But honestly, I've not spent weeks in physio and the gym getting myself fit to go and mess it all up in my first week back.' He flashed those infuriatingly sincere eyes at her, and Nikki was forced to believe him.

'Right. Lecture over. Any questions?'

'Can't think of any, although I'm delighted to see Dave Harris is with CID now.'

'He sailed through the interview board, I'm glad to say. His experience and local knowledge are a great asset.'

Joseph nodded. 'Plus he's a really good bloke. So, what are we working on at present, ma'am?'

'Nothing heavy, unless you count the mountain of paperwork that the last month generated.' She grimaced, then pulled a thin file across the desk. 'Frankly we're about as quiet as I can remember.' She opened the folder. 'A spate of small fires. Most likely arson.'

'Kids?'

'We thought so, but now we're not so sure. The last one took out a lock-up at the back of the big garage on Monk Street. It was lucky that Trumpton got there smartish, or there could have been a major incident, what with dozens of motors and the petrol reservoirs.'

Joseph frowned. 'What makes you say it's not kids?'

'The fire investigation officer said an accelerant had been used, but he swears it wasn't just bored yobs. He said there was a 'professional' feel to it.'

'A serious fire-starter does not bode well, ma'am.'

Nikki nodded. 'I know. But that was two weeks ago, three fires in as many nights, and now it's gone quiet. I don't know whether to be relieved or worried.' She closed the folder. 'Other than that, Cat and Dave are working on a cannabis farm investigation, but they are pretty close to a conclusion, then we have all the usual suspects; car ringing, break-ins, the ever-present drug trafficking, a bit of fraud, but nothing worthy of mention.'

'So basically it's same old, same old, other than the fires,' Joseph stretched. 'And which one of those tasty delights have you got lined up for me, ma'am?'

'Actually it's none of them,' she sighed. 'Well, not just yet anyway. You're with me for a few days.'

'What kind of investigation?'

'There isn't one.' She exhaled, and wondered how to explain her latest problem.

'The super wants us to help him. The auditors are in, and apart from drowning in a sea of paperwork, some faceless civilian in a comfy office has decided that our area is way over and above the national average for sudden deaths.' She leant forward and rested her elbows on the desk. 'They're scared shitless that the media will get hold of the statistics and have a field day with them. The super wants them checked, and fast.'

Joseph looked perplexed. 'But what's that got to do with us? It's a medical issue, surely?'

'I thought that to start with, but as I looked deeper I realised that it's not just 'sudden' deaths, where the doctor signs the certificate and that's that. There's an awful lot of occasions where we've classed them as 'suspicious' deaths and involved forensics.'

'To what outcome?'

'Shown up as suicides mainly, and although it's nowhere near the levels seen a while ago in Wales, it's still unsettling.'

'I thought the suicide rates were falling in the UK?'

'That's what the Government Statistics Office says. In fact, a few years back, the east of England was reported to have one of the lowest rates in England and Wales. I think that may be why *our* figures stood out like a bloody beacon.'

Joseph frowned. 'Is there any particular age group or gender involved in these figures?'

Nikki shook her head slowly. 'No. And I'm at a loss to find any kind of common denominator amongst them.' She finished her coffee, then said, 'Sorry, I know this is not CID work, but Superintendent Bainbridge really needs us to help him find some answers for his little bureaucrat.'

Joseph shrugged. 'Then let's do it.

'It's not too depressing for you, is it? All things considered?'

He smiled warmly at her, and she understood why there were so many cow-eyed women dribbling their way around the station today.

'I'm fine with it, ma'am. In fact, I'm so glad to be alive, it's actually a pretty good assignment for me. If I were depressed, then maybe not, but . . .'

Her phone rang and interrupted Joseph. It was a harassed Rick Bainbridge. She listened to what he had to say, murmured her assent and hung up.

'Gotta go. The super wants an update on my findings so far.' She gave him a rueful smile. 'Such as they are. Oh, and he sends his regards and his apologies for not getting down to see you, but I suspect that the auditor may have nailed him to his desk.' She handed Joseph a sheaf of papers 'Copies of everything I've managed to dig up. See what you think and we'll toss some ideas around when I get back.'

* * *

Joseph trawled through the articles for over an hour, and as he did his upbeat mood began to disappear. He'd been in some pretty dark places in his life, maybe a lot more than most, but he had never considered taking his own life. Now, as he read reports from a myriad of agencies and help organisations, he was sickened to realise just how many people actually did.

The figures seemed staggering. One suicide in the UK every eighty-two minutes? Surely that couldn't be right? He placed the paper down and stared at it. And why should the Greenborough area be worse than any other? He frowned. Maybe it wasn't. Figures could be manipulated to fit any given situation, and although stats were not his favourite pastime, he was quite good with them. So, in the absence of any proper police work, perhaps he should spend some time hunting out anomalies, or grey areas that had been engineered to represent something other than what they really were.

With a small sigh, Joseph opened a second folder and removed the sheets of statistics. Suddenly those old movies that he had become so fed up with recently, were actually starting to look really good.

CHAPTER TWO

Charles Cavendish-Small pointed upwards dramatically. 'And this ladies, gentlemen, and children, is the high-spot of our tour.' He paused, hoping that for once someone would understand the pun. They rarely did, and he wondered why he bothered. 'The tower. It was built in three stages, beginning with Early English and ending in Perpendicular. Historically, each stage represented the growing wealth of our town, and from the viewing platform you will get a most rewarding and magnificent view across Greenborough, the river, the surrounding Fens, and out to the Wash.'

The guide stepped lightly across the stone floor, careful to avoid walking on the memorial stones, and indicated towards an archway. 'If you would like to climb the steps, please follow me, but be warned, they are steep, and they are the only route up to the tower. There are small side recesses to wait in should others be using the steps to descend.' He glanced around at his small party. They all looked pretty healthy, although two of the old dears from the History Group would be soaking their knees in Radox for a few days afterwards. Nothing too awful had ever happened on his tours, but his fellow guide, Arthur, had had to cope with two panic attacks and a severely twisted ankle in just one weekend last summer.

'If anyone is in any doubt about their ability to climb, or has blood pressure or heart problems, please wait here, or feel free to go to the church café for a drink. We should be approximately half an hour. Thank you.'

With a slightly theatrical flourish, he swept his charges towards the screened archway. 'Follow me, and take great care. We don't want any accidents.'

There had been the usual gasps of amazement when the group stepped into the viewing area and looked out across the great tapestry of the flatlands. And today the visibility was particularly good. Clear bright blue sky, white fluffy clouds and a golden sun.

Charles sometimes looked at his visitors with less than delight, but he loved his beautiful parish church, and he loved this magical view across the county. On days like today, you could see as far as the north Norfolk coast.

He did a quick head count, assured himself that no one had been left gasping on the stairs, and began to identify various landmarks.

'Please? What is that?' asked a foreign tourist with a heavy Germanic accent.

Charles followed the pointing finger and smiled. 'That is the ruin of the Fenland Abbey of St Cecelia. Little is left except that wonderful high arch and the remains of the chapel.'

'And is that the docks?' asked one of a small party of school children, pointing to a series of cranes.

'Absolutely, young man. This end for the fishing boats and the new part is the Port of Greenborough. And, oh yes! If you look towards the estuary you can just see the masts of a cargo ship making her way towards the Wayland River.'

People pointed, took photographs and generally chatted amongst themselves, all agreeing it was certainly worth the climb. Charles let them enjoy the view for a while, then began to organise their descent.

'Right, if we are all ready. I'll . . .' he paused at the top of the stone stairwell and looked down pensively. It should be clear. There were no more tours today. He listened again, but someone was definitely on their way up, and pretty quickly at that.

'Sorry, folks. Can you all stand back for a moment, there's someone . . .' Before he could finish, he was elbowed firmly in the solar plexus, and found himself doubled over on the floor, gasping for breath.

'Hey! You can't . . . !'

A face, contorted beyond anything that Charles had ever seen, hung over him.

The man had burst through the opening from the stairs, and scattered the little group like nine pins. Now he was suspended over Charles like a hideous gargoyle from the ancient architecture that had somehow come to life and was bent on devouring him.

Pure, mind-numbing fear kept Charles a prisoner, then a terrified scream from one of the youngsters broke the spell.

This had to be a panic attack. But if it was, it had to be the very worst kind, and if he didn't calm the man, and damned quickly, someone was going to get hurt. The last thing Charles needed was a frenzied dash for the stairs.

'Keep calm everyone! It's okay! Really,' he gasped. 'Let me help you.' He held out his hand to the man. 'Please! Sit down here with me. Come on, you can do it.'

For one second, Charles thought he had got through. Then with a strangled scream, a sound that Charles would hear every night for years to come, the man turned and ran to the high stone balustrade, climbed up onto the ledge, and without a moment's hesitation, threw himself over.

Silence engulfed them all, then one of the children began to whimper and Charles scrambled to his feet and rushed to look over the wall. A couple of the group appeared at his shoulder, while others took the children and tried to calm them. All Charles could do was stare down at the broken figure below them.

The man had fallen the equivalent of nine floors, before hitting the wall that flanked the waterway. To Charles's horror, as they looked on helplessly, the lifeless body slid slowly from the wall, and dropped, like a sack of unwanted rubbish, into the sluggish tidal waters of the Wayland River.

CHAPTER THREE

'Ma'am!'

Nikki closed the superintendent's door, and looked up to see Joseph hurrying down the corridor towards her.

'Sergeant Conway's just asked me to tell you that there's been an incident. I'm afraid we have a jumper.'

Nikki's heart sank. 'Not the multi-storey car park again?'

Joseph shook his head. 'St Saviour's Tower.'

'Hell-fire! When did this happen?'

'Uniform have only just had the shout, guv. The duty sergeant said if you wanted to attend, he wouldn't deploy another senior officer.'

'Tell him we are on our way, then meet me in the yard. I'll go pick up my keys from the office.'

* * *

A blue-and-white cordon had been put across the entrance to the church grounds, and Nikki could see uniformed officers posted at the entrances and footpaths. A cluster of people were gathered by the main church door, some sat on the steps and others paced nervously up and down the path. A WPC was talking with them and had her arm tightly around a child of about eight or nine. Three more youngsters sat huddled close together on a low wall close to where the policewoman stood. Nikki took in the pale faces, slack mouths and wide, frightened eyes, and to her distress, realised that the children must have witnessed the fall.

'Over here, ma'am.' Joseph indicated towards a small group of figures leaning over the river wall. 'The doctor's there, and it looks like Yvonne and Niall must have been first on scene.'

Nikki felt relief to see WPC Yvonne Collins and PC Niall Farrow in attendance. They were a crew that she had something of a liking for. They had worked with her on several occasions and she thought that the older woman and the younger man made a good combination.

'What have we got here?' she asked.

'White male, ma'am. Jumped from the viewing platform.' Niall stared up at the tower almost disbelievingly.

'Into the river?'

'No, Inspector.' The doctor, a usually jovial man, who carried a little too much weight around his girth than was healthy for him, turned and approached them. 'Hit the wall first, I'm afraid. Snapped his back like a dry twig. You can tell by the way he's lying.'

'He's out of the water then?' asked Joseph.

The doctor nodded. 'Sort of. It's a bit difficult to see him from here. He went in, but immediately drifted into the mud around a submerged derelict boat. The tide's on its way out, so he'll be going nowhere.'

'Have you been down there, Doctor?'

'Yes, close enough to check everything that I needed to, but you'll need a few strong backs to get him out, I can tell you!' He brushed mud from his trouser legs. 'And yes, before you ask, he is most certainly dead.'

'Well, we'd better take a look, Sergeant.' Nikki walked towards the wall.

'Ma'am?' Yvonne Collins followed her. 'Forgive me for sticking my oar in, but will forensics be taking some photos before they get him brought up?'

Nikki frowned. 'It's the usual procedure. What's bothering you, Constable?'

'I don't know, ma'am, but I'm sure this isn't straightforward. Yes, he jumped. There are fifteen witnesses to testify to that, but . . .' She paused, then looked directly at Nikki. 'They all say he was either scared to death of something or someone, or he was completely off his head.'

'Sane rational people don't often throw themselves from high buildings, Yvonne.'

'But the children, ma'am. I keep thinking about the children.' Yvonne held her stare. 'Determined suicides, those who plan to jump, are usually very deliberate and very organised. They would never pick a time when the platform was full of tourists and little kids, now would they?'

Nikki groaned inwardly to think of children witnessing such a horrible thing. 'Then he *had* to be high on something. Oh hell, poor choice of words, but he must have been wasted to do a thing like that.'

'Probably was. But when you talk to the witnesses I think you'll agree that there is a very odd feel about this, ma'am.'

'Okay, I hear what you say and I trust your intuition, but before I do anything I need to go see this poor sod for myself.'

'Niall will help you down, ma'am. There's some slippery steps, and believe me, they're lethal. Then you have to hang over a narrow ledge, an old walkway of some kind. Our man is in the mud that's dredged into the bottom of that old boat.'

It took a few minutes to get down to the water level, and Niall steadied her as she leaned around the slimy brickwork of the ledge.

'I can see hi . . .' Nikki's words froze in her throat, and her mouth dried to chaff.

Lying in the reddish-brown river mud, his body impossibly twisted, and his face half submerged in a brackish puddle of water, was a man she knew.

Her mind flashed up a picture from earlier that day. A man in a scarlet rugger shirt and dark jog pants. A man waving happily as he rode off home. The man who had just offered to paint her gate. 'Martin?' Her voice crackled with emotion. 'Oh no!'

'You know him?' Joseph moved to her side, his hand on her shoulder. 'Guv?'

Nikki shrank back away from the water, but the sight of the filthy scarlet shirt stayed with her. 'He's my neighbour. He was coming for coffee at the weekend.' She knew the words sounded crass, but it was all she could think of. They were going to catch up. That's what she'd said.

Joseph exhaled loudly, and when she turned to him, his expression was full of concern.

'It's okay, it's okay.' Nikki gathered herself. This was a seemingly impossible thing to happen. Martin had seemed so . . . she tried to find the right word, so *normal.*

'Who is he, ma'am?' asked Niall softly.

Nikki straightened up, and took a deep breath. She might be a hardened police officer, but a shock was still a shock. It was just that she knew how to deal with her emotions quicker than others. 'Martin Durham, of Knot Cottage, Buckledyke Lane, Cloud Fen. He lives alone on the edge of the marsh. As far as I know there is only his sister to notify. Both his parents are dead and he was un-married. The sister's name is Elizabeth. She lives with her partner somewhere in Old Bolingbroke.' She turned to the police constable. 'And I want to be the one to go out to his cottage. Sergeant Easter and I will go directly after we've finished here.'

'Yes, ma'am, I'll radio it in straightaway.' Niall Farrow scrambled back up the wet steps to where his crewmate waited.

Nikki stared from the greenish waters of the River Wayland, up to where WPC Yvonne Collins was leaning over the wall, her hand outstretched to Niall. Yvonne's keen policeman's nose had been right. Maybe something terrible in Martin's life had driven him to kill himself, but he would *never* have done it in such a manner to cause suffering to others, especially children. She might not know him intimately, but she knew him better than most.

'Right, well, we'd better get a SOCO down here, then get uniform to sort out recovery.' She looked intently at Joseph. 'I am going to be *so* interested in what the post-mortem shows, especially the toxicology report.'

CHAPTER FOUR

As Nikki drove the familiar marsh lanes towards Cloud Fen, she knew that something had changed forever. Knot Cottage had always been simply 'Martin's place.' That was what the local villagers called it. Half of them would be hard-pressed to tell you its postal address.

'So what was this guy like?' asked Joseph.

'Dependable. Help anyone. Loved the marshes.' Nikki saw a picture in her mind of her peeling and weather-beaten garden gate, and wasn't sure if she'd ever have the heart to get it painted again.

'But still a bit of a loner?'

She frowned. 'Not really. Yes, he lived alone and he didn't talk about himself much, but he joined in with village stuff. And he was a regular at the Wild Goose.'

'Forgive me for saying, but where exactly is this 'village' you keep mentioning?'

Nikki smiled and slowed down as a long-eared hare bounded out into the lane ahead of her. 'Ah, well, Cloud Fen Village is kind of scattered, and there's not much of it anyway. It's like so many of these outlying communities, the cottages are few and far between, the post office that doubled for the corner shop was closed years ago, and all that's left is the chapel, with a service every third Sunday in the month, and the Wild Goose.' She watched as the hare dashed off into one of the great potato fields that edged the road. 'Frankly, we are lucky to still have the pub, the way things are going.'

'It is kind of yokel-ish, isn't it?'

'Careful, Town-Boy! You're talking about the place where I was born!'

'Sorry.' Joseph hung his head in mock shame. 'Do we go past your place?'

'Cloud Cottage Farm? No, we turn off just before it. But you can see it from Martin's. It's only a short way back across the marsh.'

'I wonder what will happen to the cottage?'

Nikki wondered too, but before she could answer her radio call sign blared out.

'A silver Suzuki Grand Vitara 4x4 registered to Martin Durham has been found abandoned not far from the church, ma'am.'

'Abandoned?'

'Seems that way, ma'am. We've had reports of the same car being driven erratically a few minutes prior to Durham entering the church. One witness says it looked as though he were having some kind of seizure, contorted face and all that.'

Nikki slowed to negotiate a corner, then said 'Okay, just get the car to the pound and secure it. I may need a SOCO to check it out for me. Thanks. Over and out.' Nikki relayed what had been said to Joseph and for the next five minutes they drove in silence, until she pulled the car into Buckledyke Lane

'Wow! What a place to live!' exclaimed Joseph. Then added quickly, 'And I mean that in a good, if somewhat remote, sort of way.' He stared across the vast expanse of marshland, to the distant horizon that shimmered and sparkled like a strip of silver foil.

'You should see it at sunrise,' said Nikki softly. 'My childhood bedroom looked in this direction, and my father told me I was truly blessed to wake to this sight every day. I never really appreciated it when I was five, but now I know he was right.'

'The cottage looks very neat, guv. Are we going to have to force an entry?'

Nikki threw him a withering look. 'This is a Cloud Fen, two up, two down cottage, Sergeant. We turn the handle and open the door. And if he's actually locked it for some reason, the key will be under the door mat.'

'You don't lock your doors?' asked Joseph in amazement.

She began to walk slowly up the path to the front door. 'I do these days. But then a farmhouse may be considered fair game for rich pickings. Not that there are any, but the thieves wouldn't know that until they got in. I think it's being a copper, I feel it my duty to think about security.'

'And the flak would be pretty heavy if your colleagues knew you went out and left the place wide open.'

'There is that, of course.' She arrived at the door, then veered off right along a narrow path and went around to the back. 'No one uses front doors out here.' She smiled. 'If you're going to tread mud in, do it in the kitchen, not the best room.'

She moved slowly across the backyard, then paused. She'd been in here so many times that she knew exactly what she would find even before she opened the door.

'Shall I?' asked Joseph. 'This can't be very pleasant for you.'

'No, I'm fine. It just seems so odd, I'm having trouble getting my head around it.'

'Maybe he will have left a note. That may explain things better.'

Nikki shrugged. Somehow she knew there would be no note. Just a mystery, and even if it never became a police matter, it would be one she would have to solve.

The door was unlocked.

'Surely, if you were going to go out, never to come back, you'd lock the door?' mused Joseph, half to himself.

'Would it matter? If things meant so little, and you wanted to die, would you care?'

They stepped onto the quarry-tiled floor of the kitchen, and a feeling of warmth greeted them. Partly because the place was a little time warp of old country living, clean, fresh and welcoming, and partly because a heavy iron pot was simmering gently on the solid fuel stove.

Joseph looked at Nikki and bit his lip. 'I don't think we are going to reason our way out of that one, do you, guv?'

She didn't answer. Something had happened to Martin Durham, between the time that he had spoken to her, and his fateful trip to St Saviour's Tower. Something devastating. 'You take the ground floor, Joseph. I'll check upstairs.'

'Are you looking for anything in particular, guv?'

'Just a good reason for a sane, happy man to top himself.'

'Oh, simple then.'

Nikki climbed the stairs. She had only been to the upper floor once before. It must have been many years ago, because her daughter Hannah was still coming home on the school bus, and she'd been keeping an eye open for the familiar blue-and-white coach that stopped at the end of Buckledyke Lane. Martin had picked up some kind of bug, but had been too proud to ask for help. She had had a bad feeling that all was not well, and called in. Lucky she had. An hour later an ambulance was tearing towards Greenborough General with a blue light flashing.

The main bedroom was like the rest of the cottage. Well cared for, and although a little basic, with old wood floors and heavy, plain wooden furniture, it was clear that the man loved his tiny home. There was just one photograph on his bedside table. Two smiling women, arms around each other's shoulders, one very much like him, and the other considerably younger, with a cheeky grin. Elizabeth and Janna.

Nikki picked it up, and shook her head. She'd better look for his address book and get Elizabeth's number. Even if uniform had already traced her, Nikki knew her well enough to want to offer her condolences. She replaced the frame exactly where it had sat, and stared at the woman's face. I have a feeling that you aren't going to know any more about this than I do, she thought. This death was not planned.

'Guv,' Joseph called up the stairs. 'There are an awful lot of prescription drugs in a cabinet down here. I think you should take a look at them.'

'On my way.' Nikki slid open the drawer in the bedside table. Neat lines of tablet boxes filled the space. 'Oh shit!' She closed the drawer and went to see what Joseph had found.

'I'd say this guy was very ill, wouldn't you, ma'am?' Joseph was standing in a small shower room that Martin had obviously had built onto the back of the cottage, and was pointing to the interior of a large glass-fronted cabinet. Without even looking closely, Nikki knew that the stacks of boxes were from a pharmaceutical company.

'Are they all legitimately his?'

'The labels are all marked up Martin Durham.'

'Then you're right. He must have been very poorly. But he never said a thing.'

'Which could explain a lot. Maybe he went into town for a hospital appointment, and got really bad news. News that he just couldn't handle.'

Why couldn't she believe that? It was a perfectly logical suggestion. 'Check it out, Joseph. And go out to the car and get some evidence bags. We'll need these.' She pointed to the boxes. 'Do any of the drugs mean anything to you?'

'There are a lot of antibiotics, ma'am. Penicillin, Amoxicillin, but I'm afraid the others mean nothing.' Joseph knelt down and studied them. 'This man was clearly reliant on medication big-style.'

'We'll have to talk to his GP, and get his hospital notes released.'

Nikki watched Joseph go out, and looked around the familiar old sitting room. In the past, they'd sat around the open fire, drunk hot chocolate and played Scrabble, Martin, Hannah and herself. Hannah had always liked him. She would be very sad if she knew what had happened, but Nikki would not be telling her. Her precious daughter was in a coma, and when Nikki talked to her, she told her only happy things.

'Shall I bag them all, or one of each kind, ma'am?' Joseph broke her reverie.

'Bag them all. And there are more upstairs beside the bed, get them too. Was there any post, by the way?'

'Nothing recent. A bit of junk mail and a bill or two.'

'Bank statement?'

'No, and his writing desk, unlike the door, *is* locked, and I couldn't find a key.'

Nikki looked around. Had she ever seen Martin at the desk? Maybe. Where would he hide a key? Nikki looked inside a vase, moved a few books, then shook her head. 'His sister may know, if not, I'm afraid we'll have to force it open. Meanwhile, and until I've spoken to Elizabeth, I'm going to secure the cottage. We may have to get a team in to check it out, but your serious illness theory may close this case without further investigation.'

Joseph nodded, but unenthusiastically. 'You're not convinced are you?'

Nikki puffed out her cheeks and shook her head. 'It may have a bearing on it, but no matter how bad the news that he received was . . .' Like Yvonne, she was thinking about the children. '. . .he simply could not have done it in the way that he did.'

'But he *did* do it, ma'am.'

'Yes, he did, Joseph, and *we* have to find out why.'

CHAPTER FIVE

'Sorry, but it all looks pretty straightforward to me, Nikki.' Superintendent Rick Bainbridge leant back in his chair and stared at her. 'He must have been so doped up that he didn't realise there were people already up on the viewing platform. If he were out of his head he may not have even seen them.'

'He saw them alright, sir. WPC Collins has given me the statements that she collected. Everyone said he appeared terrified of something, and one little lad said that Martin "was afraid of *them*, especially the tour guide, when he held his hand out to him to help him."'

The superintendent shrugged. 'Well, I don't know what to deduce from that comment, if anything. The poor little kid was probably traumatised. And it must have happened so quickly, it's a wonder anyone had time to take note of anything.'

'Actually the witnesses were unusually consistent in their statements, sir,' said Nikki testily. 'And I would not disregard what the boy said. Children can be very perceptive.'

Rick Bainbridge threw her a worried look. 'I think maybe you're a bit too close to this, Inspector. *If* it needs investigation, and I hope for our budget's sake that it doesn't; I'll give it to one of the other teams.'

'I'm fine, honestly, Super.' Nikki tried to keep her voice neutral, even though she was anxious not to lose the investigation. 'And there's little we can do until the tox screen comes back. I'll just check out the usual avenues while we wait. There may have been money worries, or some personal issues that, along with the heavy medication, just triggered something. The coroner is going to want everything we can get together for the inquest.'

'Okay. Stick with it for now, but don't forget, people aren't always what they seem. He may have been a good neighbour, but just how well did you really know him? Don't forget, you'd been living in the town for almost a year before you went back to Cloud Fen. Things change. People change.'

Nikki nodded. 'You're right, sir. And don't worry, I'll check everything as I would any other suspicious death, I won't get phobic over it.' She threw him what she hoped was a sincere smile and said. 'Maybe I'm just sensitive to this because of those statistics you've got me working on.'

It was the super's turn to agree. 'Ah, yes. At best they don't make easy reading, then this happens to a friend. It's understandable. Just don't look for things that aren't there.'

'Of course not, sir. So, if that's all?'

'Yes, yes, go. I have to get back to the damned auditor anyway. Just keep me up to speed, Inspector.'

Outside the door, Nikki heaved a sigh of relief. She would have to tread warily and endeavour to hold her tongue a little more. Her gut instinct screamed that something was horribly wrong about Martin Durham's death. Something so wrong, that she couldn't even bring herself to say the word suicide. Whatever, she would get to the bottom of it, and the easiest route was to keep the investigation closely under her control.

* * *

Joseph looked up as the boss came back into the CID room. 'How did it go, guv?'

The DI raised her eyebrows. 'In professional terms, Sergeant, I nearly screwed up.' She flopped into a chair. 'He reckons I'm too close. I only just managed to convince him to leave it with me, but I'm going to play things closer to my chest in future.'

Joseph nodded. 'Well, you've just had a call from Elizabeth Durham. She is devastated, but she wants to talk to you. I said we'd call on her first thing tomorrow morning, if that's okay?'

'Absolutely. Did you get the full address?'

Joseph glanced at his notebook. 'Yes, ma'am. Monk's Lodge. I've got directions.'

'Good. We'll go immediately after the morning briefing.'

'So what can I do now?' asked Joseph.

'I've got some paperwork that won't wait another day, so perhaps you would ring Martin's GP and go have a word with her? I'm pretty sure he saw Dr Helen Latimer. Her practice covers most of Cloud Fen. Her surgery is in Church Gate. The number is in the book.'

'I'm on to it, ma'am.'

* * *

Helen Latimer confirmed that she was Martin's doctor and she reluctantly consented to see him before her four p.m. surgery began, as long as he could get there in time. He checked his watch, quickly calculated how long their earlier trip to Cloud Fen had taken, and decided it should give him at least twenty minutes with the GP. Just enough time if he got a move on. As he grabbed his jacket and car keys and hurried from the office, Joseph felt a surge of what he could only call happiness. The case might be a sad one, but it felt *so* good to be back at work again.

The traffic out of the town was sluggish, although Joseph knew that once he reached the roads that led to the marshes the congestion would disappear.

But right now, he was stationary. Not something that his tight timetable had allowed for. As he tapped his fingers impatiently on the steering wheel and waited for his lane to start moving again, he caught sight of a group of men running along the curb. From their clothes, he thought they might be land workers, and they were trying to cross the busy road by dodging in and out of the slow moving vehicles. Several of them were laughing and shouting in an Eastern European language. Suddenly one of them ran around his car, then leaned across and slapped his palm loudly against the windscreen, then stared through it.

Joseph automatically recoiled at seeing a man's eyes only inches away from his own. Then he almost leapt backwards in his seat, his heart hammering in his chest.

He released his belt, swung around and tried to see where the man had gone, but he was already on the far pavement and hurrying away.

Joseph threw open the door of the car, stood up and stared after the retreating figure, but in seconds the man had disappeared.

A horn sounded loudly behind him, and he flopped back behind the wheel and put the car into gear. As he moved forward he decided that he *had* to have been mistaken. Apparently everyone has a double, and he'd just had the misfortune to see one.

As the lights changed and the road opened up again, he decided he had totally overreacted. The man had been running around with a pack of foreigners, ergo he was also a foreigner. So that settled it. How stupid could you get?

He indicated off the main road and headed for the marshes. A long straight drove-road extended out ahead of him for as far as the eye could see. He put his foot down, and as the car surged forward, he felt as if he had taken back control of himself. He even managed a small laugh at his own stupidity. What on earth would a man who he had last seen in another continent twelve years ago, be doing playing chicken in Greenborough High Road? It was unthinkable, and plain idiotic. He slowed the car as he approached a hump-back bridge over a water way, and tried to get his mind back to the late Martin Durham.

The boss was convinced there was something not right about the manner of Durham's death, and even though he had unearthed that cache of prescription drugs in Knot Cottage, Joseph was starting to believe that she might be right.

When he finally arrived at the small converted bungalow that served as a surgery, Joseph had forgotten about his earlier case of mistaken identity, and his focus was fully back on the job in hand.

If Dr Helen Latimer had sounded brusque on the phone, her manner softened considerably when she met Joseph in person.

'I'm so sorry, Sergeant. The news came as something of a shock. I'm afraid I may have sounded rather short. It wasn't intentional.' She smiled at him apologetically. 'Can I get you a coffee, or a tea?'

Joseph accepted the offer, and looked around the consulting room as Latimer went to organise the drinks. It was like being in someone's sitting room. No modern medical equipment, nothing other than a desk, a computer, two chairs and an examination couch. There were no nasty posters either; the ones that show reddish-brown muscles stretched over skeletons, or eyeballs protruding from bony skulls. Dr Latimer seemed to prefer watercolours of the Cornish coast, and studies of black Labradors.

On that basis alone, Joseph decided that he'd quite like her to be his GP.

The doctor passed him a mug of coffee and sat down. He decided she must be in her late thirties, early forties, but was a strikingly good-looking woman, with shoulder-length, wavy chestnut hair and deep brown eyes. Her skin had a rich olive tint that made him think she may have some Mediterranean origins.

He took his time and carefully explained everything they knew about the incident, and when he had finished, Helen Latimer shook her head emphatically and said, 'No way! Absolutely no way in a million years! I *know* Martin, and yes he did have medical problems, but his illness was managed and his drug regime well maintained.' She held out her hands, palms up, and said, 'I don't understand.'

'You seem to be the third woman involved in this that categorically refuses to believe Martin Durham was capable of doing what he did,' said Joseph.

'Who else are we talking about, Sergeant?'

'My boss, DI Galena, and the WPC who was first on scene.'

Helen Latimer gave him a strange enigmatic smile. 'Nikki Galena is your boss?'

'This is my first day as a permanent member of her team, Doctor, although I *have* worked with her before.' He returned the smile, with what he hoped to be an equally cryptic quality.

'Mm.' She nodded. 'And as I remember, she and Martin were close, but she moved to the town, didn't she?'

'The DI recently moved back to Cloud Fen.' Joseph grew serious. 'She spoke with Martin this morning. She said he was on really good form.'

'Then what in heaven's name happened?' mused the doctor.

'We rather hoped that you may be able to help us there.'

Helen Latimer shook her head. 'Sorry, but all I can do is release his medical records to you. The coroner's going to need them anyway.'

'Why did Martin need so many drugs?'

'His immune system was damaged by illness and cancer treatment that he suffered in his early twenties.'

'What sort of cancer?' asked Joseph.

'Cancer of the spleen.'

'Was there a chance that it had returned?'

'Definitely not. They performed a splenectomy, and he had yearly re-assessments. I have always been kept well informed by the oncology clinic.' She sat back and gave Joseph a rather sad smile. 'Regarding his immune deficiency problems, I have only been his doctor for just over a year, so frankly I was maintaining an already carefully planned drug regime. It's actually quite ironic, but we had been discussing a complete review. New drugs are being developed all the time, and I was anxious that he have the most efficient medication for his needs.'

'And was he happy about that?'

The doctor frowned. 'Not initially, I have to admit. He seemed very reticent to alter anything, but last week he turned up for an appointment, all chirpy and bright, and said he'd like to go ahead.'

'And did you?'

'Heavens, no! I needed to do a lot of research into his past history and prior medication before I'd even consider making changes, Sergeant.' She gave Joseph a mildly reproachful look. 'I would have needed to run all my suggestions past his consultant. This is complex, and not a thing that I would undertake lightly. I hadn't even begun the process.'

'I see. And there was nothing else that you felt may be bothering him?' asked Joseph.

She shook her head. 'As your boss said, the last time I saw Martin Durham, he was in fine form. In fact, he seemed so well I wondered if I should be even considering changing his medication.'

'If it ain't broke, don't fix it?'

'Exactly. But this time it was Martin who said we should explore new therapies. He was really enthusiastic. Considering his earlier reluctance, I was quite surprised.'

'Mm, I wonder what prompted the change of heart?'

'I guess we'll never know now, Sergeant, and I'm afraid you will have to excuse me, I have patients waiting, and I still need to organise those medical records for you.'

Joseph stood up and held out his hand. 'I appreciate your time, Doctor Latimer.'

'You're welcome. And do ring me if you need anything else.' She paused, 'Or if you discover anything that you think I should know about.'

'I will, thank you.' Joseph turned to leave.

'Oh, and good luck working with DI Galena, Sergeant Easter.' There was a slight chill to the words.

As Joseph approached the reception desk, he wondered what the history was between Helen Latimer and his boss, because the undercurrent was practically pulling his feet from under him.

Half an hour later, Joseph left, with a large sheaf of notes in a thick brown envelope under his arm. He was sure it would mean very little to him, but it would certainly be of great use to the pathologist.

As he climbed into the driving seat and did up his safety belt, he was suddenly shocked by a vivid flashback to the face in the windscreen. Just for a second, it was there again. Rough, coarse skinned, uneven teeth, ice-blue eyes and unwashed, dull blond hair. My God, it was so like him, it was scary.

Joseph shook his head free of the unwanted vision, and jammed his key into the ignition. He didn't want to admit it, but he was obviously still a bit shaky. The hospital had said it would take time, so maybe he was not quite as fit as he had first thought. Or maybe it was just first-day nerves. A friend of your boss, turning up dead on your debut morning was not exactly what you would choose.

With a sigh, he drove away, with even more questions swirling around in his head than when he arrived.

CHAPTER SIX

As evening settled over the fen, lights came on in the scattered assortment of houses and cottages. Nikki looked from her upstairs window, across the shadowy marsh lanes and fields, and felt a deep sadness that Knot Cottage remained in darkness.

She sat down heavily on her bed and wondered about the super's words. Maybe you really didn't know the people around you, even the ones you felt quite close to. She had known Martin for some fifteen years, and had never had an inkling about his illness.

She let out a long, audible sigh. Everyone had secrets. There were certainly things about her that Martin would never have known. In fact, there were things about her that only a very small handful of people knew.

And then there was Joseph. His past was a closed door. A locked room. Bolted and secured as tightly as a Bank of England vault.

She stood up and went downstairs. She needed a drink.

The kitchen still had a faint smell of paint, not unpleasant, just fresh and clean. She had been surprised how well the old place had scrubbed up, and even though today's dreadful events had placed a heavy blanket of melancholy over everything, she was still glad to be back home on Cloud Fen. And she was glad that Joseph had decided to join the team.

She splashed wine into a glass, sipped it slowly, then placing the glass on the old scrubbed pine table, the one she had sat at to eat her eggy soldiers as a small girl, she thought about Joseph. Maybe she should have spared him the grim task of suicide statistics on his first day. He had seemed really subdued when he returned from his trip to see Helen Latimer. Nikki gave a little snort. But then who wouldn't? Dear Helen could be a caustic cow sometimes.

She took another sip of the Merlot and tried to decide what to eat. Food was never high on her list of priorities, and it was ten to one that it would be yet another omelette. Unlike Martin. He had always prepared and cooked delicious meals for himself. She saw again the pot simmering on the old stove. She had looked in it, and noted the fresh vegetables and thick meaty stock. Martin took great care of his diet. Something she rarely seemed to find time for.

Taking eggs from a chicken-shaped pottery container, she broke three into a glass bowl, added salt, pepper, a few herbs and a splash of milk, then whisked it together thoughtfully. Helen Latimer might be a bitch, but she would surely have been as charmed as every other woman in the county by Joseph Easter's sexy good looks. Surely even Helen wouldn't have upset him on first meeting. So why did he seem so distracted, so troubled? She should have asked him, but he seemed keen to get away, and she couldn't blame him. It had been a pretty depressing day, all in all.

Nikki removed a fork from the cutlery drawer, then served up her meagre supper on one of her mother's best plates. There was something enormously reassuring about having familiar old things about her again. Her rented flat in Greenborough had been basic, minimalist, Spartan. She smiled to herself. Who was she kidding? Depressingly austere was closer to the truth. Still smiling ruefully, she switched on the radio and tuned it in to Radio 4 Extra. She badly needed something to lift her spirits, and a hammy old wireless show might do the trick.

She ate the eggs, and half-heartedly began to listen to a classic episode of *Hancock*, but after a while she switched it off. It seemed somehow disrespectful, knowing what had happened earlier that day, and as she washed up, she found herself hoping that Joseph had not returned to work too soon.

The tinkling sound of a windchime from the floor above, distracted her from her worrying thoughts. She glanced at the clock. The tide had turned, and was bringing in a strong blow off the sea. She had better go up and latch the windows, just in case there was a summer squall.

In her bedroom, she paused to once again look in the direction of Martin's place — and found herself rooted to the spot.

A tiny point of light was moving around inside Knot Cottage.

Nikki blinked a few times and refocussed her eyes. There was no doubt, someone was in Martin's cottage, and whoever it was had no sodding right to be there!

With a muffled curse, Nikki raced down the stairs, grabbed a flashlight and her mobile phone and raced from the farmhouse.

There was no way she could take the car, whoever was there would hear her coming and leg it. She had no choice but to go on foot and she covered the quarter of a mile in record time.

At the gate she sunk down for a moment into the deep shadows and caught her breath. Keeping perfectly still, she watched the darkened cottage carefully. Whoever was in there might not be alone. Her ears strained to make out sounds, but there was little other than the whisper of the wind across the marsh and the eerie call of a night owl.

With great care, she crept towards the side of the cottage, and made her way round to the back door. It was open just a crack. No doubt to facilitate a speedy exit if required.

Rustling sounds were coming from inside. As if someone were leafing swiftly through a newspaper, trying to find a particular article. Nikki stood behind the door, and tried to see exactly where the intruder was.

He was still in the sitting room, so whatever he was looking for was obviously proving more difficult to find than he had expected. She stared in, but could only make out a black shape behind the fine light point of the torch, and he was hunched over Martin's dining table.

Nikki tried to think. It seemed to her that she had two choices. Rush in and challenge him, or keep low and follow him when he came out. Sadly, although following him could mean catching whoever it was red-handed, it could also mean she could lose him completely, especially if he had a vehicle concealed nearby.

Which left little choice. Nikki swung a hefty kick at the door, reached inside and with a loud shout, flicked on the light switch.

It had been a pretty good idea, and it would have worked, if the intruder had not tripped the fuses on the electric meter when he broke in.

By the time she realised what had happened and switched on her flashlight, the man was upon her.

Nikki fought back. She had never backed off from a fight and rarely came off second best in a tussle, but circumstances were not in her favour. Her assailant caught her a crushing blow in the ribs, one that totally winded her, and by the time she had regained her breath, he was gone. She staggered out after him, but heard the sound of a powerful motorcycle engine roar into the night, and realised that there would be no chasing him.

Cursing and swearing her way to the meter, Nikki flipped up the switches, and squinted as the light came on.

'Shit! Shit!' she shouted out loud.

The sitting room was wrecked. Martin's precious belongings lay broken and shattered in untidy piles across the carpet.

She looked around in both dismay and anger, and found herself fighting back tears. 'I just hope you never found whatever it was you were after, you bastard scumbag!' She tried to wipe the salty water from her cheeks with the sleeve of her blouse. 'Bastard!'

Still cursing, Nikki pulled her mobile from her pocket, breathed a sigh of relief that it was still working, and quickly punched the speed dial number for the police station.

CHAPTER SEVEN

The main car park of the Greenborough Fitness Club and pool was deserted. Joseph parked close to the door and pulled his gym bag from the seat beside him. He had taken to getting there just before six thirty when the club opened. He liked the calm of the place in the early morning, and plunging into an empty pool had a decadence that he secretly enjoyed. He'd always tried to find time for a swim, mainly early like this to prep him for the day ahead, but sometimes he'd go in the evening, to wash away the stresses of a gruelling shift. Greenborough club had quite limited facilities but as he was somewhat limited himself, that suited him perfectly.

He cruised steadily up and down in the warm water and tried to forget that he'd had a sincerely crap night. His sleep had been interrupted by disturbing dreams that had left him feeling uneasy and edgy. Martin Durham's peculiar death had not helped, and neither had that weird incident with the man in the High Road.

He switched from breast-stroke to crawl, and tried to concentrate entirely on his breathing. It didn't work, so he flipped over, stared at the ceiling to keep in lane, and propelled himself backwards for a few lengths. Part of him wanted to see that jaywalker again, to see him properly, note the differences, then laugh at himself for being such a prat. And another part of him was loathe to meet the doppelganger of such a brute of a man.

Joseph turned in the water and ducked under. The rushing in his ears whisked away the unwanted thoughts, and holding his breath, he swam underwater until he touched the wall.

He had another fifteen minutes before he had to hit the shower room. He hauled himself out of the pool, rinsed himself off under one of the poolside showers, and walked along the wet tiled floor to the steam room.

A thick steamy cloud made it impossible to see if he were alone in the small room, but a movement on the top seating ledge told him he wasn't.

'Mind if I join you?' he asked his unseen companion.

'Be my guest. I'm practically expiring! I'm sure they rent this out at night to a lobster boiling company!' A tall figure leaned forward, then slipped down to the lower ledge.

A tiny shiver rippled through him, as her leg lightly brushed his shoulder as she climbed down.

'I swear they've turned the temperature up this morning.'

Noting it was the woman from the car park, Joseph silently agreed that it was becoming extremely hot indeed in the tiny enclosed space.

'Bryony.' The woman held out a well-manicured hand. 'I've seen you here before.'

He took her hand, and was surprised by the firmness of her grip. 'Joseph. Pleased to meet you.'

The woman stood up. 'Sorry, Joseph, I hate to be rude, but I've got a busy morning lined up. See you again, no doubt?'

Joseph flashed her his brightest smile. 'I hope so.'

After the glass door had closed, he let out a long, low whistle. He really would need a cold shower today, and the steam had nothing to do with it.

* * *

'Well, you look a damn sight happier than you did when you left last night,' murmured Nikki as he entered her office.

Joseph raised his eyebrows. 'And you look like you've had a run in with the riot squad!' He stared at the purple shadow that was staining one cheekbone, and did not miss the fact that she was protecting her rib cage. 'What happened, ma'am?'

She stood up and winced. 'Come with me to the super's office. He wants the gruesome details too and I don't know if I have the energy to say it all twice.'

He walked beside her along the corridor to the lifts.

'Some bastard broke into Martin's cottage last night.' Her voice was low, and full of contempt.

'You're joking!'

'Do I look like I'm joking, Sergeant?' she growled.

'Sorry. It was only an expression of incredulity. I wasn't questioning you.' He shook his head in disbelief. 'Are you okay?'

'I'll live.' She pressed the button for the lift. 'But I cannot tell you how much I'd like to meet that intruder again.'

'Preferably in the custody suite.'

'I'm not too worried where it is, Sergeant. I just want the opportunity to even the score.'

Joseph couldn't ignore the dark shade of the old Nikki Galena in those words, but chose to hold his tongue.

The lift sighed to a halt, and they made their way to Rick Bainbridge's office where Nikki filled them in on what had occurred.

'Sounds like an opportunist to me,' speculated the super. 'Bad news travels fast. Maybe someone got to hear of Durham's death, knew the place would be empty and ransacked it.'

'Sorry, sir, but whoever that was, was looking for something specific.'

'And what the devil would that be?'

'Initially, a key, sir.' Nikki bit the inside of her cheek. 'Joseph and I looked for it earlier, only we *replaced* the vases and the ornaments that we searched, we didn't smash them to pieces.'

'A key to what?' asked the super.

'Martin's desk. It was locked when we were there.' Her expression hardened. 'It's matchwood now.'

The super's brow knitted into a wrinkled frown. 'But what was he looking for?'

Nikki shrugged. 'I've no idea.'

'Whatever it was, it was very important to him,' added Joseph. 'After all, you called out that you were the police, and he still thought it was worth knocking seven bells out of you.'

'Thank you for reminding me of that, Sergeant,' said Nikki nursing her side. 'And another thing, it wasn't a lucky wallop either. The intruder knew exactly where to hit me to incapacitate me.'

'So what are you saying, Nikki? That Durham was involved in something dodgy?'

'I don't know what the hell I'm saying!' Her face was a mask of confusion. 'I just know that a kind and generous man, someone I thought I knew, has committed a terrible act, and I have the horrible feeling that nothing is quite as it seems at Knot Cottage.'

The super allowed her outburst to abate, then said, 'Have you had your injuries checked out?'

She nodded. 'The FMO was treating a prisoner when I came here last night. It's only bruising. It'll pass.'

'So where do you want to go from here?'

Joseph threw her a warning glance. She needed to cool down, or the super would give the case to another team. He saw her close her eyes for a moment, and he knew that she had understood his meaning.

'We'll just continue gathering evidence for the inquest, sir.' Her voice was calmer. 'And as soon as the sergeant and I have spoken to Martin Durham's sister, we'll make a careful search of Knot Cottage.' She took a deep breath. 'I know that I disturbed him, and I'm still not entirely sure that he found what he was looking for.'

The super nodded. 'Then you'd better get a man out there to keep an eye on the place. And we *should* watch your home too, but finances probably won't stretch.'

'There's been an officer at Martin's since last night, and I can take care of myself, thank you, sir,' said Nikki, then she gave him a half grin. 'It may have been pitch black but the intruder didn't get away scot-free. In the scuffle I managed to grab a few strands of his hair. It's gone to the lab for DNA testing.'

Joseph smiled broadly. 'Good on you, ma'am! If he's on the database, we've got him.'

'And even if he isn't, if we get a suspect, we can place him at the scene of the crime. Good work.' The super stood up and pulled a face. 'Now, I've got an appointment with the auditor from hell, so if that's all?'

'Right, sir, we'll get out to Old Bolingbroke.'

'Just remember to report in later, Inspector.'

'Wilco, sir.'

* * *

'I'll drive, ma'am,' said Joseph tactfully. 'Help me to get a feel for the area.'

Nikki agreed, knowing full well that he was thinking only of her, which was great because her side was killing her.

'We take the main road north, out of Greenborough, and pick up the A16. I'll direct you in as we get closer.'

Joseph pulled out of the station yard, and slipped easily into the light traffic flow. 'So, you know Elizabeth Durham?'

'Not well. I've met her a few times. She came over as being a very genuine, friendly person. She and Martin were close. He told me they were inseparable during their college days.'

Joseph slowed down at a pedestrian crossing and waved a small group of children across. 'Students together? What did they study?'

'I'm not sure really, although Elizabeth is some sort of tree person,' said Nikki, trying to remember the full title of her chosen profession. 'Well respected, apparently.'

'I guess you're not talking about a lumberjack or a tree hugger?'

Nikki smiled. 'I'm not sure about her personal habits, but she is, let me get this right, an arboriculturist. Martin called her a landscape architect.'

'Funny that. There aren't too many trees here on the Fens.'

'There are where we are going. It may only be a twenty minute drive but you'll notice a big difference in the countryside. It's less agricultural closer to the Wolds. Lots more trees.'

'And you say she lives with her partner. What does he do?'

'*She*. Her partner is Janna Hepburn-Lowe.'

Joseph threw her a swift glance, then returned his eyes to the road. 'From *the* Hepburn-Lowe family?'

'Yup. They've been together for years.' Nikki groaned and tried to ease herself into a more comfortable position. 'Do try to avoid bloody manhole covers, Joseph. My ribs feel like they've been kicked by a horse!'

'Sorry. Go on.'

'Janna's another nature lover. She owns a massive garden centre quite close to where they live.' She tilted her head to one side. 'And it wasn't Daddy's millions that provided it either. Janna actually worked there as a kid, Saturday job or something. Loved it so much she finished up buying it when the original owners retired.'

'Good for her,' said Joseph, then his face clouded over. 'But I guess that rules out financial worries on Martin's part. If he *was* in debt and his sister loved him, she'd hardly let him get suicidal over money troubles. Not when your partner is loaded.'

'Exactly.' She pointed to a large sign. 'Get in the right hand lane, right at the roundabout, and you're on the road to the A16, okay?'

'Roger, ma'am.'

Nikki shifted again, trying to keep the seatbelt away from her bruised side. 'You know, I have a really bad feeling about all this, Joseph, and it is nothing to do with knowing Martin.' She stared out of the car window. 'That man who trashed Knot Cottage? He was a pro, I'm sure of it.'

'Then it's good that we have uniform watching the place until we get there. It shouldn't be too difficult to spot your man's modus operandi for his search, even if he tried to make it look like the super's opportunist burglar.'

'Did he get what he was after, I wonder?' sighed Nikki.

'And what could be *that* important?' countered Joseph.

Nikki sat back, and felt a steely determination creep over her. 'I don't know yet, Joseph. But I'm damn sure that I won't rest until I find out what the hell's going on.'

Joseph nodded emphatically. 'I don't doubt you for one minute, ma'am. And for what it's worth, I'm with you all the way.'

* * *

Elizabeth Durham opened the door to them herself, and although it was a very long time since they'd last met, Nikki recognised her immediately.

On the surface, the woman covered her grief well, but the dark-rimmed eyes, the slight tremors of the hands, and the occasional lapses in concentration, gave her sorrow away as clearly as if she were wearing widow's weeds.

She invited them into the lounge, a large, airy, high-ceilinged room that opened into a splendid, well-stocked garden room. 'I still can't believe it,' she said, after the introductions had been made. 'And I don't understand.'

'No one does,' said Nikki simply. 'We are all at a loss to know what could have caused him to do such a thing. And Elizabeth, I am so very sorry. Martin was such a good friend and neighbour.'

She wordlessly shrugged her acceptance of the condolences, then suddenly looked exhausted and lowered herself down onto the deep cushions of the sofa. With a flourish of one hand, she indicated for them to do the same, and she watched them as they chose two chairs opposite her. 'Can I get you some refreshments?'

Nikki and Joseph both declined. It seemed almost too much to ask. As if that one small act of boiling a kettle might cause the floodgates to break.

'When will I be able to have him back? To organise his funeral?'

Nikki swallowed. 'I'm afraid that depends on the coroner, Elizabeth. The inquest opens the day after tomorrow, but it will be adjourned, awaiting all the reports.' She gave her an apologetic smile. 'It's a complicated case, with both witness statements and a lot of forensic reports. It will take time to prepare, and there will be a lot for him to consider.'

'So it may be held up for some time?'

Nikki chose her words carefully. 'Maybe, or he may allow you to bury him.'

'But my brother wanted to be cremated. Oh, it will be a cremation, definitely.'

This was not going well. Elizabeth was a highly intelligent woman, but shock had blurred her normally sharp mind.

'The thing is . . .' Joseph's soft voice had taken over. 'The thing is, Ms Durham, that we are all *very* worried about Martin's sudden decision to end his life. We need to explore every avenue to understand what happened, and until we are satisfied with our findings and a satisfactory explanation has been reached, we cannot allow Martin's body to be cremated.' He paused. 'For your sake, and for your brother, we need to provide you with answers.'

'The coroner may feel that you need some sort of closure,' added Nikki gently. 'So he could grant you permission for a burial, then later, when a verdict has been reached, Martin's wishes could be followed.'

Elizabeth's eyes filled with tears. 'Dig him up?'

'I know it sounds awful, but it's done very discreetly, with the utmost care and compassion,' added Joseph. 'And please don't concern yourself. It may never come to that.'

'Where is Janna?' asked Nikki, concerned that Elizabeth was alone.

A small smile spread across her face. 'She's slipped over to the garden centre while you are here with me. She needs to tie up a few things with her manager. She's taking some time off so that I don't have to deal with this alone.'

'That's good.'

'She's a good person,' said Elizabeth. 'And she's worried sick over me.'

'Would it be too soon to ask a few questions?' Nikki did not want to cause any more distress, but she still needed to tell Elizabeth about the break-in at Knot Cottage.

'No, I'll do all I can to help.' She visibly rallied. 'And I'm sorry about just now, I don't know what came over me.' She looked at them in turn, then abruptly stood up.

'First, some coffee. Why don't you both go down to the garden room? There's a lovely view over the gardens, and you can just see Janna's pride and joy in the distance. I'll fetch the drinks, and then I'll do my best to answer your questions.'

Nikki followed Joseph down three shallow steps, and into the big conservatory. The scent of jasmine and some other sweet, oriental flower hit her immediately. 'This is beautiful!' she whispered.

'This is expensive!' returned Joseph. 'Very, very expensive.' He pointed to a panel on the wall. 'State-of-the-art automated blinds, automatic humidity and temperature control. Very nice indeed.'

And the exterior of the property was like manicured parkland. 'How the other half live,' she breathed. 'And I guess that is the fabled garden centre.'

At the bottom of the rolling lawns, and on the far side of a long pasture, sunlight was glinting off a massive glass structure.

'This lodge was the gatehouse for the original estate.' Elizabeth stood at the top of the steps. 'We added the garden room, plants being a passion for us both, and we've drawn up plans to build a Victorian-style orangery.'

'That would be some project to undertake,' said Joseph.

'If we ever find the time. But excuse me, the coffee will be ready.'

Nikki glanced impatiently at her watch. She wanted to talk to Elizabeth, but she needed to get back to the cottage to try to find out what had been stolen.

'Black or white?' Elizabeth placed a tray on a decorated rattan table, picked up the cafetière, and poured the coffee.

Nikki decided that there was no time left for procrastination. She took her drink, sat in a big cane chair by the window, and said, 'When did you last see your brother?'

'About a week ago. He came for supper a couple of times a month.'

'And how did he seem?'

'Top form.' She sipped her drink tentatively. 'That's what makes it all so hard to understand. We both commented on how, oh, how *happy*, he seemed.'

'More than usual?'

'Maybe. Or perhaps he was just pleased because a paper he'd written was coming up for publication shortly.'

'Oh really? On what subject?' asked Joseph with interest.

'Salt marsh ecology, management and restoration.' She gave them a weak smile. 'Sounds pretty heavy, doesn't it? When Martin was younger he wanted to be a forensic botanist, but his illness put paid to that. When he recovered, he did continue to study biology and botany, and the marshes provided him with constant interest.'

'I knew that he was pretty interested in the local plant life, but I had no idea he was *that* knowledgeable.' Nikki was starting to wonder if she actually knew anything about Martin Durham. 'Did he have any money worries?'

'My brother was not rich, but he was financially secure, and the cottage was his, no mortgage. He had no debts either. So no, that was not the problem.'

'And there is nothing that you can think of that may have been bothering him?'

'I've gone over and over this, since the moment I heard he was dead, but there's nothing, absolutely nothing.'

'Did he mention anything to you about changing his medication?' asked Joseph abruptly.

Elizabeth's hand trembled for a moment, then her jaw clenched. 'What do you mean?'

Nikki stared at her. Why should that question bother her?

Joseph gave her an innocent look. 'Sorry, but we understand that he was keen for his GP to revise his regime?'

'Oh, that! Yes, I believe she had suggested new drugs were available. I'm not sure if he'd decided to go ahead though.'

'And I hate to ask this,' added Joseph, 'but did he ever take any recreational drugs?'

Elizabeth Durham suddenly laughed out loud. 'Martin? That's a joke! He was phobic about his medication! He took nothing that could upset the balance. Not even a herbal remedy. Ask anyone at the Wild Goose, he'd gone there for years, and I guarantee you, he never took one sip of alcohol in all that time, so drugs? No, Sergeant. He wouldn't have dared!'

'I'm sorry, but I had to ask,' said Joseph quietly. 'Because he was not acting rationally when he went to St Saviour's Church.'

'I should say not. He killed himself, didn't he?' said Elizabeth icily.

'There is another problem, Elizabeth,' interjected Nikki. 'Knot Cottage was broken into last night. I accosted the intruder, but sadly he got the better of me.' She indicated to her bruised face.

'Oh!' Elizabeth's hands flew up to her mouth. 'How could they? Some thugs, I suppose? Looking for money for drugs! It's always that these days, isn't it? Oh, poor Martin, he was so particular about his home.'

Please! Don't worry about me! thought Nikki, but said. 'I believe the intruder was after something in particular. Would you have any idea what that could be?'

Elizabeth's eyes narrowed slightly. 'No. He had nothing of great value.'

'What about his papers, maybe the one about the salt marsh? Would it have any monetary significance?'

She shook her head. 'No. Years of work, yes, but it's not about making money.'

Nikki felt a mild sense of discomfort surrounding Martin's sister, but pressed on. 'So there would have been nothing of importance inside his locked desk, then?'

'Nothing that I know of,' replied Elizabeth shortly.

'Well, thank you for your help,' Nikki stood up. 'I'm sorry if we distressed you.'

'Will you keep me notified of any developments?'

Nikki nodded. 'Of course, and we may need to speak to you again. Right now, we are going back to Knot Cottage.'

'You know Martin thought a lot of you and Hannah,' Elizabeth said suddenly. 'He was very upset when Robert left you, although he never liked the man, I'm afraid.'

'No one in their right mind liked my ex-husband, Elizabeth,' said Nikki with a grimace. 'The only good thing about him was his daughter.'

'And how is Hannah now?'

'No change, although they are talking about sending her to a clinic in Belgium, in Liege.' Nikki didn't want to talk about Hannah, and stepped a little closer to the door. 'They offer no promises, but they understand her problem better than most.'

Elizabeth seemed to sense her discomfort, nodded sadly and changed the subject.

'When do you think I will be able to go over and clean up? I'd like to go soon. Martin would hate it to be in a mess.'

Nikki understood what she meant. His place was always immaculate. Too immaculate, she wondered? 'We'll ring you.' She took a card from her bag and handed it to Elizabeth. 'My mobile number and direct line is on that. If you think of anything, no matter how insignificant, contact me, okay?'

* * *

Joseph drove carefully through the gate, making sure to avoid a large uneven manhole, and onto the main road. 'What was that all about?'

'Pass. She was fine, although naturally distraught about her brother, until you mentioned the drugs, then she nearly disappeared up her own bottom. But why?'

'Not sure, but I got the distinct impression that she knew exactly what was in that locked desk.'

'Which is more than we bloody do,' muttered Nikki. 'And I've been wondering about his obsession for cleanliness, he's always been that way and I never really thought much about it. Now I'm wondering if he was scared of infections. What with having to take all those tablets to keep healthy.'

'Probably was,' Joseph nodded. 'I'm sure I would be.'

Nikki clutched at her waist as they approached a level-crossing. 'Shit! That's tender!'

'Then I suggest we find somewhere to grab a hot drink, a sandwich, and you take some very strong painkillers before we go on to Knot Cottage.'

'I agree, and I know where we can get all that for free,' she grimaced through the pain. 'My kitchen.'

CHAPTER EIGHT

Knot Cottage had thrown up nothing of interest. The only papers left, in a small stationery drawer in the broken desk, were some diet sheets and lists of vitamin and mineral supplements.

Only one thing had claimed Nikki's attention, and that was an old photograph. One of Martin, Hannah and herself, collecting samphire out on the marsh. Wind rippled their hair into ringlets, and tugged at their clothes. She remembered the day, and the buckets of the fleshy-leaved plant that her aunt wanted for pickling, but she couldn't for the life of her recall who had taken the picture. It had made her feel both nostalgic and mildly confused as to why Martin had kept it.

Now the photo sat on her desk. She rather liked it, and it would mean nothing to anyone else, so for now at least, it would stay with her.

Joseph was sorting the paperwork they had brought back, and she was re-reading the witness statements, when the phone rang.

'Mr Cavendish-Small, what can I do for you?'

The man sounded on edge, which Nikki thought to be quite understandable considering what he'd been through.

'I just keep feeling that it was all my fault, Inspector, but I was terrified that my sightseers may rush for the stairs, you see. And that would have been a terrible disaster, and there were children to consider.'

'How could it possibly have been your fault?'

'Because I reached out to him. And he recoiled, as if I were the devil incarnate.' The man paused, then said, 'One of the kiddies said the man was afraid of me, and I believe the boy was right, but what could I have done to scare him so badly that he . . .'

'Listen to me, Mr Cavendish-Small. It was absolutely nothing to do with you. We don't know what upset the balance of his mind, but I assure you, it happened to him long before he ever got near that viewing platform.'

'Common sense says that you are right, Inspector Galena, but you didn't see his eyes! I'll never forget them. They looked like the sort of thing you see in horror films, not in your own parish church.'

Nikki felt desperately sorry but could not console him. How could she? It must have been quite horrific. 'All I can say is that it wasn't your fault, sir. That poor man was just very sick. Beyond anyone's help. The most important thing is that no one else was hurt, and that was down to you. You did very well under dreadful circumstances, sir.'

The man's voice seemed to lack all power, and he said, 'Thank you, Inspector, it's kind of you to say that, but I still believe I may have been to blame.'

Before Nikki could reply, she realised that Charles Cavendish-Small had hung up. She replaced her phone, stared at the old photograph propped up against her monitor screen and thought, Oh Martin, what have you done?

* * *

Joseph was having trouble concentrating. For some reason, every time he found himself with a few moments to himself, his mind wandered to the woman from the pool. Bryony, she had called herself. He didn't think he'd ever met anyone with that name before. He wondered what she did for a living, and he also wondered if she were married. Because that would be where his fantasy ended. He didn't do married. In fact it had been years since he did anything that involved a relationship of any kind. He had one failed marriage of his own, and one difficult daughter living in another country. And it still hurt, so . . .

He picked up his mobile phone from the desk and went to find the boss. He needed some work to keep his mind from straying.

In the corridor he was practically leapt on by Cat Cullen and Dave Harris. He knew from their beaming faces that they had just had a really good result.

'Wacky baccy farm all sorted?' he asked.

'Not just one! Three of them, Sarge!' Cat's eyes sparkled.

'*And* we got all but one of the little scrotes who were running them,' added Dave.

'Drinks are on us tonight, Sarge, over in the Hammer at seven. Can you make it?'

'I'll be there, and good work. The guv'nor will be well pleased.'

'We'll just need to get the paperwork done, and we are free to help you out, Sarge.' Dave gave him a shrewd look. 'I hear not everything in the garden is blooming?'

'And that the guv took a beating?' added Cat in little more than a whisper.

Joseph nodded. 'There's a bad feeling about this enquiry all right. Even I'm unsettled by it, and I never knew the poor guy who topped himself.'

'Well, as from tomorrow we are all yours. Maybe four heads will be better than two.' Cat skipped off like a little kid going to a party. 'Don't forget! Seven o'clock at the Hammer!'

'Is the guv'nor okay, Sarge?' Dave had real concern in his voice.

'Very sore, in more ways than one. The bruises she can handle, but she's far from happy that the assailant decked her.'

Dave smiled. 'Ah yes, that would smart. But as long as she's not badly hurt.' He moved off down the corridor. 'See you later, Sarge.'

The DI wasn't in her office, and Joseph really didn't feel like going back to the suspicious death reports, so he headed for the vending machine outside the mess room. The guv'nor's sandwich had worked at the time, but he felt a strong desire for a chocolate boost.

As he strolled along the window-lined corridor, he thought about her home on the fen. It was the kind of house he would have loved to have brought up lots of kids in; and at least three dogs and a cat. She'd always referred to it as a cottage, but it was a proper family farmhouse, and it seemed all wrong for her to live there alone.

He pushed some coins into the machine, pressed a button and waited. At least it would be a better bet than the slum of a town flat she'd rented, in order to be closer to the drug dealers. Cloud Cottage Farm was a lovely old place, and he sincerely hoped she'd be happy back there. If he were honest, he'd never really felt comfortable on the wide open flatlands, but seeing Cloud Fen today, he had to admit that there was an airy kind of magic to it, and it was slowly winning him over.

He picked up his Snickers, peeled off the wrapper and balled it up. The bin was a little further along the corridor, and he aimed, threw, and missed. With a snort of disgust he picked it up and placed it inside, glancing out of the big picture window as he did. There was not much to see. Just a narrow lane that ran along the side of the station and down towards the river. It was fairly regularly used, but right now there was only a dog walker and a couple of old men, deep in conversation.

He bit into the chocolate, and thought about Bryony. Maybe he should ask her to go for a drink with him. It couldn't hurt, and if she said no, well at least he'd tried.

Joseph sighed, and watched as the dog walker disappeared, and a woman with a shopping trolley took his place.

With something of a shock, he suddenly realised that he didn't want Bryony to say no. Since his last case his priorities had changed. He thought of Nikki Galena, all alone in that big house, and he knew that he didn't want to be like that. He wanted someone to share his life with. He didn't want to just exist and work, he wanted to live.

He straightened up, and smiled to himself. He'd go to the pool tomorrow and he'd sound her out. Then if she happened to be unattached, well, just a drink, no one could take offence at that, now could they?

The thought had barely had time to compute through his brain, when everything froze. He was no longer aware of anything going on around him. He heard nothing, and saw nothing, other than the man who was standing down in the lane, staring up at him, his right hand touching his forehead in a smart salute.

Joseph almost gagged on the chocolate.

It was him. Not a double, not a figment of his imagination. It was Billy Sweet.

* * *

'Joseph? You okay?' Nikki stood just metres away from him, but he didn't seem to notice her. For a moment she thought he was ill, then she saw his expression. She tried to read what she saw, but it was difficult. Confusion, disbelief, and what looked like fear, all clouded his handsome face.

'I . . . I thought . . .' He turned to the window and stared anxiously out.

'What, Joseph? What's wrong?'

'There was a man in the, uh, lane.' His speech was stilted. 'Someone I once knew.'

Nikki raised her eyebrows. 'And presumably someone you didn't like very much?'

Joseph's expression hardened. 'I hated him.' He suddenly leant back against the wall and shook his head. 'That's a word I never wanted to hear myself say again. I thought I'd learnt all about forgiveness. But then I never thought I'd see *him* again.'

'Who is he?' asked Nikki.

'A bad man,' answered Joseph slowly. 'A very bad man.'

Nikki walked over to the window and looked down into the empty lane. 'And you are sure it was him?'

'It was him.'

'Where was he?'

'Directly below us. Staring up here. At me.' His face screwed up. 'But how would he know I was here?'

Nikki frowned. 'With all this glass, if he kept watch on the station for a while he'd spot you sooner or later. Let's check out the CCTV. What's his name, by the way?'

For a moment Nikki thought that Joseph was not going to be able to speak. He was certainly having trouble naming the devil.

'Billy Sweet,' he murmured. 'But don't be fooled by the name. He's pure evil.'

'Come on. Let's go to the control room. See if we can find him.' Nikki led the way, and having told the civilian in charge what area they wanted to trace, sat down in front of the computer screens and waited.

'Two old gits having a barney, and some old biddy with a shopper, now where is our man?' She stared at the monitors. 'Ah, there, is that . . . ? No, it's a bloke and a dog.'

'Where did you say he stood?' asked the CCTV operator. Nikki looked at Joseph, who explained again.

'Then he must have got into the blind spot, Sergeant. There's one area where the cameras aren't aligned properly. I've been asking maintenance to sort it for weeks.'

'But surely we'd see him walking into the lane?' asked Nikki.

'Not if he came up Hour Glass Alley. It converges into the area with no coverage.'

'Fat lot of bloody good that is!' growled Nikki. 'These really are sodding useless! When you need one, they are either vandalised or there's no one available to watch them.' She turned to Joseph. 'Sorry, Sergeant. But your man got lucky.'

Joseph exhaled. 'Maybe. Or . . .'

Nikki observed him carefully. Whatever this Sweet character had done in the past, it was having one hell of an impact right now, and she didn't like it. She had never seen him so rattled, and the last thing Joseph needed was some creepy blast from the past ruining the life he was just getting back together.

She stood up and walked to the door. 'Coffee, in my office. We need to talk.'

In the short time that Nikki had known Joseph Easter, he had demonstrated incredible self-control. Being an impatient person herself, there had been times when his laid-back approach had made her want to tear his head off his shoulders. And he never talked about himself. The tiny pieces of his life that she was acquainted with had not been shared without considerable pain. The one thing she did know was that he had once been a soldier, a special forces operative. And she had the distinct idea that Billy Sweet came from that area of his past.

She stirred her coffee thoughtfully and contemplated the word *eggshells*. 'Right. Before you tell me to butt out, my friend, I'm going to play devil's advocate here. What I say may not be my true opinion, but hear me out.'

Joseph looked at her over the top of his coffee mug, and nodded silently.

'Clearly you haven't seen this person for years. Could you possibly be mistaken?'

'He looked exactly the same as I remember him, and his face is etched on my memory for reasons that I'd prefer not to discuss, ma'am,' said Joseph stonily.

'Well, that's odd for starters. He should have aged.'

'Maybe he had. I didn't see him for more than a second or two.'

Nikki decided not to press the point that if he'd only seen him fleetingly, he could well have been wrong. 'Moving on. Is it probable that this man should turn up in Greenborough?'

'No. Highly improbable.' Joseph ran a hand through his hair and shook his head slowly. 'I thought about that the last time I saw him and . . .'

'You've seen him before?' she exclaimed. 'You never said!'

'It was when I was driving out to see Dr Latimer.'

'I *knew* you were troubled by something when you came back! I thought Helen had upset you.'

Joseph told her about his encounter, then sat back and shrugged. 'I'd convinced myself that it was just some guy that reminded me of Billy Sweet. But now, I'm sure it was him, ma'am. Dead certain.'

'Does he have some sort of unfinished business with you, Joseph?'

Joseph's eyes narrowed. 'I don't know. Maybe he knew that I suspected him of some terrible things, maybe not. The other men he served with didn't want him near them either. He was fearless, but he was a psycho, ma'am. And a loose cannon like that could cost you your life, or that of your comrades. But no, the last I heard he had shipped out and joined a private security force, by that time I was in Civvy Street. End of story, or so I thought.'

'You once told me you had a bad mission, was he part of it?'

Joseph closed his eyes. 'I can't go there right now, ma'am.'

Nikki knew the answer. 'Okay. So what do we do next?'

'I don't know.' He scratched his head. 'Why on earth would he be here?'

'I suggest we ask him.'

His eyes widened. 'And how are we going to do that? He's like a will-o'-the-wisp. Here one moment and gone the next.'

'Well, did you notice his clothes?'

Joseph thought for a minute. 'Dark zipper jacket, thin nylon material, black jeans and a T-shirt. Pale, dirty white or grey, maybe. Shoes were some kind of suede trainers, really grubby.'

Nikki nodded. 'Good. Excellent, in fact. Let's go back to the control room and get them to track him. Hopefully there's more than one camera in this town that is actually working, so they should have a good chance of spotting him. Especially if he decided to play chicken in the middle of the Greenborough High Road yesterday, don't you think?'

'Good point, ma'am. And I appreciate your concern, but this is hardly a police matter. We've got a lot of work to do on Martin's case.'

'Naturally the investigation comes first, but I don't want some creepy shit freaking out my detectives! So we deal with him, then get on with our own work, okay?'

Joseph stood up, looking slightly less harassed. 'Let's do it.'

* * *

'What do you mean, inconclusive?' Nikki felt her temperature begin to rise.

'Sorry ma'am, we found the incident that Sergeant Easter described, but the footage is too grainy to identify anyone specific. It's certainly not clear enough to lift an image.'

'Oh great! Okay, let me have a tape of it anyway. Thanks for trying.'

The woman left and Nikki sank down in her chair. If they had managed to get a mugshot of the man, she could circulate it and get him brought in. Joseph could then have looked at him close up, and that would have been that. Either a simple case of mistaken identity or Joseph would have to take an unwanted trip down memory lane.

She gnawed on the inside of her cheek. Just say Joseph was correct and this Billy Sweet really was rampaging down a Lincolnshire High Street. What the hell did he want? It had to be something to do with Joseph. She wondered what Billy Sweet had done. If the whole unit despised him, it had to be something pretty grim.

'Ma'am? You wanted me?' Cat Cullen leant around the door. Her recently emerald green striped hairstyle was now reduced to just white blond spikes.

Nikki grinned at her. 'Very good work with the cannabis farms, Detective. An excellent result.'

'Ta, guv. Dave and me are pretty chuffed with ourselves.'

'You have every right to be.' Nikki jabbed her thumb in the direction of a chair.

'I want you to do me a little favour before we discuss your next investigation. You've spent a lot of time on the streets recently, would this man mean anything to you?' She handed Cat, Joseph's written description of Billy Sweet.

'Phew, that could be half the guys that I've been hanging out with, but it really doesn't sound like anyone I could name. Want me to make enquiries, guv?'

Nikki nodded, then looked up as the CCTV operator appeared in the doorway and handed her a CD.

'Stick this in the machine, Cat. It may help, although I'm told the quality is crap.'

Cat took the CD and switched on the viewer. After a few moments they were watching three lanes of painfully slow moving traffic.

'This will never make the Cannes Film Festival, ma'am. When does the action start?'

'About now I should think. There's Joseph's Ford, at a standstill in the middle lane.'

'And what are those yobs doing?'

'They are the ones that we are interested in. Watch Joseph's vehicle. One of those men apparently hammered on his windscreen, then ran away.'

'Wow!' said Cat. 'If that's their idea of fun, they really need to get out more.'

As Joseph had described, the group of men ran in and out of the traffic, dodging and weaving as the vehicles moved forward or stopped. Then one of them broke away and dived in front of Joseph's Ford.

'The quality *is* crap. You're right.' Cat leaned in closer. 'What's he doing?'

'Looks like he's slapping the windscreen. Now he's leaning over the bonnet and staring inside.'

'What an arsehole,' Cat frowned. 'And now he's off.'

Nikki stared at the screen. No question, the man was unidentifiable. But now she looked at Joseph. He had jumped out of his car and was staring around anxiously, trying to see where the man had gone.

'The sarge overreacted a bit, didn't he, guv?' asked Cat. 'It was only some prat, doing what prats do.'

Nikki didn't answer. She'd been thinking exactly the same thing, and whether the man was Billy Sweet or Lord Lucan, Joseph clearly believed he had seen a ghost.

'Go out for the afternoon, Cat. Ask around. See if this description rings any bells with anyone, and concentrate on the West Street Quarter, those other men were apparently foreign.'

'Sure. No problem. And if I find him?'

'Ring me, and steer well clear. Understand? No contact with him. He may be an innocent party, but just as easily, he may be very unpleasant.'

As Cat stood up to leave, Nikki added, 'And keep this just between us for the present, okay?'

Cat tapped the side of her nose. 'Got it, ma'am. I'll be silent as the grave.'

As the young detective closed the door, Nikki looked back to the photograph of Martin Durham. She was getting sidetracked by Joseph's problems, but Martin was dead, and Joseph was alive and troubled.

Somehow she'd find time for both.

CHAPTER NINE

The Hammer and Anvil pub was packed with celebrating police officers and civilians.

'They don't need much encouragement, do they?' yelled Dave, above the ear-splitting noise of voices and music.

Joseph forced a grin. He had not wanted to come, but he was part of the team now and he didn't want to let Cat or Dave down. 'What are you having, mate?' he asked.

'I'm fine, Sarge. I've got a pint and that'll do me.' He pointed towards the bar. 'The first drink goes on the DI's slate. And as that doesn't happen too often, I'd have a large one if I were you!'

Joseph eased between the packed tables, and found that the bar was least crowded right at the far end. As he shouldered his way into the queue he decided that this kind of gathering really wasn't his thing. He'd do the rounds, smile, speak to everyone he knew then quietly disappear.

'As I stand *no* chance of ever reaching the bar, would you be kind enough to get me a G & T while you're there, Joseph?'

He spun around and saw Bryony standing behind him.

'My pleasure! Although I could be some time by the look of this lot!'

'I'll be over by the door to the restaurant. It's quieter there. Do you need a ball of string to find your way back to me?' she asked with a smile.

'Don't worry. I came first in orienteering.' He returned the smile, then added, 'although I was only twelve at the time.'

She melted into the crowd, and when Joseph had recovered from the surprise at seeing her, he wondered if she were alone, or maybe waiting for someone. Did women go to rowdy pubs alone these days? Maybe they did. He was pretty out of touch with the social scene.

Finally, with their drinks firmly grasped in both hands, he found her.

'What on earth is going on?'

'The Old Bill are celebrating slinging a few more villains in the slammer.'

Her brow wrinkled, and he thought it made her look even more attractive. 'What?'

'Arrests. We've made some good arrests today.'

'Ah, so you are a policeman.'

Joseph smiled sheepishly and hoped that she wouldn't throw up her hands and run screaming from the pub. ''Fraid so.'

'Ah, I wondered what you did for a living.'

Relief swept over him. So she'd been thinking about him too.

'Actually, we've met before. Before the fitness club, I mean, but I don't think you'd remember me. You were pretty poorly.'

It was Joseph's turn to frown. 'I must have been half dead not to remember you.'

Bryony laughed. 'You probably were! It was at the hospital a few months ago. I was visiting my brother. It was Curlew Ward, wasn't it?'

He nodded. 'But I'm really sorry. You see I don't remember much about the first few days there. I was pretty out of it.'

'It's all right. Are you fully recovered?' She laughed again. 'Silly question! You'd hardly be 'slinging villains in the slammer' if you were still incapacitated, now would you?'

'Probably not, although I am very passionate about my job.'

'I like passion.' Bryony grinned broadly, picked up her drink and raised it in salute. 'Cheers, Joseph.'

'Indeed.' He clinked his glass against hers. 'This is too weird. You know I'd fully intended to accost you at the pool tomorrow, and ask you if you'd like to go for a drink, and voila! Here we are!'

'Funny that. I had the same plan. Although I was going to give you one chance to get in first, for the sake of your male pride.'

Joseph felt his stomach give a little lurch. 'So I assume you would have said yes?'

'Assume nothing, Joseph. It doesn't pay.' She looked him full in the eyes, 'Except on this occasion.'

'I'm glad to hear that, Bryony. So, how come you're here tonight?'

'Don't ask!' She gave him a mock frown. 'Today has been a catalogue of disasters. Although this seems to be making up for it somewhat.' She sipped her drink. 'For my sins, my boss has organised myself and a work colleague to arrange a charity event. We are supposed to be scouting out suitable pubs for a scavenger hunt.'

'My boss never gives me jobs like that! Some might say that was a very enjoyable task.'

'And it might have been, if we hadn't picked one that was evacuated because a fire alarm went off, another that was full of hairy bikers, and in the one before this; my friend had a pint of lager tipped all over her and went home in a huff! This was the last one, so I thought I'd check it out and get it over with, and found all this going on!' She pulled a face. 'I was just on my way out, when I saw you.'

'Detective Sergeant Joseph Easter to the rescue, madam!' He held out his hand.

'Bryony Barton, ex-damsel in distress. Thank you!' She took his hand and bowed her head, then laughed out loud.

'Can we go somewhere quieter? Or is it obligatory to stay until you're rat-arsed?'

'Not in the slightest. But tradition demands that I must just congratulate the arresting officers, then I'm all yours.' He stood up. 'Excuse me, I'll be back in five.'

* * *

Niall leant on the bar and dug Yvonne sharply in the ribs, 'Gossip Alert! Gossip Alert!'

'For God's sake, Niall, mind my drink! You know, for a trendy young geezer, you are the biggest old woman on the force!'

'Shut up and look! The Sarge is chatting up that super-cool bird in the blue dress!'

'Are you sure she's not chatting him up? He *is* probably the best-looking bloke in Greenborough.'

Niall snorted. 'I'm devastated! I thought you loved me, Vonnie!'

'Of course, I do! In a motherly kind of way.' Yvonne placed her glass on the bar and tried not to stare across to where Joseph Easter sat talking animatedly to the striking-looking woman. Good luck to you, she thought. After all you've been through, you deserve a bit of fun.

Niall was still talking. 'Well, I don't know what the DI will make of that! Dear me! Whatever is he thinking of?'

Yvonne threw him a puzzled look. 'What are you rambling on about? Half a shandy and you're practically incoherent! You can't be suggesting that Holy Joe and Old Nik are an item, are you? Are you quite mad?'

'Oh Vonnie! Don't be naïve! They are meant for each other!'

'Huh? The sergeant and the DI! I've never heard anything so barmy!'

'Five squid says she's going to be pissed off as hell when she finds out about this!'

'You're on, honey-child! Although I'm going to hate to take your pocket money quite so easily.'

'Where is DI Galena anyway?'

Yvonne took a big gulp of her wine. 'I saw her going into the super's office just before we left, but she'll be along soon.' She glanced back and raised her eyebrows. 'Uh-oh, looks like the good sergeant has tired of our company already. And who could blame him! That woman has one heck of a good figure!'

'I'll second that!' whispered Niall.

'Put your eyeballs back in, Niall, and try to stop drooling.'

'Sorry, Mother. Fancy another?'

'My turn.' Yvonne took her purse from her bag, and watched with a smile as the sergeant escorted the woman to the door and they both disappeared into the street.

* * *

Joseph took Bryony to a small Italian restaurant, where they shared a carafe of house red, and ate a chef's special of four cheese ravioli and a salad. At around ten she said she had an early start the next day, so Joseph walked her down to the taxi rank.

'Will you be at the pool tomorrow?' he asked hopefully.

'Not tomorrow, I have to go to Gainsborough for a meeting, but I'll be there on Friday.'

'I'll see you there then.' For a moment he felt like a tongue-tied kid, scared to say the wrong thing, but desperate to get the girl to see him again. 'And when I do, perhaps you would accept an invitation to dinner on Saturday evening?'

'Ask me on Friday, Joseph. And thank you for being my saving grace tonight.'

'Anytime.'

A taxi moved slowly up the rank towards them. 'My number.' He handed her a card, and gave her a brief peck on the cheek. He wanted to kiss her, really kiss her, but . . . then it was too late. Bryony was leaning towards the driver's window and telling him an address on the far side of town, one that Joseph immediately made a mental note of. He opened the door for her and watched her get in.

As he closed the door, he glanced across the road to the railway station buildings, and saw a man standing in the shadows, watching them intently. He was hardly visible, but Joseph caught sight of a dull gleam of pale hair in the orange glow of a street lamp

'What's wrong, Joseph?' asked Bryony. There was a tinge of concern in her voice. 'You're as white as a sheet.'

'A man. Over there.' He pointed.

'Where?' She cast her eyes this way and that.

'He's gone. You didn't see him?' Joseph tried to get the panic out of his voice.

'Sorry, no. Who is he?'

'No one.' He covered his anxiety with a smile. 'No one at all. See you Friday. Take care, and thank you for tonight.'

Bryony looked at him for a long while, then smiled back. 'Goodnight, Joseph.'

As the car pulled away, she called from the open window, 'Got a good memory? Remember this!' Then she called out her telephone number, and the window closed and she was gone.

Joseph grabbed a pen from his pocket, wrote the number on his hand, and watched the car until it turned on the High Street. Then he sprinted across the road. He paced up and down the railway approach, looked in every hiding place, and tried doors to see if any were open, but the station was deserted.

This time he really wasn't sure about what he'd seen. The shadows had concealed the figure. All he knew was that *someone* had been there, and he had slipped out of sight quickly enough for Bryony not to see him.

After one last look around, Joseph gave up and walked back towards the taxi rank. As he got close, he decided that he could not face being shut inside a cab. It was a fair distance, but he'd walk. He had so much on his mind, he could do with the time alone to try to make sense of things.

He pushed his hands deep into his pockets and strode off in the direction of his lodgings. As he walked into the night, all he wanted to think about was Bryony. But try as he might, every time he remembered the outline of her face, it was overpowered by the ugly, uneven features of Billy Sweet.

CHAPTER TEN

'Good morning, Sergeant.' Nikki's voice echoed across the CID room. 'My office, please.' Joseph felt distinctly as if he'd been summoned for a caning by the head mistress.

He closed the door and looked at her speculatively. 'Ma'am?'

'A friendly word to the wise, my friend. Next time you plan an assignation, try to arrange it in a different pub to one that contains half the Fenland Constabulary! I've heard nothing else since I got in!'

'But . . . !' Joseph spluttered, 'But I never . . . it wasn't an assignation, ma'am! She was there by chance, and I know her from the fitness club. Like me, she swims most mornings. That's all.'

'Oh really? But you'd left before I even made it as far as the pub front door, and together, I hear. Or has the grapevine got it wrong?'

'Well, yes, I mean, no.' Joseph felt like a total idiot. For some reason, he hadn't thought about what his colleagues would say the next day, and clearly, they were saying a lot. He looked up miserably, and saw his boss grinning at him.

'Well done! At least that may quell some of the other things they say about you! Those mess room gossips won't have a leg to stand on now, when they call you Holy Joe or Mr Goody Two-Shoes.'

'Thanks for reminding me, ma'am. But I thought they'd already given up on that.'

'They probably have. I wouldn't know. I don't pay the slightest attention to them anyway.' She smiled up at him. 'Why should I? While they are sniping at you, they are leaving me alone. I just couldn't resist having a little dig myself. Frankly, I'm pig sick that I missed seeing her. Quite a looker, I hear.'

Joseph groaned and sank down into a chair. 'I'm beginning to wish I'd given last night a miss.'

'No, you're not, and you know it,' she leant forward. 'What's she like, Joseph?'

A small smile spread across his face. 'She's gorgeous.'

'More. I need details.'

'Well, her name is Bryony Barton, she's thirty, and she works for the Public Analyst, here in Greenborough. Funnily enough, she saw me first when I was in the hospital. Her brother was in the same ward.'

'And she has a good sense of humour, likes the theatre, dogs, and walking barefoot in the sand at sunset?'

Joseph tried to look aggrieved, but it was so rare that DI Galena openly enjoyed something so much, he didn't have the heart to stop her.

'Well, we did talk, and we seem to have quite a lot in common, but . . .' Joseph stopped as Cat Cullen appeared in the doorway.

'Ma'am. Sorry to interrupt, but . . .'

Joseph had expected Cat to take the mickey out of him more than anyone, but to his surprise, her expression was serious and her tone unusually grave.

'. . . some kids have found a body.'

The boss sighed. 'Great. As if I hadn't got enough on my plate with Martin's death. What do we know, Cat?'

'A male, guv. Found in some wasteland off Beale Street. Throat cut.' She threw a sideways glance to Joseph, and he didn't like the look on her face. 'Thing is, and obviously I haven't seen him yet, but he fits the description of the man that Sergeant Easter is looking for.'

Joseph felt a spasm grip his gut. Sweet? Dead?

He closed his eyes. When he'd left the army, he'd spent a lot of time trying to make his life right again. Trying to understand things on a deeper level. And he'd succeeded. Not through religion, although a lot of his fellow officers thought that was the case, but with a more spiritual approach to life.

He opened his eyes again. So why did he feel such delight in hoping that another human being was dead? It went against everything he believed in.

'Joseph?' The DI was staring at him. 'I said, I think you need to see this.'

'Yes, of course, ma'am.' He stood up. The answer to his own question was clear. Billy Sweet wasn't a human being. To be classed as that, you needed to belong or relate to the nature of mankind, and there was nothing kind about Sweet. He took a deep breath. 'Let's go.'

* * *

The body was still in situ, although an awning had been hastily erected around it to protect the scene and block it from view.

Joseph, the DI, and Cat carefully picked their way over stones and rubbish to the covered area.

'Ah, the good detective inspector! And my old Fenchester friend, Joseph! How are you, dear boy?' Without waiting for an answer, the tall, beanpole of a man pushed his wire-rimmed glasses further up onto the bridge of his hawk nose, and beamed benignly at Cat. 'And we must not forget you, lovely lady, although we haven't yet been introduced.' He peered at the DI.

'Cat Cullen meet Professor Rory Wilkinson. Home Office pathologist. Forensic science wizard, and the possessor

73

of the darkest sense of humour imaginable. And another ex-pat from Fenchester.' She gave him a grim smile.

'You forgot your usual slanderous comment about allegedly being a raging queen,' he added, sounding slightly put out at the omission.

'Sorry, and that. So what have you got for us?'

'An interesting one to be sure. But not pleasant.'

'Murder can be pleasant?'

'Murder can be many things, Inspector,' said the pathologist enigmatically. 'But this is not some crime of passion, or a fight that got out of hand. This is an execution. Now, if you'd all like to follow me?'

Joseph didn't want to follow him anywhere. Joseph wanted to turn his back and walk away. The word execution had sent a ripple of horror down his spine. He had seen too many executions, and he still saw them, when sleep would not come or when a nightmare took possession of his slumbers.

Rory Wilkinson moved beneath the cordon, lifted the canvas flap to the awning, and invited them inside as cordially as if it were a garden party. 'Mind yourselves, the ground is somewhat uneven, and the copious quantity of blood doesn't help either.'

Joseph breathed in, held his breath, and moved reluctantly into the temporary shelter.

No one spoke immediately. Even the garrulous pathologist seemed somewhat in awe of his newest acquisition.

The man lay on his side, his knees bent, ankles tightly tied with some kind of thin rope, and his hands tied in the same manner behind his back. He had been made to kneel for his last moments on this earth. His throat had been sliced from ear to ear, and he had fallen sideways, allowing his lifeblood to ooze into the weeds and the detritus of the waste ground.

Bile rose in Joseph's throat. This was something that belonged in his past. Something he had prayed that he would never see again.

He swallowed, and steeled himself to look at the body.

A black nylon bomber jacket, old jeans, a T-shirt, though the blood had made its original colour impossible to see, and scuffed and worn trainers.

Unsteadily, he took a few steps backwards, then ducked out under the canvas to drag in some gulps of fresh air.

The dead man was ugly, had a rough cut thatch of corn-coloured hair, uneven features and pale blue eyes, but he wasn't Billy Sweet.

* * *

Nikki sat in the car and stared across at him. 'You are sure?'

'Absolutely. I've never seen that man before.' Joseph looked pale and gaunt. 'Although there is a resemblance.'

'Could it have been the man that you think has been following you?'

'No, ma'am. The man I saw was Billy Sweet.' His lips drew tighter. 'But thinking about it, the dead guy may have been the man I saw hanging around the station buildings last night. Beale Street is only a few minutes from there.' He rubbed hard at his temple. 'If only there had been some kind of identification on him,' muttered Joseph. 'It would have given us somewhere to start.'

Nikki shrugged. 'No such luck. We'll just have to wait for the fingerprint check, a photo image identification, and failing all that, DNA tests.' She took a deep breath.

'And you have to consider that this may have nothing whatsoever to do with you, or this guy who has been watching you.'

'Billy killed him.' Joseph's voice was little more than a monotone. 'I've seen his work before.'

'You mean this Billy Sweet has already killed in this manner?' asked Nikki incredulously.

'Oh yes.' Joseph gave a small humourless laugh. 'It was a kind of hobby of his.'

'You're making me feel sick,' said Nikki through gritted teeth.

'So now you know why I'm half out of my mind at the thought of him being here in Greenborough, amongst people I care about.'

'And the only connection that we know about, to Billy Sweet and Greenborough, is you, Joseph.' Nikki bit on the side of her thumb nail. 'I think it's time to take this back to the station. We'll set up the murder room, then go over everything that we know so far. And Joseph . . . ?' She looked at him with real concern in her eyes. And although she did not want to compound his problems, she knew that she had to ask some questions that he would find hard to cope with. 'You do know that we are going to have to go over some pretty unpleasant stuff, don't you? About your past.'

Joseph slumped back into his seat, as if all his energy had sapped away and left only a limp shell. 'Then we're going to need a very large bottle of Scotch and a tape recorder, because if I do manage to talk to you, the story will be told once and only once, okay?'

'I'll buy the whisky,' said Nikki flatly. 'And for your sake, I think this part will be best dealt with away from the station, don't you?' She gave him an enquiring look. 'So, your place or mine?'

'Have you *seen* my place, ma'am?' he answered, showing a hint of the old Joseph.

'Then Cloud Fen it is. After we've done the preliminaries back at the nick. Seven o'clock, and bring a toothbrush. You won't be driving afterwards.'

CHAPTER ELEVEN

Nikki left the others preparing the murder room, went to her office and closed the door. She needed some time alone to try to get her head around what was happening.

Martin Durham's unexplained suicide still haunted her. Over and over she saw him, riding off down the lane on his bicycle, waving to her. He'd said he had something to tell her, "a little bit of interesting news." His face had been alive, bright. Then apparently he had prepared a stew for lunch, jumped into his car and driven to Greenborough, where a few hours later he lay dead in the stinking mud of the Wayland River.

Nikki gave a shaky little sigh. She'd read somewhere that suicide was a permanent solution to a temporary problem. Could something *that* terrible have happened between the hours of 7.30 a.m. and midday? Something awful enough to make Martin Durham kill himself?

She reached across and picked up the old picture that was still propped against her monitor. She felt sad now that she had seen him so infrequently while she was staying in the town. He had been a great support to both her and Hannah when her ex-husband Robert left home. Not pushy, not intrusive, just there. And now he'd gone, and she owed it to him to put the record straight. She didn't want him written off as some flaky saddo, because he was far from that, and maybe she was the only one who would have the incentive and the wherewithal to bring the truth to light.

'Hang on in there, Martin,' she whispered. 'Things have gone a little mad here right now, but I'll find out what happened, I promise.'

'First sign of madness, Nikki, talking to yourself.'

She had been so engrossed in her own thoughts that she hadn't even heard Rick Bainbridge enter her office. She grinned ruefully, 'And what is the second sign, Super? Because I'm sure to be displaying it.'

'I'm not sure. Something about looking for hairs on your palms, I think.' He stared at the picture that was still in her hand. 'Who's in the photo?'

She passed it across for the superintendent to see. 'My old neighbour, Martin Durham, Hannah and I.'

'I never realised that you were that close.' He scrutinised the snap, then handed it back to her.

'We were just good neighbours, sir. Kind of there for each other. Cloud Fen is a small, outlying community; it's what you do.'

'Then no doubt his loss will hit hard.'

Nikki nodded. 'He was a good man, he will be missed.' She stared up at the superintendent and was pretty sure it was not Martin that he wanted to talk about.

As if on cue, he sat down and said, 'But that's not why I'm here. I want your honest opinion on Sergeant Easter.'

Nikki was somewhat taken back. She had been sure it would be a request for a report on the dead man, but Joseph? 'Why? What's wrong?'

The super's brow wrinkled into furrows. 'I'm concerned that he's come back too soon, Nikki. I saw him yesterday and I didn't like the look on his face. He seemed totally distracted by something.'

Nikki thought quickly. If Joseph's possible involvement with the dead man came to light too soon, the superintendent would have them off the case before she could draw breath. 'Ah, I see the grapevine hasn't stretched its sticky little tendrils in your direction yet, sir.' She mustered a broad smile, 'Our Joseph has got a new flame. And if the rest of the station is right, he has every right to look preoccupied, sir. Apparently she's a stunner.'

'Joseph?'

'The one and the same.'

'Good Lord!'

'My sentiments precisely. But don't worry about him, sir, he's still on the ball regarding his work. He's been nose to the grindstone ever since he started.' She lost the smile. 'And we *are* busy, sir, what with Martin, and now the death in Beale Street.'

'Mm. That was my next question. Is this execution-style murder true, or have the rookies hyped it up?'

'It's true, sir.' Nikki decided to keep her information to the minimum for the time being. 'I've never seen anything like it before. Professor Wilkinson has said he will prioritise the post-mortem, so we should get his preliminary report pretty quickly.'

'And we have no idea of the man's identity?'

'None, but hopefully we'll get some answers soon. Everyone is geared up for the investigation, and the murder room should be ready by now.' She looked at him seriously. 'I'd better get back out there, sir. I'll keep you updated of everything as we go along.'

'Good. And let me know if you need more detectives. Some of the enquiries being dealt with at present can afford to go on the back burner.'

'Thanks, Super. I'll ascertain where this is going, and let you know.' She looked at him hopefully. 'Do you think Sergeant Conway could spare me a couple of bodies for some leg work? Yvonne and Niall would be a great help if they were free?'

The super shook his head, then gave her an exasperated half-smile. 'Oh, alright, I'll do my best, but no promises,

Nikki. You know that CID should work closely with uniform, not just commandeer their staff, as and when.'

'I'd really appreciate it, sir.'

'As I said, no promises.' He walked to the door, then turned back, a disbelieving smile playing across his face. 'A real stunner, you say?'

'Absolutely, sir. Haven't seen her myself, but the words that are being bandied around are pretty descriptive. 'Stunning' was the mildest of several very colourful, and graphic adjectives.'

'Oh, I can imagine exactly what kind of words the mess room have come up with, and most of them quite unrepeatable, I should think.' He shook his head again. 'Poor old Joseph!'

Nikki raised her eyebrows. 'Hardly! If what I hear is right, it's lucky old Joseph!'

* * *

'Ma'am?' Joseph looked at her, a puzzled expression on his face. 'What's with the super? I could swear he winked at me?'

'Oh dear, you may have me to thank for that.'

'Thank you for what?'

'Just think about it, Sergeant. What have half the station been talking about, until we had a murder land on our patch, that is? Just believe me, what I told the super is all for the best.'

Joseph shook his head, and remained totally bemused.

Nikki turned to Dave. 'Are we all set up?'

'Yes, ma'am. And you've just received a note from Professor Wilkinson.' He handed her an envelope.

'Okay, get everyone together, and we'll take a look at what we've got so far.' She tore open the envelope and looked at the copperplate script that was Rory Wilkinson's everyday handwriting.

My Dear Inspector. As you were tactful enough not to demand an immediate answer to that age old question, "Can you give me a time of death?", I have made it my business to provide you with a little gift, my closest 'guesstimate,' pre-post-mortem findings, of course. I believe our man was executed, and there is no doubt that is what happened, between ten and eleven o'clock last night. It was quite warm last evening, and although the rigor mortis was advanced, it had not reached the point of full body rigidity. Our insect friends were naturally enjoying themselves enormously, but the eggs had not hatched into maggots, so we are looking at the fact that he had been dead for less than twelve hours when he and I were introduced.

I can also confirm, even without detailed examination, that your killer is right-handed. The incised wound was made by the killer standing behind the victim, and the cut extends from high up close to the ear, sweeps downwards across the throat, then back up again. The cut is left to right, indicating a right-handed assailant. It was a clean, efficient, and highly effective move, so alas, I suspect this is not the first time that this person has used this particular procedure.

See! It pays not to hassle your friendly pathologist at the scene of the crime!

My opinion and prelim report, will be on your desk tomorrow, God willing.

And now back to my cold cadaver,

Felicitations

Rory. MD, BCh, MRCP, FRCPath, Life-time Member of the Judy Garland Fan Club, etc. etc.

Nikki smiled to herself. Professor Wilkinson had a reputation for stalling if pressed over the elusive time of death, although it hadn't been easy, she had purposely refused to ask him his opinion. She now had her answer and more.

She looked up and smiled smugly, as the door opened and Yvonne Collins and Niall Farrow walked in. Things were progressing exactly as planned.

'Okay, guys, find a seat and we'll recap on what we know.' She walked to the front of the room. 'And until we get the forensic reports back, we'll stick to the facts. We can throw ideas around when we know more.'

Nikki drew in a deep breath. Joseph's involvement would stay in the background for now, with one small exception, his jaywalker. 'Right, last night between the hours of ten and eleven p.m. . . .' She clearly described everything they had found on the filthy wasteground in Beale Street, and when she paused to gather herself, a low murmur of disbelief greeted her.

'Dear God,' muttered Niall. 'Sounds like something from Vietnam, not Greenborough.'

Nikki silently agreed, then continued. 'He had no identification on him, but his description is approx.. five foot ten, naturally blond hair, blue eyes and no distinguishing features other than a small scar on his wrist. No visible tattoos or birthmarks, although the full examination may show something. We have him as about thirty-five, maybe younger.' She listed his clothes, and watched as they all scribbled down what she said. 'Now,' she looked at her team. 'We are already running a fingerprint check and his picture will be circulated, but I don't need to tell you that we need to get on top of this really quickly. Whoever killed him is a highly dangerous individual, and we have no idea if this is just a one-off, a personal vendetta, or the start of a killing spree. Whatever, we don't want what appears to be a professional hitman on our streets for long.'

A murmur of agreement ran around the room.

'So, we need CCTV checks for that whole area, including the station. Officers out asking questions of local residents and workers, not that there are many as that spot is pretty low density housing, and we need a real push on identifying the dead man.'

'I was in the vicinity of the station last night, ma'am,' said Joseph slowly. 'I saw a man loitering in the shadows and went to investigate, but he had disappeared. I'm not saying it was the same person, and the street lights drained everything of colour, but I think he had blondish-fair hair.'

Nikki nodded. 'Hopefully there may be some working cameras that will show him up.' She was glad Joseph had mentioned the fact that he was there *before* the CCTV check began. 'A completely separate incident occurred the day before, again involving Sergeant Easter. Some men were messing around on the High Road, dashing in between cars. One of them hammered on the sergeant's windscreen as he was going out to Cloud Fen to conduct an interview. We've got them on camera, but it's very poor quality. The thing is, the man was of the same build and description, and wore similar clothes. May be coincidence, may not.'

She looked up and saw Joseph looking at her apprehensively, but she had no intention of telling anyone about the man he had seen in the alley, or of his fears about knowing the identity of an evil man in their midst. All in good time. She wanted to hear the history of Billy Sweet, and get Joseph's involvement with him clear in her head long before she discussed it with the team.

'Okay, sort out who does what between yourselves. I know we are pretty well stuck until we get some reports and some answers back, but do what you can, and try to get some sleep tonight. We could be pretty busy until we catch this killer.'

She turned to Joseph. 'Come with me. There are a few details I need to discuss while the others organise themselves.'

In her office, she told him about the super noticing that he wasn't himself.

'He must have seen you after you spotted your mystery man in the lane. He thought you'd come back too soon, and I have to say that you did look like shit.'

'I probably did.' Joseph sighed. 'Ah right, so you told him I was love-struck?'

'It was the first thing that came into my mind, and it worked. So, if he winks at you again, don't worry, he's not a friend of Dorothy. Just run with it, I need you here with me, not being sent on extended R & R again.' She scratched her head thoughtfully. 'By the way, did your new woman, what's her name . . . ?'

'Bryony.'

'Oh, yes, Bryony. Did *she* see this shadowy figure?'

'No. He disappeared as soon as I pointed towards him.'

'Shame, it would have helped to have another pair of eyes see him.'

'Tell me about it,' he grumbled. 'But she was in the cab by that time, and the station buildings were not in her line of vision.'

'When are you seeing her again?' The words were out of her mouth before she could stop them. 'Sorry, Joseph, it's none of my damned business what you do. Hell, I must have sounded just like your mother!'

'Believe me, you are nothing like my mother.' Joseph gave her a rueful smile. 'And to be honest, I'd planned on seeing her at the pool tomorrow, work permitting. And I was going to ask her out for dinner on Saturday evening, but now I'm not sure if I should be planning anything, with Billy Sweet out there.'

She looked at him for a while, then gave a little shrug. 'I'm not sure what I'd do. But as I said, it's none of my business and I shouldn't have asked.'

For some reason that she couldn't explain, not even to herself, she really didn't want to know about Bryony. 'Now, I'd really better chase up these fingerprints.'

He stood up to go.

'Do you like pasta?' she asked suddenly.

'My favourite. Why?'

'Tonight. My cooking skills are hardly legendary, but my pasta is reasonably edible. And if it is rubbish, hopefully enough Scotch should make it seem passable.'

'I'm sure it will be great,' said Joseph. 'Did you mean it about the toothbrush?'

'Oh yes. No way are you leaving Cloud Fen tonight, Sergeant. And I haven't just spent a fortune doing up the guest room to have no one stay in it!'

Joseph didn't answer immediately, but just nodded as he went out, then turned and said. 'Thanks, I do appreciate it. This won't be easy.'

Nikki felt a pang of sadness. She'd been in some seriously bad places herself in the past. 'I know, Joseph, and if there was any other way, but . . .'

'If people are going to die, I have no choice, do I?'

'I'm afraid you don't.' She touched his arm lightly. 'But that doesn't make it any easier, does it?'

'No one in their right mind would want to walk back into a nightmare. Let's just hope it turns out to be a cathartic experience, shall we?'

Nikki watched him leave and shivered, because she knew that whatever kind of experience Joseph was going to have, it was going to be far from cathartic.

CHAPTER TWELVE

Joseph crunched the gears, and uncharacteristically swore out loud. He should take more care on these lethal marsh lanes. They concealed insidious little bends that sneaked out of nowhere and with the tall, reedy marsh grass on the boggy verges, and the deep ditches either side . . . ? He shivered. If you finished up in a ditch, you could be there for a week before someone found you.

With an effort, he pulled himself together and tried to relax. Pretend it's just supper with a good friend. A few drinks, then a few more, and let the alcohol loosen the tongue. Share some deep secrets, have another drink, and crash out. Simple.

He laughed bitterly. He hadn't done that for many a year, not since . . . he abruptly brought his thoughts to a halt. It was far too soon to be going there.

Joseph slowed down and made himself take in the view over this weird water-world. It certainly was a strange place, and he wasn't sure if he loved it or hated it. For one thing, it was rare to find a place that completely wrecked your sense of perspective. You could go up on the sea bank, and if the east wind would allow you to stand upright and see clearly, you could stare into infinity. Or so the long, straight paths that disappeared into the horizon would have you believe. The marshes, the rivers, the great endless fields, and the ever-present 360 degrees of sky, could reflect and magnify your moods like no other place he had ever been, and he had travelled more than most. If you were sad, the remoteness echoed your misery, but if you were happy, the sheer magnitude of the sky above, the clouds forming new landscapes every moment, could lift you to unimaginable heights.

With every trip he made, he felt more confused about it. He smiled to himself. One thing was certain, DI Galena loved it. She was a different person when she was out here. She belonged, and Joseph could *feel* her closeness to the place.

He dropped a gear and eased around one of those long, and incredibly deceiving bends, before continuing his train of thought.

The boss and Cloud Fen. It was quite strange. Nikki Galena was a tough, independent woman, and a bloody good copper. She might have tempered down her tunnel-visioned obsession for ridding the streets of drug dealers, but she was still steely and driven. Someone who you would place in a city, or at very least a town like Greenborough, not out here in these misty groves of solitude. Maybe she needed them, to rid her mind of the grim happenings that her job insisted she deal with on a daily basis. Maybe this was her security blanket. Perhaps she wrapped herself in the sea-frets to free herself from the dreadful things that man did to man. A place of escape.

Joseph smiled and sighed. In the distance he could see the outline of Cloud Cottage Farm, and he felt both relieved that he'd survived the marsh lanes, and apprehensive about what the night may bring.

The farmhouse looked welcoming. Evening sunlight glinted off the windows, and he thought that it would be good to arrive home each night, and find something like this waiting for you. Good, but not perfect, because after years of being alone, he was coming to realise that *alone* wasn't what he wanted. It suited the boss, and until recently, it would have suited him. He turned onto the lane that led to her home, and wondered why his change of heart? It had to be his brush with the Grim Reaper.

Joseph slowed down and saw the gates were wide open for him. It was time to let the melancholy stuff go. Time to paint on another face.

He swung in and parked around the back of the property, next to a big old red brick barn. He jumped out, took a deep breath of the ozone-laden air, then went round and retrieved a bulging plastic bag and a small overnighter from the boot. At least he had the first part of the evening planned, even though he knew it was purely a diversionary tactic. He would salvage the meal. If the boss was such a pants cook, she would relish his help, and he loved to cook. Chopping and dicing, blending and sautéing was *his* way to unwind, to escape.

He walked around to the back door, recalling what she had told him about no one using the front, and vaguely wondered why he had bothered to lock the car. As he waited for her to answer his knock, he decided that some therapeutic cooking would definitely serve him well, because if there were ever a time when he needed to relax, it was now.

* * *

'Okay, so where did you learn to do all that?' asked the boss, clearly impressed. 'And so quickly! I'd still be reading the instructions on the pasta packet.'

Joseph glanced down at the old pine table, now colourful with bowls of steaming pasta and sauce, green salad, tomatoes and olives, and richly aromatic garlic and herb bread.

'College. I'd seen some of my fellow students' pasty faces and pimples, and decided that I was going to pass out with diplomas and degrees, not malnutrition and scurvy.' He picked up a bottle of Merlot that had been left to breathe while he cooked. 'Red okay for you, ma'am?'

'Red, pink, white, all okay for me, thank you.' The boss sighed happily and took two glasses down from a Welsh dresser. 'And we're off duty tonight, Joseph. So on this occasion, Nikki is fine.'

He poured the wine into the glasses, and held his up to hers. 'Cheers, Nikki.'

'To you, Joseph.' The crystal made a small ringing sound. 'You have no idea how much better this meal is than the one I had planned.'

'I doubt it, ma . . . Nikki. I'm sure you are a perfectly good cook, it's just not your thing, that's all.'

'Not quite what my daughter used to tell me, but hey! Let's eat!'

Half way through the meal, Joseph lay down his napkin. 'I just wanted to say thank you for not making me fess up to my past in front of the team.' He sipped his wine. 'Frankly, I don't think I could have done it.'

'That would have been incredibly insensitive,' said Nikki. 'I may be a hard-arsed cow at times and I want to catch the killer, but not at the expense of my sergeant.'

Joseph nodded. There was something about the atmosphere in the old kitchen. They were sitting talking, as dozens of others must have done over several generations, and it felt warm and intimate. 'You do know that you are probably the only person I could share this with, don't you?'

Nikki looked at him across the top of her glass. 'Well, I guess we've been through a couple of pretty emotive situations in the short time we've known each other.' She smiled at him. 'And you were the one to accompany me 'down where it's twisted and dark' when I needed to offload. So I guess it's just a reversal of roles this time.'

Joseph decided that he felt very comfortable in this old room with the pine furniture, the Butler sink, the pottery chickens and the ancestral memories. He poured some more wine, and they finished their supper.

'Does cognac keep?' she asked, as he stacked plates into the dishwasher.

'Not in my house. But that's just due to my propensity for fine brandy. Why?'

'When the builders were clearing the attic to work on the wiring and the insulation, they found some old boxes belonging to my father. I brought them down to sort out and found an unopened bottle of cognac.' She raised an eyebrow at him. 'Worth a try, do you think?'

'Is it ever! What's on the label?'

'Several layers of dust, I should think.' She opened the larder and removed a tall straight bottle with two rather scuffed and faded off-white labels on the front.

Joseph carefully took it from her and his eyes widened. 'We can't drink this!'

'Oh, gone off has it? Then we'll revert back to the whisky and I'll pour that down the sink.'

'No!' Joseph almost choked at the threat of tipping the spirit away. 'This is a Croizet 1961! It's rare, Nikki, and would probably cost you over £300 to buy!'

'God, my father is a sneaky old devil! What on earth was he squirreling that away for?' She stared at the bottle in disbelief, then grinned and said, 'Oh well, at least its drinkable. I'll get a couple of balloon glasses, then we can do it properly.'

Joseph touched the bottle with something like reverence, then laughed out loud at his boss's total disregard for the heritage of such a fine spirit. But who was he to complain? He'd tasted some fine brandy before, but this would be a first.

Nikki returned from the lounge, glasses in hand. 'You do the honours, Joseph. The way I look at it is this; I never even knew it was there. My poor father doesn't know what year it is any more, sadly he doesn't even know his only daughter, so he won't be objecting. And if I'd never returned to live here, then that bottle would either have been left in the attic for some other bugger to lift, or taken to the dump, so . . . ?'

'Let's say the house is welcoming you home, shall we?'

'I like that. Want to go through to the sitting room, or would you rather stay here?'

'Stay here.' He replied without even thinking. 'I love the feel to this room.'

'That's what my mother always said. She said it felt safe, and even if she was on her own, she felt as if the family were around her.'

As Joseph carefully unsealed the bottle, he knew exactly what the perceptive woman had meant. 'Okay, here goes nothing!' He poured the amber liquid into the brandy balloons and gently sniffed one of them. 'Oh my! That is something else. Let's hope its anaesthetic properties are as good as its bouquet.'

Nikki took hers from him and sipped it tentatively. 'No way would I pay three hundred quid for it, but it is very nice. Thank you, Daddy.'

Joseph was lost for words. He just sat there smiling inanely and wishing he had been born to an indecently wealthy French family.

The silence that engulfed them was as comfy as a pair of old slippers, and Joseph suddenly knew that he had run out of excuses. There was nothing left to come between him and the horrors of his past.

'You said that when you go through a difficult time with someone, you feel very close to them afterwards, or words to that effect.' He stared into the glinting crystal goblet. 'So I think you'll understand when I say that it was like that with my army comrades. They say you're brothers in arms, but that doesn't even get close. Those men are everything to you. You love them in a way that . . .' he paused looking for the right words, but not truly finding them. 'You've got to have been part of something like that to know just how much your mates mean to you.'

He took another sip of the cognac and looked across at his boss. He had the feeling that she was going to be a good listener. It took a very special person just to listen, and not butt in, criticize or compare your story to something from their own past.

'It was never my intended career, but I loved being a soldier, Nikki, and I was a good one.' A sigh slipped from between his lips. 'A natural.'

'I can believe that,' said Nikki softly. 'I've seen how you react under pressure.'

He nodded, and wondered how long he could make one sip of that rare cognac last.

'You already knew that I was with UK special forces. But I was actually part of an elite team that dealt with very delicate special ops. And I thrived on it, Nikki, until Billy Sweet poisoned everything.'

He gripped his glass tightly, and his next drink was more of a slug than a sip. He knew that Nikki's company, his relaxed surroundings and the brandy were making the telling of this story as easy as it would ever be, but he still wanted to run away before he had to fully enter that dreadful pit of memory.

Nikki seemed to sense his difficulty, and reached across to refill his glass. 'You had a bad mission, didn't you? Where were you?'

'Africa,' he whispered.

There was no turning back. Joseph set his jaw firmly forward. 'I know it's Sweet that you are interested in, but to appreciate what happened, you have to know a bit about what we were doing.' He took a deep breath. 'Four of us were sent out to the Democratic Republic of Congo to look for a small unit of men who had disappeared without a trace.' He swallowed hard, as the filthy smells and the stinking heat rushed back at him. 'The country was a living nightmare. Hell on earth. Massacres, child soldiers, systematic rape, and a refugee crisis that helped to destabilize the whole of the eastern Congo. It was worse than anything I'd ever seen, and I'd been in some shit-holes before.' He swirled the cognac around and around in the glass, and tried to lose himself in the topaz vortex. 'No matter what I say, Nikki, it could never convey how terrible it was, but try to imagine this. In the area where we were deployed, three quarters of all the children had disappeared. Three quarters!' He closed his eyes and tried not to hear the heart-rending wails of the women.

'So why were the first group out there?' prompted Nikki, trying to keep her voice steady,

'It was to do with precious metals and minerals. The whole place is a great big geological treasure chest, but greed and the conflict have just left it like one blasted, shameful battlefield. The group had been sent to a village called Zutu. There was a mine there, one that was being overseen by European scientists and engineers. It had rich seams of valuable minerals. Not just gold, copper or diamonds, even though they were common enough, there were mining minerals like niobium, pyrochlore, coltan, and germanium. All needed by hi-tech industries, like for nuclear reactors or space technology.' Joseph shivered a little, even though the kitchen was still warm. 'We knew that one of the scientists had been murdered, and two engineers were missing, that's why the first group went out. To get the remaining staff to safety, and find and bring home the missing men.'

'But they disappeared too?'

'They accomplished their mission, retrieved the hostages and got the rest of the staff extracted by helicopter, but they went back to Zutu.'

Nikki frowned, but said nothing.

'They contacted HQ with their coordinates saying that they had discovered something else, something that intelligence had not briefed them about.' Joseph shifted uncomfortably in his chair. 'After that, they sent just one communication, regarding a neighbouring village called Ituga. A terrifying report about women and children being taken as slaves and forced to opencast mine minerals, sometimes with their bare hands, and give everything they found to their rebel captors. These women were also expected to prostitute themselves, and if they refused you can guess what happened to them. The unit's plan was to recon the other mine, assess the potential for an evacuation, and either request assistance or deal with it immediately. It was a covert mission, and imperative that the identity of the sponsor was concealed. It couldn't be known that the British government was involved, not in that hotbed of political shit.' He drank more brandy. 'My team was Kilo Charlie Zero. We were a four man patrol, and we shipped out as soon as communication with Ituga broke down.'

Joseph stood up and walked slowly around the kitchen, touching ordinary homely objects, as if trying to ground himself in the present. 'We found the unit in a cave close to the mine. Three of them had been butchered, and the fourth was sitting there with the bodies, too traumatised to speak.' He ran his hand across the cold surface of a marble chopping block. 'I'd served with one of them before, Terry Bourne, he was a fine soldier, and an extraordinary human being.' A picture of the tousle-haired man with a boxer's nose and a big smile came unbidden into his thoughts. Rough and tough on the outside, but inside, a rare gentleman. 'We radioed our findings in, got the bodies to a place of safety ready to be brought home, and took the remaining soldier with us. We requested a helicopter evacuation for him and our dead, but there was heavy rebel fighting close by and they couldn't comply. My commanding officer made the decision that we go in and finish the job ourselves.'

'Find out what was going on at the Ituga mine?'

'Yeah, and send back full intelligence,' Joseph sighed, 'And that's where it all went pear-shaped.' He flopped back down into his chair. 'I'm not sure if any of us really knew what happened, but we got a radio message telling us that a group of rebels had been seen bringing in a new batch of women and children. According to our information, they were being held in a large hut prior to selection for duties, and the rebels were regrouping ready for their next sortie in a cave close to the perimeter of the mine.'

Joseph licked his lips and steeled himself to speak. 'Our intel was wrong. It was the women who were in the cave that we attacked. Somehow in the bedlam that followed, we managed to get only two of the women out, most of them died.' He glanced across at Nikki's face. It was set as if in stone, and he had no idea what she was thinking.

'And the children?' She finally asked.

'There were no children this time.'

Nikki's face softened. 'Thank God for small mercies. And Billy Sweet? Where does he fit in?'

Joseph took another gulp of his drink. This was the worse bit. The bit he had relegated to the deepest, darkest part of his memory. The accidental killing of the women had been devastating, life-destroying. But what had come next was the stuff of nightmares. He rubbed his hand across his mouth.

'We were hopelessly outnumbered, and we'd lost the element of surprise. We fell back, taking the two women and the silent soldier.' He stood up again, and began to pace. 'As night fell, we found a deserted building, an old shelter, a store of some kind. It was way outside the perimeter and well hidden.' Joseph saw it in his mind's eye, saw the sun-bleached wood and the corrugated metal sheets that served as a roof, and suddenly he was there, back in Africa.

'All clear!' he called out, as he checked the last part of the deserted shack. He relaxed a little, but kept his rifle at the ready. 'Get the women inside; it'll get cold pretty quickly.' He stood back as his comrades entered the building.

'It's going to be a long night, Bunny.' His friend, Cameron McBride, hitched up a rag of material that was hung at the glass-less window and tried to decide how best to keep guard until morning. 'The terrain sucks. Too many dead spots for snipers to hide in. Two hour watches, two men awake at all times, I reckon.'

'Yeah.' They called him Bunny because of his surname. He was the Easter Bunny.

'I'll take the first watch.'

'Me too,' added Teddy Churchill, wiping grime and other unspeakable substances from his boots.

'I'll sort out some rations, get the women and this lad fed.' Kenny Williams' dirty face crinkled up in frustration. 'Daren't risk a fire though, its cold grub or nothing.'

Joseph's stomach was in no fit state for food, hot or cold, and he was grateful to get outside into the night. The bloodbath in the mine was still playing itself out in his head. How could everything have gone so wrong?

95

He was still hearing the screams echoing around in his mind, when Teddy sidled up to him and whispered.

'There's movement down on the track, 500 metres south.'

They moved together into the darkness and watched the narrow road.

Joseph flipped down his night-vision sights, and saw figures huddled in the scrubby trees that flanked the track. 'Go get Cam and Kenny.'

Moments later, the four soldiers eased themselves further down the incline, to get a better look at their ghostly intruders.

They watched for a while, then Cam tapped his arm and gestured towards the shadows. 'They are women! Thank God! Some of them must have escaped!'

'Are they alone?' whispered Kenny.

'Can't see.'

'Bait,' murmured Teddy grimly. 'It's a trap.'

Joseph suddenly froze. 'Or a lure. To get us away from the shack.'

Cam inhaled sharply, then said, 'No, the squaddie's with them, the girls will be alright. He's a mess, but he's still a soldier.' His confidence faded. 'Surely they wouldn't . . . ?'

'I'm going back.' Joseph knew something was terribly wrong. 'One of you come with me.'

As he began to climb back up towards the shack, he felt Cam move in behind him. 'Bad vibes, man.'

Joseph didn't answer.

Like wraiths in the night, they drifted up to the door, and slipped inside.

The coppery, metallic smell hit them instantly, and it was something they were both horribly familiar with. Then they heard the sound. A weird, sing-song keening; like nothing Joseph had ever heard either before or since.

'Oh God, oh God,' whispered Cam.

The women were dead. They had been hogtied and their throats neatly slit. And sitting on his haunches in front of them rocking backwards and forwards, was the young soldier. When he realised that he was no longer alone, the horrible noise that was issuing from his throat ceased, and for the first time since they arrived in Ituga, he spoke.

Actually he screamed. 'They made me watch! The bastards made me watch!'

Joseph stared at him,

'They were waiting! They came in! They came in as soon as you'd gone!'

'And you let them do this!' Cam's voice was even louder.

'I couldn't do anything,' blubbered the young man.

'And they left you alone, did they? I don't fucking think so!' Cam sneered at the soldier. 'You ran away, didn't you? You shitty little coward! You left these women to be slaughtered, and you hid!'

Until then Joseph had said nothing, then he asked, 'What's your name, soldier?'

'Sweet, sir. Billy Sweet. And I didn't run. They held me and made me watch, I swear. Then something scared them. They pushed me to the floor and ran off.'

Joseph's powerful flashlight lit up the man's eyes, and he shivered. It might have been the trauma he had suffered, or it might have been the light, Joseph was never sure, but the soldier had the unblinking pale eyes of a fish. Cold, dead eyes.

Suddenly Joseph was back in the kitchen, his breathing laboured, and Nikki was beside him, pressing the glass into his shaking hands.

'Take a sip, Joseph, go on. It's okay. *You're* okay, honestly.'

He took a long shuddery breath. 'Yes, I am aren't I?'

'Are you up to finishing the story, or . . . ?'

'I've come this far, let's get it done with.' He fought to control the shaking. 'When it was light, I searched for signs of intruders. There were none. I looked for a knife, but the terrain was too difficult. You see, the others believed he was a coward. I believed he was a murderer.' He stretched, trying to unknot his cramped muscles. 'A week later, I went back to that area to help mop up the rebels, and I heard talk. Talk about a baby-faced white soldier who had killed his own comrades.' Joseph looked at Nikki. 'I knew then I'd been right about Billy Sweet.'

'*He* butchered his friends?' Nikki's voice rose several octaves. 'And the women?'

'I believe so. But no witnesses came forward, and there was no proof. He was sent for psychological evaluation, given a long holiday somewhere nice, and allowed back on active duty two months later.'

'My God! How come they didn't see through him?'

'Psychopaths are brilliant and convincing liars.' Joseph shrugged. 'Ironic, isn't it? It was me that finished up on the scrapheap. I couldn't cope with what had happened at the mine. Those poor women died, and we killed them. They were supposed to be the rebels.' He gave one last sigh. 'Billy Sweet marched back to war, and I threw my rifle into a river and went home.'

'You never saw him again?'

'Just once. A week or so before I got my honourable discharge. I was helping out at a training camp in the Brecon Beacons, and I heard a group of soldiers complaining about one of the men. I heard them mention the name, and I *had* to go take a look at him. That's how come I know his face. He'd changed, of course. I don't think he was ever as young as he seemed. He'd got older, got tougher, and uglier. But his eyes were just the same.'

'Did he see you, and did he recognise you?'

'Oh yes. From the derisory smile on his evil face, I'd say, most definitely.'

Nikki looked across at him, her face drawn and sombre. 'And you believe that that was the man who jumped in front of your car in the Greenborough High Road?'

When he answered, the words were slow and deliberate. 'Yes. The man I saw was Billy Sweet.'

* * *

They talked on until one in the morning. They talked about families, about his soul-searching journey after he left the army, about the police force, and of living on the fen. She talked about Martin, and she even managed to let Joseph talk about Bryony, although she still felt that inexplicable feeling of discomfort deep inside when he mentioned the other woman.

Whatever, it was good to have him there. She had told the super that she could take care of herself, and she had never been frightened to be alone, but like it or not, Cloud Fen was a remote spot when there was a violent thug on the loose, and Joseph's presence was a distinct comfort.

She had given him the guest room, the room that had been hers as a child, and told him to try to catch the sunrise. The dawn over the marsh was as beautiful as anywhere in the world.

As she slipped into her own bed, she thought about Joseph, lying just a few feet away from her, and sighed. She hoped he would see the sun come up, sending dazzling flame fingers across the oily dark waters of the marsh. He could do with some bright light to warm the sadness that lived inside him.

CHAPTER THIRTEEN

Joseph had certainly seen the sunrise, as he had seen every other hour of the night. It had nothing to do with not being tired. He had been exhausted, totally drained by everything that he had dredged up from the mud of his past. He was simply scared to sleep. He knew only too well the nightmares that were lurking in his head, waiting to crawl and slither into his dream sleep.

So he had got to see the dawn. And as Nikki had said, it had been spectacular. For a moment or two he had been able to lose himself in it, as the deep, blood-red orb that was the sun broke free of the dark horizon. He wished he could stay there, basking in its breathtaking beauty, but there was a killer close by, and the time for relaxing would only come when Sweet was behind bars, or beneath the ground.

Joseph had showered and gone downstairs to find Nikki, already dressed, and trying to prise a hunk of burnt toast from the toaster with a knife. He had declined the offer of a cooked breakfast and settled for coffee and a cold croissant, then after thanking her for both her hospitality and the incredibly good brandy, drove away from Cloud Fen and headed towards the swimming pool. He had time for a half an hour's swim before he started work and it might help to wash away the shadows that still clung to him.

He had just completed his twentieth length, when the changing room door opened and Bryony walked in. She waved brightly and went to one of the poolside showers, allowing him time to take in the sight of her.

She was wearing a black sports swimsuit with a scarlet flash down the sides, and looked every inch the athlete. He ducked under the water for a moment and tried to understand why he felt such an idiotic delight in her being there.

'Hi, you!' she said as she broke the water inches from his face.

'Glad you made it,' he said, pushing his wet hair back from his face.

'As if I'd miss the chance of seeing you.' She grinned at him, then rolled over on her back and glided effortless up the half empty pool. 'Keep up, slowcoach!'

He pushed off and took a few powerful strokes, but he was still not even close to her. Bryony was completely at home in the water and moved through it with both grace and ease. He was not a bad swimmer, although nothing like he had been, even so he was not rubbish, but right now he felt like a lumbering whale next to a dolphin.

It took him about ten minutes to find a stroke that enabled him to keep up with her, and even then he was sure that she was slowing down to let him catch her.

The water felt good, and he didn't want to leave, but the big clock at the end of the pool was telling him otherwise. 'I've got to go.'

'So soon?' Water glistened on her smooth skin, and Joseph silently cursed the fact that he had to work.

'We've got a lot on, I'm afraid.'

'Big case, Mr Detective Sergeant?'

Joseph bit his lip and thought, yeah, big as they come and the timing stinks. 'Something like that.' He swam on his side towards the steps. 'So how about Saturday? Are we on for dinner?'

Bryony swam towards him and planted a light kiss on his cheek before plunging down beneath the bright blue water and swimming off.

'Take that as a "yes", shall I?' He called after her, then realised that he was not supposed to know where she lived. 'Where shall I pick you up?'

'I'll meet you at seven, outside that dreadful pub of yours,' she shouted.

He waved to her and pushed open the changing room door. That was just fine, but this time he'd make sure it was not heaving with policemen.

* * *

'We've got a match, Joseph.'

Nikki was already in the murder room, and sifting through a pile of fresh reports.

'On?' He threw his jacket over the back of his chair and moved to her side.

'Our execution victim. His name is Chris Forbes. His fingerprints turned up on the police computer. Nothing heavy, just some trouble over taking a car without the owner's consent.'

'Was he a local, ma'am?' asked Joseph.

'Yes, he's from the Carborough Estate. Bit of a rough family, but other than that one incident, he seems to have been clean.' She paused, then added, 'So why did he finish up dead?'

'I would think wrong place, wrong time. He simply had the misfortune to bump into something nasty in the night.' Joseph's eyes narrowed. 'None of Billy's other victims had done anything wrong either.'

'Maybe. The family has been informed and there's a liaison officer with them. Dave was in early so he went straight over, we'll talk to them later.' Nikki looked at him pensively. 'And Joseph, I suggest we keep everything that we discussed last night, just between us for the time being. And you need to try to keep your emotions under tight control, even if you see this man again.' She shook her head. 'Otherwise everything will have to come out in the open, and I don't want you to have to face all that, not officially, unless there is absolutely no other way.'

Joseph nodded. 'If we catch him it will be a different ball game, but until then I'll do my best to keep a lid on my reactions.' He gave her a relieved smile. 'I really appreciate that, thank you.'

'No problem. Now grab a pile of these reports and help me check them, and a very strong coffee may help.' She held out a sheaf of paperwork.

Joseph took them and grinned. 'Can you believe that brandy?

'I can't believe we drank half a bottle of the stuff, that's for sure!' She grimaced, 'Or maybe I can.' She flopped into a chair and looked up at him with a pained expression. 'You didn't actually go swimming earlier, did you?'

'Yup.' He felt a thrill run through him as he recalled those soft lips touch his cheek, 'And I'm glad I did.'

'Ah, Bryony.'

Joseph smiled and nodded, although he wondered if he had imagined a slight hint of disapproval.

'Then just keep your wits about you, Sergeant. Don't get too distracted.' Her old tone was back, so he just grinned and went to get the coffee.

As he placed the cups under the dispenser and waited, he glanced through the reports. Nothing leapt out, other than a memo from the SOCO who had checked Knot Cottage.

He returned to the murder room and put the drinks on the desk. 'You were right about whoever turned over Martin Durham's drum. The SOCO says it was a pro.'

'I said he was!' His boss frowned angrily. 'Your average blagger would never have disabled me that easily.' She scanned the memo and made a snorting noise. 'No trace evidence found at scene. No fingerprints, footprints, stray hairs, no bloody nothing.'

'Are we surprised?'

'No, not at all. I just half hoped that we wouldn't have to wait for the DNA on that hair that I managed to yank from his scalp.'

'Makes it even more important that you did.'

'I suppose. I just wish things happened as fast as they do in *CSI* or *NCIS*.'

'I don't think the Fenland Constabulary's budget could run to a dedicated state-of-the-art forensics lab like Abby Sciuto's. We are lucky to have *cars*, even if half of them are clapped out! Sadly this is the real world.'

'And it's a psych ward run by the inmates.' Nikki threw up her hands. 'We've got this fabulous building, cost a fortune, and we have to sign in triplicate and wait for three weeks if we need a new stapler!' With a disgusted grunt she picked up the telephone that had shrieked out from the desk in front of her.

'Yes, DI Galena here. Oh, hello Rory.' She listened for a moment, then holding the receiver between her chin and her shoulder began sorting through the remaining reports. 'Got it! Yes, hang on.' She opened the thin envelope and began to read. After a second or two she said, 'But I don't understand.'

Joseph looked at her. Her voice had dropped to little more than a sigh.

'That seems impossible, Professor.' After a while she thanked him and hung up. 'The tox report on Martin. His bloodstream was flowing with doxepin hydrochloride, in the form of a drug called Sinepin. The professor thought he should draw my attention to it prior to delivering his full opinion.'

Joseph frowned. 'I don't remember seeing any drugs of that name at Knot Cottage.'

'There weren't any. I have a list of all the medication that he was legitimately taking, and all bar one were present in the report, and Rory is very concerned.'

'What kind of drug is this Sinepin?' he asked.

'No idea. The professor is bringing his preliminary findings over at lunchtime and he'll give us the details then.' Nikki picked up her coffee cup and stared into it. 'They couldn't have been recreational. Martin *never* took drugs. Hell, I've spent half my life with drug users, I'd have spotted signs.'

'They sound like prescription drugs,' said Joseph. 'So how did he get hold of them?'

The boss shrugged. 'This is getting more shitty by the hour.' She looked worried. 'And we should be getting our heads around Chris Forbes' murder.'

'I've been thinking about that. The type of rope that was used may be of help to us.' He sucked in air, then lowered his voice so that only she could hear him. 'Soldiers always have string or twine in their kit. I'll be interested to hear what kind it is.'

The boss said nothing, but just nodded.

'And the knots the killer used. I should have been more attentive, but the shock of seeing the body in that position, I just . . . I just had to get out of there.'

'Don't be too hard on yourself, Joseph. It's hardly surprising, is it?' There was compassion in her voice. 'But if you can, check the photographs as soon as we have them, I'm sure the report will pick up on the way the victim was bound.'

'I'll certainly be able to tell you if it was a military-style attack.'

'Let's just wait and see, shall we? Part of me is still hoping that this is nothing to do with you.' The boss gave him an unenthusiastic look. 'Although the other part is pretty sure that's not the case.' She closed a file with a snap. 'But let's not jump the gun. Hard evidence is what we require.'

Joseph nodded, then looked up as the door opened and Dave Harris walked in. His face was drawn and his eyes deep and sad. 'That's one side of police work that I hate.'

'Don't we all,' said Nikki. 'So, anything helpful from the parents?'

Dave sat down heavily and shook his head. 'All but useless, guv. Chris Forbes lived at home, he was thirty-four, but he was not bright, if you catch my drift?'

'Learning difficulties?' asked Joseph.

Dave nodded. 'Not severe, but his younger brother said that the lift never went up to the top floor. Chris was happy in his own little fantasy world, and sadly the family were happy to let him live there.'

'Something they are no doubt regretting,' murmured Nikki.

'He didn't work, and spent most of his time in pool halls with his drop-out mates. To be honest, I don't think he was bad, just highly impressionable and very trusting.'

'And no one took him too seriously, I suppose?'

'That's the point, Sarge. Who listens for long to a Walter Mitty? His brothers admitted that he'd been going on about some "brilliant bloke" who bought him drinks, but as none of them had actually met him, and as they didn't give a toss who Chris was drinking with, we have no description.'

'Where did he drink? Or play pool? Maybe we can track this new friend that way?' said Nikki.

'The Plough on River Street was his local, guv. Cat's checked it out already. He *was* there with a stranger recently, but no one took any notice of him. The description was hazy, just kind of ordinary, non-descript, and he always wore a knitted beanie hat.' Dave pulled a face. 'The only thing that did come up was that Chris called this new friend by a nickname.'

'And that was?'

'He called him Snaz, ma'am.'

Joseph fought to stifle an involuntary gasp, and when he glanced up he saw Nikki staring at him.

'Well, that's a start, Dave. Go grab yourself some breakfast, okay?'

As the door closed, she raised her eyebrows enquiringly. 'Right, Joseph, what spooked you?'

Fighting to keep his voice level, he said, 'The Russian special forces soldiers are called *Spetsnaz*, ma'am. Billy Sweet held them in pretty high regard, and he always referred to them as the Snaz.' He looked at her enquiringly. 'Now where do you sit on the subject of coincidences?'

* * *

An hour later, Cat knocked lightly on Nikki's door and stuck her head around. 'Got a minute, ma'am?'

'Only if you've got me something on Chris Forbes' friend Snaz?'

'I went back to the Plough, ma'am, to see one of Chris's old friends. This bloke Liam mentioned seeing Chris with a stranger outside a dodgy pool parlour down by the docks. A dirty dive called the Paper Wall.'

'Want me to check it out, ma'am?' asked Joseph.

'No offence, Sergeant, but I think we'll leave it to Cat. She has the knack of blending in rather well in dubious joints, don't you, detective?' She smiled at Joseph. 'Sorry, but she'll get more than you from their kind of clientele. You look a tad too wholesome for the Paper Wall.'

'You make it sound as if I should be selling *War Cry*,' said Joseph huffily.

'If the cap fits, mate!' laughed Cat. 'You leave this one to me. I have a rare talent for disguise when undercover.'

'I know, I've seen you in action, remember?' Joseph closed the report he'd been reading.

'So, what am I trying to find out, while I'm stamping on the cockroaches?'

'If anyone can give us an ID on a man with the tag, Snaz.'

'You do know they won't have CCTV, and their security consists of an eighteen stone, tattooed woman who looks harder than Desperate Dan?'

'You mean Gloria,' Nikki smiled. 'Yeah, start with her. As long as she wasn't already juiced up by the time Chris and his new friend got there, she would have clocked them alright. Get round there as soon as they open, okay?'

'Can't wait.'

'Well, if that's the case, why don't you rope in Yvonne and Niall and go around *all* the local pool halls and pubs to try to find someone who can finger this mystery man that Chris had been spending time with. We need a face, Cat.'

'No problem, ma'am.' Cat gathered up her jacket and headed for the door. 'Time for a swift change of clothes, and then show us committed.'

Nikki glanced up at the clock. Professor Wilkinson should be with them shortly with the preliminary reports on Martin's death, and it was a report that was worrying the life out of her. Strangely, even the execution of Chris Forbes couldn't rid her of the constant nagging anxiety about her old neighbour and his horrible death.

'More coffee, ma'am?' asked Joseph.

'Make that three. Rory has his black, no sugar.'

A few moments later Rory Wilkinson stuck his head round the door, and waved a large white paper bag. 'I come bearing gifts! And I don't mean gruesome goodies from the path lab either.'

No matter how grim her thoughts had been, this unorthodox forensic genius always managed to bring a smile to her face. 'Then welcome, Professor. Grab a seat. Joseph is already getting refreshments.'

'Which should go nicely with these.' He tore open the bag and revealed three enormous chocolate éclairs. 'Called in at the *boulangerie* en route. *C'est manifique, n'est ce pas?*'

'Oh Lord! I should say so! If Joseph doesn't get a move on he'll be unlucky.'

As if on cue, Joseph shouldered the door open and entered carrying three large mugs of coffee. 'Haven't missed anything, have I?'

'Nearly, but not quite,' said Nikki, looking longingly at the thick chocolate covering the cream-filled choux pastry. 'Right, so are these to help sweeten the mood, knowing about your other gift, the one in the giant brown manila folder?'

'Ah, so astute! Every inch the detective, ma'am.' He grinned. 'But no, actually I missed breakfast and I'm starving.' His face became a little more serious. 'Although I have to say, the tidings that I bring are by no means straightforward.'

'As if I thought they would be,' sighed Nikki, taking a bite out of her éclair. 'So, whenever you are ready?'

The pathologist put down his coffee mug, dabbed at the corners of his mouth with a white handkerchief, and sat back. 'Well, Mr Durham died as the result of his fall from the church tower, this we know. His injuries were a little different to those normally expected from a fall from such a great height, because of the fact that he hit the wall and not a flat hard surface. He shattered his spinal column at the areas of the second, third and fourth lumbar vertebrae, severing the spinal cord and shearing through the arteries.' Rory pointed to the folder. 'There's much more, of course. It's all in there. Crushed ribs, massive head injury and intracranial bleeds, caused as his head was swung down against the wall when his back broke. Liver damaged, et al., but this is to be expected, wholly understandable, and it's none of this that worries me.'

Nikki was feeling a mild nausea sweep over her. This was an old friend that Rory was describing, and it didn't make pleasant listening. She tried not to think of broken, splintered bones and quickly said, 'It's the toxicology report, isn't it?'

Rory nibbled delicately on his éclair and nodded, 'Mm, exactly.' He removed a thick batch of papers from his file, skimmed through them, then laid them on the desk and looked up. 'I'll try to simplify this for you. And please don't think that I'm insulting your intelligence, dear hearts, but forensic toxicology is complex, and it's still one of the most difficult tasks to prove death by poisoning.'

'He was poisoned?' asked Joseph, almost choking on his coffee.

'Oh no, well, not in the way that you mean, but, there again, one *could* say that . . .'

'Rory?' Nikki bit her lip. 'Come to the point.'

'Sorry. What I mean is this; Martin Durham killed himself by leaping from the tower. Fact. He did this because he was under the effect of a powerful hallucinogen. Fact. But did he purposefully take the drug himself, or was it administered to him by person or persons unknown? Unproven.'

'Tell us about the drugs,' said Joseph. 'He had a real cache of them at his home.'

'And thereby hangs another mystery,' replied Rory. 'But let's take this one step at a time, shall we? We took samples from his blood, urine, stomach contents, liver, what was left

of it, and his vitreous humour. You see, you are not just looking for the toxins, you are looking for their effects, in the form
of metabolites. So, using a combination of mass spectrometry
and gas spectrometry we isolated and identified samples of all
his prescription drugs, bar one. *Plus* another substance, the
one that turned out to be doxepin hydrochloride.'

Nikki stared across the desk at Rory. 'You just said, "bar
one". Why would he take all his meds and leave one out? Is it
something that he didn't need to take regularly?'

'Oh no, it's part of his daily regime.'

'And the other one? The hallucinogen? What would that
be taken for?'

'It's used, quite legitimately, as an anti-anxiety drug, an
antidepressant. It's similar to Amitriptyline. But, as with a
lot of chemicals, it's not the drug itself, it's the quantity that
is taken. And this was a dose large enough to trigger an acid
trip in an elephant.'

'But Martin never used recreational drugs. He didn't
smoke and he didn't drink.'

'Then that could have made its effect on him even more
severe.'

Joseph placed his mug on the desk and stared at it.
'There were no pharmaceutical company boxes or bottles in
Martin's home that were antidepressants, of that I am sure.
And as his GP never mentioned them, how did he get hold
of them, and why take it anyway? By accident?'

'That's possible, of course,' said Rory. 'But frankly, I
doubt it. It's the missing tablet that has me foxed.' He pushed
his glasses further up onto the bridge of his nose and peered
at Nikki. 'From what I understand, Martin Durham was a
meticulous man, and very careful with his medication. You
knew him, so am I right?'

'Bear in mind I never knew he took medication, but
otherwise, most certainly. His house was spotless. He cooked
wholesome food and exercised regularly.'

'I deduced that much from the state of his body and the
contents of his stomach.' He puffed out his cheeks and made

a low, whistling sound. 'So why miss one tablet? Anyone who takes pills regularly has a specific routine, and if those tablets are life sustaining, you are very particular indeed.'

'Common sense would dictate that somehow he took the Sinepin accidentally, believing it to be his other tablet,' said Joseph thoughtfully. 'Do they look alike, Professor?'

'Not at all. The antidepressant is a brightly coloured gelatine capsule, the colour varying as to the strength of the dose, and his own drug was a small yellow tablet. No way would he have confused them.'

'Then he was deliberately given it, by someone else,' muttered Nikki. 'Maybe the man who ransacked his cottage?'

'This is ludicrous!' exclaimed Joseph. 'We are talking about an ordinary man. Someone who lives in a small village, in a time-warp cottage, with a love for the marshes, and not a scrap of scandal to his name. Why on earth should he be targeted, maybe even killed, by some shady professional hitman? It just doesn't make sense.'

'We need to find out more about Martin's past,' said Nikki flatly. 'How much do we really know about the people around us? Not much, I'm willing to wager.'

Rory nodded. 'For what it's worth, I really think that's where you *should* start. If he were given that drug intentionally, then you *have* to find out who is behind it. This time just one man died, but he could have taken any one of those poor souls up on the viewing platform with him. And there were children there, weren't there?'

Nikki nodded dumbly. She knew a bit about hallucinations. She'd seen enough junkies on bad trips. Kids whose senses were telling them lies, making them believe all manner of nightmares. A string of questions flooded into her mind. What on earth had Martin become involved in? What could be so awful that he should be sent to such a terrible death? Or was she just being paranoid? There were most likely other far more common-or-garden reasons for what happened, and maybe the break-in was just that, and the intruder really did just land her with a lucky punch. Maybe.

'And then there is my other little mystery regarding his medication.' Rory adjusted his glasses again. 'I did a little ferreting of my own, because I was puzzled to see that most of his tablets were issued by Dr Latimer of Cloud Fen, and two others came in plain white boxes with the tablet name and dosage on the side, but no maker's name. They most certainly did not come from any of the suppliers that I know.'

'Internet?' enquired Joseph. 'Isn't that where people self-medicate themselves these days?'

'Ah-ha! Two minds! But no, dear Joseph. Sadly my mini-investigation has proved us wrong. I've no idea where these drugs come from.'

Nikki looked towards Joseph. 'Time for you to take another trip to Dr Latimer's surgery, I think.'

The pathologist smiled, 'I have my doubts that she will know any more than we do, but I'd be interested to see her expression when you tell about this little conundrum. And I have to leave this with you now.' Rory pushed the file across the desk to her. 'Don't read it after dark.' He took another, thinner file from his bag. 'Now we come to the unfortunate Mr Christopher Forbes. And this is much more straight-forward. A deliberate and ruthless murder, carried out with minimum fuss and scarily skilfully executed.'

'A professional?' asked Nikki, before Joseph could speak.

'Most definitely. Knew exactly the right amount of pressure to use, and the correct angle of the blade for a clean and fatal cut.'

'A contract killer, then?'

Rory took a deep breath. 'I'd say this man had more of a military background. Hitmen prefer guns. It's impersonal. A gun distances the killer from the victim. You have to be very sure of yourself, and very cool, to use a knife. Not many people have the nerve to get *that* up close with their prey.'

Nikki looked at Joseph, but his face was set in stone. She knew he'd just had the confirmation he'd been waiting for.

'And there was very little trace evidence on the body. Probably nothing, after we've eliminated the few odd hairs on his clothing. Frankly I'm not expecting much at all.' Rory stretched. 'The only thing that we have with a connection to the murderer is the rope that he used to tie the man, and sadly it's pretty common stuff. The kind you can pick up in any marine chandlers or outdoor pursuit store.'

Nikki heard Joseph murmur the word 'damn' under his breath.

'So apart from a positive gallery of photographs, that is all I have for you at present, and I need to get back. So, it's over to you, my friends.' Rory stood up. 'And *do* let me know what you discover about that mysterious missing pill. It's the sort of accursed thing that bugs your every waking moment, and then robs you of your sleep.'

'Isn't it just,' said Nikki vehemently. 'But I'll get to the bottom of it, Professor. I promise you that.'

'Oh, I'm sure you will, Inspector dearest, just don't take too long. I shall be positively haggard with worry! And you've no idea just how much I value my beauty sleep!'

With a curt bow and a flourish of his hand, he was gone, and Nikki and Joseph were left in the silent office. Rory's exit had taken with it every ounce of humour and life from the room.

Suddenly Joseph stood up. 'I should go and see Dr Latimer.'

Nikki frowned at him. 'In a moment, but don't you have anything to say about Chris Forbes' death?'

'What's to say, ma'am? He was killed by a military-trained operative. I knew that.'

'We'll find him, Joseph. Someone at the Paper Wall will give us an ID, then we can look for him in earnest.'

'*I* can give you an ID, ma'am, but if he doesn't want us to find him, we won't find him. End of.'

'This isn't the jungle, Sergeant, it's a market town in the Fens! You can't sneeze here without half the town offering you a hankie.' She looked at him long and hard. 'And we still have no absolute proof that it is Billy Sweet. This could be some nasty scam. Have you considered that there may

113

be someone out there who wants to get at you for putting their nearest and dearest in the Scrubs or somewhere equally as salubrious? An old case? Someone who has decided it's payback time? It does happen, Joseph.'

Joseph didn't answer, but just stared down at his feet.

'We have to be objective, you know that,' Nikki reasoned. 'It's like Martin's death. I *knew* him, and my gut tells me that someone engineered his demise deliberately, but I have to consider that it may have just been a terrible accident. Maybe some half-brain in the Wild Goose thought he looked a bit down, and stuck a little helper in his orange juice, who knows? Maybe something went wrong in the pharmaceutical factory, perhaps a rogue tablet got mixed in with others, and he'd taken it before he realised. I don't want to, Joseph, but I have to look down all the avenues.'

'I guess you're right.' His voice was low and almost husky. 'I'm sorry, ma'am, but it's hard to think about any other scenario when it all seems so clear, so vividly clear.'

'I know.' Nikki did know, but right now it wasn't helping. 'Look, maybe you should concentrate on Martin for a bit, and I head up the hunt for our assassin. I don't mean permanently, just until we've gathered a bit more information. Keep each other up to date with everything, and back each other up as and when required. How does that sound?'

'Sure.' He gave her a weak smile. 'Maybe it's for the best.'

'Okay, so bugger off to dear Helen Latimer, and the best of British.'

'What *is* it with you two?' asked Joseph, a hint of his usual humour creeping back into his voice.

'Old history, Joseph, very old history. Probably neither of us can honestly remember why we finished up as such eye-gouging adversaries, but . . .' she gave a little laugh, 'we are so used to bitching about each other that it comes as second nature.'

'Mm,' Joseph looked at her shrewdly. 'I'm willing to bet the good doctor knows *exactly* why you two don't get on. Maybe I should ask her about it.'

'Do that, sonny-boy, and you'll be back in Fenchester before you can blink!'

'Ha!' His grin widened, 'Caught you there! But when these two cases are over, I want to know *all* the sordid gossip, okay?'

'Sort this mess, and I'll be glad to sit down with the rest of that brandy, and bare my very soul! Sordid bits and all! Now, sod off, Sergeant, and find me some answers, some I can believe in.'

CHAPTER FOURTEEN

As Joseph drove towards Cloud Fen, Nikki delivered a diluted version of her report to the superintendent. She had decided not to dwell on the suggestion that Martin Durham may have met with his maker by design. It would not take much for Rick Bainbridge to remove her from the case, and any suggestion by her of foul play could be misconstrued as 'being emotionally too close.' So as far as she could, she concentrated on the death of Chris Forbes.

'Sir, we have a well-liked, although highly impressionable man, not retarded, but certainly not the brightest light on the Christmas tree, murdered by a trained killer. And we have unearthed nothing so far to indicate a motive for the killing.'

The super thought about it for a moment, then said, 'Well, it seems that he frequented public houses and pool halls, maybe he overheard something he shouldn't and the killer didn't trust him not to shoot his mouth off.'

'Possibly, sir. We'll know more when we get an ID on this man who had been hanging around with him. If the mystery man was the murderer, then it sounds as if Chris was being groomed, although for what, I can't imagine.'

'A clinical killing like this is very rare, Nikki. It's the sort of thing you hear about in war zones, not Greenborough.'

His face screwed up into a leathery mask of concern. 'As a matter of interest, what did Joseph make of it?'

Nikki used one of Joseph's own blank expressions, and said 'Much the same as you, sir. Why?'

'Just wondered.'

Joseph's past was not common knowledge, and although the superintendent knew about his background, he was unaware that Nikki also knew, and right now, she wanted it to stay that way.

'And where are we with your suicide case, Martin Durham?' continued the super.

'There is some concern over the drugs in his system brought up by the tox report. Joseph has driven out to speak to his GP about it. And nothing's shown up from the break-in at Knot Cottage.'

'Oh well, keep me up to speed on that.' He sighed and shook his head. 'And thinking about suicides, all this has rather put paid to the work that you were doing for me, hasn't it? The statistics on un-natural deaths?' His face darkened. 'You wouldn't believe it, we have an execution-style murder on our patch, and still I'm being asked for bloody useless figures and sodding reports. It's crazy.'

'We've not given up on it, sir. We'll do our best to get something together for you.' Nikki suddenly felt sorry for him. Rick had been a great copper, but slowly he had come to hate everything that promotion had brought with it. There were times when she knew that he would rather be back on the beat, than organising flow charts and initiatives, and juggling budgets. 'Don't worry, sir. Joseph is a wizard with figures, if there is an anomaly there, I'm sure he'll spot it.'

'The murder comes first, Nikki. I know that. But if you can sneak an hour or two on them sometime, I'd be grateful.'

Nikki left his office and wandered down to the canteen in search of a snack and a hot drink. Her head was a mess. Joseph was worrying her senseless and she had no one to talk to about it.

She took her lunch back to her office and half-heartedly unwrapped an unappetizing-looking sandwich. Unless there was something that Joseph wasn't telling her about this Billy Sweet, she could not fathom why some psycho should suddenly leap back from the past and start stalking him.

She chewed slowly and wondered if she should try to get some kind of trace on Sweet. Not that she had a clue where to begin. Joseph had mentioned that he had gone to work for a private security force, which sounded very much like the man was now a mercenary soldier and that meant his movements would be very hard to track. Probably impossible.

She sipped her drink. She really didn't believe that Joseph had held anything back. He honestly seemed as confused about what was happening as she did. And if he was right, and it was Sweet, why kill a vulnerable man like Chris Forbes? She picked up a pen and scribbled answers on a piece of paper.

> 1) *The super's idea. CF was silenced for knowing something.*
> 2) *The killer's a psycho, he doesn't need a reason.*
> 3) *Practice. CF was not his primary target.*
> 4) *Mistaken identity.*
> 5) *CF could have been anyone, he was killed purely to get Joseph's attention.*

Nikki ringed number 5. Then added, *To freak Joseph out.* She underlined it in heavy strokes. No matter how much she hated the thought, Joseph did seem to be the key. And if that were the case, how much longer could she keep this under wraps?

She finished her mouthful, threw the rest in the bin and stood up. She needed a recognisable face to that new 'friend' of Chris Forbes, and she needed it before the shit hit the fan for Joseph.

* * *

Joseph pulled the Ford off the main road, and headed back on himself along a narrow lane that led to a small wetlands nature reserve. He knew that he should be getting back to the station, but he felt overwhelmed by the sudden need to get away from the furore of the murder enquiry. He wanted a few minutes alone, to think. And as he had driven away from Cloud Fen, he remembered what Nikki Galena had once told him about going to the sea bank 'to get her head together.'

After half a mile he pulled into a sheltered parking area almost completely surrounded by trees and bushes. A weather-beaten painted sign told him that parking was free, although cars were left at the owner's risk. Too right, he thought. Secluded and miles from anywhere. The perfect spot for a bit of vehicle vandalism.

He locked his car and offered a small prayer that it would remain as he left it, complete with CD player, and hopefully all its wheels, then followed the path through the trees and up to the high river bank.

To his left were the lagoons, shallow watery pools frequented by waterfowl and waders, and to his right, the river bank ran for miles out into the marshes, and finally on to the estuary. It wasn't Nikki's famous sea bank, but it was the next best thing.

He looked both ways, then chose the lagoons, and seeing no one else around, wandered along the track to one of the dilapidated bird-hides.

The steps up were rickety, and the door was little better. It swung open with a creak loud enough to scare every bird on the east coast. Inside there was a weird smell of salt-damp wood and a mustiness that was less than pleasant. He opened the observation flap, hooked it up and sat on the wooden bench to look out.

At first he saw only sedge grass, reeds and the oily dark waters of the lagoons, but after a while he realised that there was movement all around him. Tiny warblers clung to the reeds, their harsh repetitive song echoing across the pools. A heron stood seemingly motionless in the shallow water, and above him a skylark's song rose and fell continuously.

He knew he didn't have long, but this was what he needed right now. A place of solitude; somewhere to put his thoughts in order. He took a deep breath, held it, then allowed his mind to go over what had just occurred at the Cloud Fen Surgery.

Predictably, Dr Latimer had been furious. She had never prescribed any form of antidepressants for Martin Durham, and flatly denied any knowledge of the other two types of tablets that he had been taking. She had stared at the photo of the plain white boxes in complete amazement, and demanded to know where he had got them from. She had then proceeded to blame Joseph and his team for not comparing Martin's medical notes with the drugs they had found at the house. It had taken a while to placate her, and even then, Joseph had finally left feeling ill at ease. Either Martin had been seeing two doctors, or he had been obtaining drugs illegally, and that just didn't gel with the kind of person that his sister and the DI had described. He had made a mental note to ring the oncology clinic that conducted Martin's yearly follow-up, maybe they could throw some light on his mixture of medication.

He stretched his aching back and watched as a curlew probed its long down-curved beak into the edge of the water searching for food. And Martin Durham was not the only problem. There was the other matter, the one he could hardly bear to think about. The fact that poor, trusting Chris Forbes might have died because of him.

He chewed on a rough nail, and tried to relax the turmoil in his head. He cursed softly. It really wasn't fair. Until the moment when he had seen that horrible face peering through his windscreen, things had been good. Really good. He had come to terms with himself. Accepted that he couldn't change the horrors of his past, but that he must not let them ruin the present or his future. He had let the bitterness of his divorce go, and made inroads to some kind of peace with his daughter. He had taken a new job with a boss that he had learnt to respect, and he'd survived an attack. Yes, things were good. Until Billy Sweet's ugly face had appeared and tainted everything.

Joseph looked down, and saw deep indentations in the palms of his hands. He had clenched his fists so tightly that his nails had almost broken the skin.

How could things swing around so quickly? How . . . ?

His mobile broke the silence, and for a second, made his heart race. He flipped it open expecting to see the guv'nor's name, but to his surprise, it was Bryony.

He stared at it, but didn't answer it. Apart from his job, she was the only happy thing in his life at present, and he was scared to get involved with her. If Sweet was after him, there would be no better way to get to him, than through a girlfriend. So for her sake he should keep his distance.

The tinny ringtone seemed to go on for ever, but finally it stopped, and the quiet in the small hut became almost deafening. Sweet was even souring his hopes and dreams.

He pushed the phone back into his pocket, then closed down the hatch. He should get back.

Remarkably the car was still there, and in one piece. 'Thank you,' he murmured to his unseen angels, and unlocked it. As he did, he heard his phone bleep, telling him that he had a text message.

"Am having a seriously shitty day. A drink would help. Would your BIG CASE allow it? Ring me. Bry"

Joseph stared at the message, his finger hovering over the reply button. If he didn't contact her, she wouldn't wait for ever. And what if he was wrong about everything? Maybe some villain from his past *had* decided to set him up for a fall. It would appear that he was still pretty shaky after his recent trauma, so perhaps he was letting his imagination get things out of proportion. By letting Bryony go, he could be ruining a chance for some happiness in his life.

He stared at his mobile phone, and felt like Don Camillo talking to JC, weighing up his worldly options against his moral conscience. With a sigh, he closed his phone and pushed his key into the ignition. JC wins. The risk was too great.

* * *

The murder room was now alive with CID officers. A series of photographs, dates, times, places and names were spread over the big glass case board. Most of it he could handle easily, but the picture of Chris Forbes' clinical assassination made him shudder every time he looked at it.

Dave Harris acknowledged him with a wave.

'Anything new, Dave?' he asked, sliding behind his desk

'Not yet, Sarge. Cat's just rung me and said they were having no luck at all. Reckoned she'd never heard the words 'average,' 'nondescript,' and 'ordinary' used so often.'

'And I suppose he always wore a hat or a hoody?'

'Exactly. Making it almost impossible to give a description.'

'Is the boss in, Dave?'

'Fuming quietly in her office. I think she'd hoped that we would have been able to circulate at least an e-fit by now.' He pulled a face. 'I hope you've got some good news for her if you're planning on going in there unarmed.'

'Thankfully I've got a few phone calls to make first.' He logged in to his computer and searched the file on Martin Durham until he found the name of the oncology clinic that he had attended. He scribbled down the number and lifted the phone.

'Oncology suite. Good afternoon. How may I help you?'

The voice sounded too young to be anything other than a Brownie, but he explained who he was and asked to be put through to whoever was in charge. After a while he was passed on to a fully-fledged Girl Guide. He swiftly explained the situation, then gave her the police station number and asked her to ring them direct to confirm his authenticity.

It took only five minutes for his desk phone to ring.

'I'd be glad to assist, Detective Sergeant Easter, but I'm afraid we do not have a patient of that name.'

'But I have copies of reports sent to a Dr Helen Latimer in Cloud Fen. Now I can understand that you would prefer not to discuss this over the phone, but . . .'

'Sorry, Sergeant, it's not that. I've checked our database thoroughly. We have never treated anyone of that name. And before you ask, I have cross-checked the spelling.'

Joseph thanked her and slowly replaced the phone. What had Helen Latimer said to him, when he first spoke to her? "I've had regular updates from his oncology clinic."'

With a frown he picked the phone back up and dialled the doctor's number. 'Yes, it *is* important.' His tone held no room for negotiation, and soon he heard Dr Latimer's voice. The woman was clearly unhappy at having her work interrupted.

'Sorry but this is urgent,' he snapped. 'I need to know if you ever recall ringing Martin Durham's oncology clinic personally.'

The woman went silent for a while, then in a considerably softer voice said, 'Now you come to mention it, there was never any need to. They always contacted me, either by phone, or by mail.' She paused. 'What's this all about, Sergeant Easter?'

'I wish I knew, Doctor. Really I do.' He thanked her and hung up. Bad mood or not, it was time to see the DI.

* * *

'Never heard of him! There has to be some mistake.'

'The administrator was adamant. I think we really need to find out a lot more about your neighbour, don't you?' said Joseph.

Nikki felt the muscles in her neck tense. It seemed as if her fears about Martin were about to be realised.

For a while she said nothing, as thoughts madly careered about in her head, then she looked down at the heap of paperwork on her desk. 'This isn't going to help either.' She tapped her finger on the files. 'The sudden death statistics that we were working on?' She gave Joseph a wry smile. 'It's all right, I'm not skiving off the murder investigation. It's just that the super is still being hounded for bloody figures, and I needed something to occupy my mind while I was waiting for Cat and her crew to get back.' She sorted out two reports and handed them across to Joseph. 'I was getting them into some form of order, and I saw a name I recognised. When I looked further, I started to feel twitchy. Look at these and tell me what you think.'

She sat back and observed him while he studied the papers. This was not the Joseph who had first come to Greenborough. That man had been calm, quietly sure of himself and completely in control. The Joseph who sat opposite her now looked drawn and preoccupied. He seemed as if his mind was in constant debate over something, and if she didn't know him better she would have said he was frightened.

After a while he looked up. 'I see what you mean, ma'am. But two other cases of suicide in very stable, apparently happy people, doesn't mean much, does it?'

Nikki shrugged. 'These are just basic summaries, no autopsies, or any other reports. I think we should check them out. Both caused something of a stir at the time, I do remember that.' She rubbed her eyes. 'I'd hate to think we missed something, and that bad things were happening to good people.'

She took the paper from him, stared at it, then dredged what she could remember from her memory. 'Amelia Reed. Age fifty-one. Bit of a local hero, in as much as she rescued and cared for stray and ill-treated animals. She drowned in her bath. No history of mental illness. There were questions as to whether it was suicide or accidental death. There were some other questions too, but I can't recall what they were. I do know an open verdict was returned.'

Joseph nodded thoughtfully. 'And the other one?'

'Paul Cousins, age fifty-two. Seen running towards the railway lines as if all the hounds of hell were pursuing him, only it wasn't hounds that caught up with him, it was the

9.45 from Peterborough. The day before he'd become a grandfather for the first time.'

'Running as if pursued,' said Joseph thoughtfully, 'Surely that's a similar scenario to Martin? And are these recent cases?'

'Within the last twelve months.'

'Maybe I should get someone to pull the full reports just in case there are any more factors that could connect them?' Joseph rubbed hard on his chin. 'Although frankly I think we may be wasting precious time.'

'Maybe, but this still has to be done.' She jabbed her finger at the statistics, 'I've no intentions of leaving the super in the brown and sticky stuff.' Nikki exhaled loudly. 'And I *know* *w*e have a violent killer out there, and he *has* to be caught. But there is something very wrong with Martin's death too, and if someone is inducing innocent people to kill themselves, then this other assassin is just as bad and equally as deadly.'

'Maybe we should hand it over to another team,' said Joseph dubiously

'And which case would you hand over, Joseph?' Nikki looked at him steadily. 'One seems to be connected to you, and the other to me.'

Joseph looked directly into her eyes but did not answer.

'Not easy is it? And although no way would I expect you to explain everything about your past to another team, I feel that I owe Martin to find out who did this to him.' She abruptly stood up and began to pace the office. 'You see I think I may have done him a disservice, unintentionally, that is.'

'Maybe I shouldn't ask this . . . ?' Joseph turned his head slightly to one side. 'And I know he was practically old enough to be your father, but was there more to your relationship than just being neighbours?'

A while ago, Nikki would have thought nothing of throwing him out of the office, but now she just shook her head, and handed him the photo of Martin, Hannah and herself. 'No never. But I think maybe I missed the signs.'

He stared at the picture. 'That he cared for you?'

'Mm. I think I was so wrapped up in my own life, my own problems, that I never saw it. That, and as you so delicately mentioned, he was such a lot older than me. I never even considered the possibility.'

'And are you basing that supposition purely on this,' Joseph passed the photo back.

'No. There's something else.' She drew in a long breath and stared at the picture. 'You know how long my daughter's been in hospital, don't you? Well, someone has been sending her a small bunch of freesias. Same day, every week, without fail. This is the first time for over a year when there have been no flowers.'

'And you think Martin sent them?'

'Who else? It certainly wasn't her father,' she said bitterly. 'That bastard visited once, then rang me and said it was all too traumatic and flew back to the States. We haven't seen him since.'

'You've tried to find out who sent them?'

'Oh yes. But they used a town florist and paid cash, via an envelope through the door. No name and no card attached.'

'It's certainly odd, but it sounds like something that will never be explained.'

'Probably not. I certainly can't ask him now, can I?'

'So what do we do about the two investigations?'

'We juggle them. The super has provided a lot of back up to help with Chris Forbes' murder enquiry, so I suggest you and I delegate as much of the leg work that we possibly can, and meantime we keep digging up all we can about Martin, and these other suspect suicides. *And* we need to see Martin's sister again. I'm damn sure she knows something that she wasn't prepared to tell us last time.'

Joseph nodded, and Nikki could see a flicker of relief in his eyes. Not that she believed it would last for long. Even if their killer was not Sweet, he seemed to be doing a good job in remaining unidentified, which kept Joseph in a permanent state of agitation. And that helped no one.

'If it helps, I'll stay on tonight and try to crunch some numbers for the super. Before all this blew up, I'd thought of a way to get a better overall view, cross forces. See what criteria they use, and how they arrive at their figures.'

Nikki hated to say 'yes' when Joseph looked so exhausted, but she had the feeling that he wouldn't rest even if he did go home. There was far too much on his mind. 'If you could, just a couple of hours would be great.' She flopped back down in her chair. 'I'll stay too, and I'll send out for a Chinese, if you like?'

'Suits me, ma'am. Mrs Blakely has threatened a corned beef hash tonight and I'm not too sure I could stomach it.'

'Mm, doesn't sound quite your thing, Joseph.'

He threw her a small smile. 'Oh I'm fine with hash generally, but I happened to see the sell-by date on the tin of corned beef. That's what's worrying me.'

'Ah, right. Chinese it is then.'

CHAPTER FIFTEEN

Cat Cullen and the others arrived back just after six. There was little to report, and nothing that would help their identification of Snaz.

'I can't believe how sodding thick some people are!' she grumbled. 'No one could give us hair colour, no distinguishing marks or tattoos, no label wear or designer clothing, and no name, other than some of them heard Chris call him Snaz.'

'And since the murder he has conveniently disappeared,' added Niall, unbuckling his heavy equipment belt.

Nikki remained impassive, she had expected little else. 'Okay, well you guys get home, grab some sleep and be back early.' She looked across at the big figure of Dave Harris, who still sat hunched over his computer, doggedly thumping on the keyboard. 'And that includes you, Dave.'

'Right you are, ma'am. I'm pretty well finished here.' He double clicked the mouse and a printer whirred into life. 'Everything I can find on Amelia Reed and Paul Cousins.' He raised his eyebrows. 'And there's quite a bit.'

Nikki took the information from him and went to her office. She had already tried to get hold of Elizabeth Durham, and been greeted by an answerphone. She had left a message asking her to get in touch as a matter of some urgency.

Now, as Joseph was flicking through reams of figures on the computer screen, there was little left for her to do but to tackle Dave's reports.

She sat back and began to thumb through them. Dave had been his usual thorough self, and even printed off local newspaper articles on the deaths. As she began to read, the stories flooded back to her.

Two deaths that had shocked their nearest and dearest to the core.

Paul Cousins' horrific method of dying had left several pasty-faced officers searching the railway line for missing internal organs, and his wife requiring long-term psychiatric treatment. Like Martin, he had no money worries, but Paul was surrounded by a close family, and the coming of the first grandchild had apparently been a total joy.

Nikki skimmed down the press cuttings, and words like disbelief, impossible, and bombshell kept reoccurring. The same words that she could use in relation to Martin.

There were similar descriptions regarding Amelia Reed, although the circumstances regarding her death were far more obscure. Did she black-out? Was she held under? Or did she drown herself? Every aspect was hacked around for weeks in the papers. As a woman, she seemed full of fire and had a real passion for helping animals. She was someone who had been known to take on gangs of badger baiters, and on one occasion, before the fox-hunting ban, a full complement of scarlet-coated huntsmen. She had climbed over walls, fences and barbed wire to rescue ill-treated dogs and various forms of livestock, and was thanked by receiving several broken bones and a criminal record.

Not exactly a scaredy-cat, were you, Amelia? thought Nikki.

She turned to another account, read it, then frowned and read it again. A neighbour had reported hearing Amelia remonstrate loudly with someone about an hour before she died, but on investigation there was no indication of anyone else ever being in the house. This was backed up by the fact that one of her dogs, a faithful and possessive Jack Russell, never barked at all during what had seemed like a heated argument.

Nikki quickly checked against the police statements, and found the name of the neighbour. She ran her finger down the details and stopped at the telephone number. This had happened a year ago, but there was a good chance that the person still lived there.

She picked up the phone and dialled.

'Mr Matthews? Excellent! Now I'm sorry to ring like this, but I was wondering . . .' Nikki explained that they were reviewing the case and needed his help. They talked for a while, then she thanked him and hung up. She could be wrong, but her gut feeling said otherwise. She grabbed the rest of the notes and hunted through for the PM results.

'Damn!' she swore out loud. Then she went over it again. There was a considerable amount of medication in her blood, but no mention of any abnormally high doses of an hallucinogen. She stared at the list of drugs, but apart from a water tablet, they meant nothing to her. She cursed again.

From Mr Matthew's description of what he had heard, Nikki could have sworn that Amelia was not arguing, but having a bad trip, shouting at demons. That would have answered the problem of no one else having been seen, and the dog not barking. But why didn't the drug show up in her blood? Maybe it was a Rohypnol type? One that did not stay in the system for long. She pushed the file to one side. That could be it, but she needed Professor Rory Wilkinson to confirm it.

Nikki's hand hung over the phone, then she stopped. Best to check out the PM on Paul Cousins first.

She scanned the report, but could find nothing from toxicology. With a small snort of irritation, she went through it again. Everything else was there, except the tox screen. 'Shit!' The one report she really needed had vanished into the wonderful never-never land of Gone Missing.

'Food's here, ma'am.' Joseph's voice calmed her somewhat. 'Shall I bring it in?'

Nikki stood up. 'No, I'll come out there. I'm just about to start dusting the ceiling with these old reports.'

'Sorry about that. I'm not doing too badly actually.' He set out several foil food trays on his desk and pulled the lids off. 'Smells good.' He passed her a fork. 'I don't think the super has too much to worry about with these statistics, you know. Whoever compiled them in the first place should be shot. On closer examination, they've omitted to take into consideration a lot of regional variables and I suspect that part of it is compiled by estimates based on out of date trends, so to be honest I . . .'

'Joseph. Speak English. And pass the soy sauce, please.' She took the sachet from him and tore it open. 'What you are saying is that the survey is crap, is that right?'

'You do have a remarkable way with words, ma'am. But in a nutshell, yes.'

'And you can prove that statement?'

'I should be able to. In fact, given a little longer I can probably produce some pretty convincing data.'

'Just enough to get the superintendent off the hook will do nicely.' Nikki eased her fork into some Singapore noodles and transferred them to her plate. 'You know what is really scary about this?'

'What the noodles?'

Nikki threw him a hopeless look. 'No, wally, the stats. If we hadn't been asked to look at them, we'd never have seen these other suspect cases.'

'And are they suspect?' asked Joseph, taking a bite out of a spring roll.

'I'd stake my pension on the fact that there's more to both of them than met the eye of the coroner.'

'That *is* scary.'

'And if we're right, will we find more?' said Nikki quietly.

'Let's sort these first, shall we?'

Before Nikki could answer, Joseph's phone rang. He flipped it open, stared at it for a while, then closed it again. As he did, his brighter mood seemed to fade.

'Bryony?' she asked tentatively.

'Bryony.' He pushed some food around his plate, but didn't eat anything.

'You think you might be putting her in danger, don't you?'

Joseph laid his fork down. 'I need proof about Billy Sweet. Without it, I'm in limbo. Damned if I do, damned if I don't.'

'It wouldn't hurt to talk to her, would it?' Nikki wondered why she was encouraging him.

'I suppose I should. I hate to keep ignoring her calls. After all, I did give her my number.'

Nikki felt a hint of something she didn't understand; something that she certainly wasn't going to start analysing right now. 'Yes. You're a lot of things, Joseph Easter, but you're not rude. So ring back and apologise.'

'Okay, I'll do it when we've eaten.'

'Do it now.'

'I need to eat.'

'Then microwave it later. Go phone Bryony.'

* * *

She watched him as she ate, and although she couldn't hear the conversation, his body language spoke volumes. Whoever Bryony was, he enjoyed her company, and from the expression on his face, she understood that the woman had forgiven his uncharacteristic bad manners.

Nikki threw away the empty cartons and her paper plate, returned to her office and wondered where that relationship was going to go.

She walked around her desk and sat down. Whatever, it wasn't her business, but this case was. And she needed to move it forward. She left a message on Rory Wilkinson's voicemail, and wondered what to do next. Elizabeth Durham was the obvious next stop, but she'd have to wait until the woman rang her.

She looked through the window in her office door and saw Joseph back at his desk, typing with one hand, and eating cooling sweet-and-sour with the other. She smiled. She should be glad for him, pleased that he had found someone. And she was. Of course she was.

With a small shake of her head, Nikki turned back to the reports and began to read.

* * *

It was almost an hour later when Joseph knocked on her door.

'I'm going to make a move, ma'am, if that's alright? I've set up a regional fact sheet. It'll take a bit longer to collate all the relevant figures, but I've got a lot of information to hand from various agencies.' He grinned at her. 'We could get a gold star from the super, *if* I get it right.'

'That's great. Good work, Joseph. Now go meet your lady.'

She wasn't sure if it was the light, but she thought she saw a reddish hue creep up his neck.

'It's just a drink. Give me a chance to explain how difficult it is when there's an enquiry running.' He looked a little like a teenager trying to explain himself. 'I'm going to try to put things on hold until . . .' he shrugged.

'I know. Until you have that proof that you are looking for.' She really did feel like his mother, and she didn't like that feeling. 'Now shut up and bugger off. I've got work to do.'

* * *

Bryony had suggested a small bar down by the river, and as it was not a regular hang-out place for policemen, he readily agreed.

She had looked hauntingly beautiful when he saw her, and he had felt a strange sadness sweep over him, because he knew that his job could prevent this relationship from ever coming to anything.

They had talked for a couple of hours, and finally Joseph confessed that he was involved in the murder enquiry that was on the whole town's lips, and that he may have to take a rain check until it was over. And then he told her that even if they did see each other, it was no picnic dating a copper. He would make arrangements, then have to cancel at the last minute. He would not get to ring her when he promised to, and sometimes he may have to work long into the night and not see her at all.

And she had simply smiled and said surely that was par for the course. If she wanted nine to five, she'd date a banker.

The only thing he didn't tell her was that he feared for her safety.

Around eleven, he called a cab and waited in the bar with her until it arrived.

'Sort your case out quickly, Joseph,' she slipped her arm through his. 'I've got plans for us.'

'I like the sound of that,' he whispered. 'And I may have one or two of my own.'

'Good. I like variety.' She laughed softly, then looked up as the taxi cab drew up outside. 'Looks like this is me. Can I drop you off?'

'No, thanks. I like to walk, and it's in the opposite direction.'

'Are you sure you wouldn't like to squeeze into the back with me?'

Joseph would have loved nothing better, but knew it was far too dangerous, for several different reasons, and all he could lamely say was, 'Soon, I promise.'

This time he kissed her. And for a moment, everything was fine in his world. As fine as it got, until he opened his eyes, and on the far side of the street he saw Billy Sweet.

'Joseph? What . . . ? Oh God, not again!' Bryony pulled herself away from him and spun around. 'Where?' she asked urgently.

'He's . . . he was right there.' He pointed towards the wall that ran along the river bank. 'Right there.'

'Then come on!'

To his horror, Bryony sprinted away from him and ran across the road. 'No!' He roared. 'Leave him!'

Bryony faltered, then turned and looked back at him appealingly. 'We can't let him get away with this Joseph, whoever he is, he can't keeping stalking you.'

'No, Bryony! He could be dangerous!' He ran across to where she stood, and put his arms tightly around her. 'At least you saw him this time.'

There was a short pause, then she said, 'Of course I did, just fleetingly. I think he went over the wall and along that towpath that runs under the bridge.'

'Did you see his face?'

'No. It's too dark.'

'And he was wearing a blasted hoody,' he whispered.

'Look, lady, do you want to go home or not? The clock's still ticking you know.'

Joseph waved to the taxi driver. 'She's just coming.' He turned back to Bryony. 'Text or ring me when you get home, okay? Just to let me know you're safe.'

She pulled her jacket around her. 'I was just going to say the same thing to you.' Her lovely face screwed up into an expression of deep concern. 'Is he something to do with your case?'

'I have no idea, Bry, but I pray he isn't.'

'Please come in the cab with me,' she urged.

Joseph walked her across the road. 'Best not. If he is watching me, I don't want to lead him to your place.'

'Then take care, Joseph. Take great care.' She kissed him again, and opened the rear door of the cab. 'Call me,' she mouthed through the closed window.

He nodded and the taxi pulled away.

Joseph walked across the road and leaned on the river wall. A little way below him the narrow towpath snaked off and under the bridge, where it disappeared into darkness. It was too late to follow him now. He might have caught him earlier, but certainly not with Bryony to worry about.

Bryony. He pushed his hands deep in his pockets and set off for home. Had he said too much? Or too little? He hadn't wanted to scare her, but then it would appear that she wasn't easily scared. Without a second thought, she had taken off like a shot from a gun. He smiled in the darkness, and she wasn't fazed by his line of work either. So maybe, when the dust settled . . . A frisson of fear snaked between his shoulder blades. He was getting ahead of himself, and there was one nasty glaring fact that he seemed to be trying to avoid. Sweet had seen Bryony. In fact, he'd seen her twice.

The shiver intensified. He'd been a fool. He should never have agreed to meet her. If anything happened to her . . . he couldn't bear to think about that possibility. Now he was desperate for her call. How long would it take? Fifteen minutes max. He bit his lip, and increased his pace. He just wanted to be back at his digs.

He strode along the river road then branched off towards Salmon Park Gardens. That was the quickest route, and now he was beginning to worry about his landlady as well. What if Sweet got in? He'd think nothing of topping an elderly woman. For her sake, he'd better stay at the nick. He was sure that the boss would make allowances for him under the circumstances. He'd pack a bag as soon as he got home, and then . . . Joseph froze in his tracks, and involuntarily clamped his hands over his ears.

Dear God! Please no! He slowly took his hands away, but still he heard it.

The empty avenue in front of him echoed with a strange, eerie wail. It was high pitched, unearthly, and horribly familiar. He'd only heard it once before, but he would never forget it. It was the terrible keening that Billy Sweet's throat had produced as he sat in front of those slaughtered women back in the Congo.

He spun around, trying to pin point where it was coming from, but then it abruptly stopped.

Joseph tensed, straining to make out any other sounds, then suddenly he smelt the stench of death, felt the humid jungle heat on his skin and heard the cries of the dying. He was back on patrol, using every sense to locate the enemy. He dropped low to the ground and crouched in the shadows, waiting.

Hearing nothing, he silently moved forward, then he caught the faintest breath of a sigh brought to him on the breeze, and it was coming from the edge of the park.

He narrowed his eyes and took careful note of the terrain, checking instinctively for obstacles and hazards. There was a jumble of shrubbery, waiting for the gardeners to prune it back, and a dense cluster of small trees forming a dark canopy. Not good, he thought to himself. Too many places to hide.

On the far side of the park, he could hear laughter. Kids yelling out obscenities to each other, then laughing again. Just stay there, he murmured, keep out of this.

He straightened up and inched further forward, looking this way and that, and feeling naked without his M-16 assault rifle.

'Oh Bunny? Bunny, where are you?'

The sing-song voice took him by surprise and bile surged up into his throat. He swung round to the direction that it came from. He'd wanted proof. Now he had it. 'Show yourself, you murdering scumbag!' he hissed.

'Over here, Bunny dear,' sang the voice, but this time it sounded more distant.

Joseph broke cover and ran towards the spot where the deranged sound had originated, but before he could reach it, he pitched forward and crashed to the ground. Something had been thrown across the path, directly beneath his feet.

He cursed, rolled over and peered around him. Then he realised that he was covered in something sticky. Something sticky, warm and reeking of copper. Or was it iron? He had never quite worked that one out. Did it matter right now? No, it didn't.

Joseph eased himself up and away from the man's body, and with a quick appraisal to check that the killer was not about to launch himself on his unprotected back, took a Maglite from his pocket and shone it down.

Corn-coloured hair, pale eyes, a grey hooded jacket, faded jeans and a throat slit from ear to ear.

There was no point in checking for signs of life. From the strange tilted angle of the head, Joseph could see into the severed windpipe. He sighed, switched off the torch, and slowly sank back so that he was sitting on his heels.

It wasn't Billy Sweet that lay on the blood-red ground, but it did look a bit like him. As Joseph pulled his mobile from his pocket and called for help, he wondered how he would feel if it *had* been the renegade soldier, the psychotic killer of women and comrades alike?

The answer was he didn't know, but however he may have felt, it had to be better than this.

He gave his location, a brief account of what had occurred, closed his phone, and sat in the purple shadows of Salmon Park Gardens and cried.

CHAPTER SIXTEEN

'Nikki? Where are you?'

She carefully negotiated a blind bend then pressed the button on her radio. 'A mile from home, Super. Approaching Cloud Fen.'

'I need you at the hospital, immediately.'

Nikki slammed on the brakes, reversed the car at speed into a farm track, then whipped it back onto the road. 'On my way, sir.'

She knew better than to ask what was occurring. Rick Bainbridge would have said if he could, but the tone of his voice had told her that it was serious, and that was enough for her.

Her headlights scored piercing darts of light across the lonely fen, and in minutes, she was screaming back down the dual-carriageway towards Greenborough.

The car park was almost empty when she got there. She left the car as close to the A & E department as she could, locked it and ran across the ambulance bay to the front entrance. She had no idea what had happened, but something nagged at her gut, telling her that it concerned Joseph. She just prayed that he had not been injured again.

She had barely set foot through the automatic doors, when the superintendent appeared from a side room and beckoned to her.

She followed him into the tiny office and closed the door. The room, a place where the triage nurse usually assessed the urgency of attention to the walking wounded, seemed crowded by the large frame of Rick Bainbridge and herself.

'Is it Joseph, sir?' That was all she really wanted to know.

'Indirectly.' The big man leaned against a trolley and folded his arms. 'It's okay, he's not injured, but he's badly shaken.' The harsh light did little for his pallor. 'There's been another murder.'

'Oh hell. Another, so soon?' She had not expected that. 'When and where, sir?'

'Just over half an hour ago, in Salmon Park Gardens.' He ran a beefy hand through his iron-grey hair. 'A white male, throat cut and no ID, as before, and Joseph had the bad luck to find him.'

Nikki closed her eyes and let the information wash over her. Joseph really did not need this right now. She thought fast. She needed to see her sergeant before the super started asking tricky questions. 'Can I see him, sir? After all he's been through he's going to need a friend with him.'

'Shortly.'

Actually, now would be good, she thought.

'I need to talk to you, Nikki.' He pointed to an uncomfortable-looking plastic chair. 'Sit down.'

It was a definite command, and reluctantly, she obeyed.

'I'm afraid, we have a problem.'

Her heart sank. This did not sound good. 'And that is?' she asked, trying to keep the anxiety from her voice.

'I asked you if you thought that Joseph had returned to work too soon, didn't I?'

Nikki nodded. 'And I categorically stated that I believed that he was fine.' She gave the man a defiant stare and said, 'And I still stand by that opinion.'

'Well, I'm afraid that I'm not so sure.' He returned her stare. 'When uniform reached the scene tonight, Joseph was in a very bad way.'

'So what! Forgive me, but two bodies and a jumper in your first days back after getting injured on duty is not what I'd call easy street, sir.'

'I agree, but when I said a *bad way*, I meant it. He seemed far more traumatised than I would have expected, Nikki.' He paused, seeming to weigh something up, then said. 'There are things about Joseph's past that you are not privy to, and let me just say that given his history, he should not have reacted in the way that he did.'

Nikki wanted to scream, but gritted her teeth and said, 'I *know* that he was a soldier, I know he was special forces, but he's still a human being, a caring and compassionate one. There's only just so much a body can take, sir. *Anybody!*'

Rick Bainbridge raised one eyebrow. 'It was my belief that I was the only one on the station to know.'

'You are, apart from me, and that's how he wants it to stay.' She gave a loud sigh. 'I'm sorry, sir, but we went through a lot together on that last case. We both shared a few secrets when it got really shitty.'

Bainbridge softened. 'I suppose you did. But I'm really worried about him, Nikki. And I'm sure you'll understand that he has to go back on sick leave for a while, and we'll need to get him re-evaluated as to be properly fit for work.'

'But that'll take forever, sir! Can't we just play it by ear, and ask Joseph how he feels about it?'

'He's on sick leave, Inspector. No buts.'

She opened her mouth to protest, then shut it again. She was going to get nowhere tonight, so she may just as well save her breath. 'Whatever you say, sir. Now can I go and see him?'

* * *

Joseph lay on a trolley and stared at them. To Nikki, his eyes seemed unnaturally dilated and his speech was slightly slurred. 'Can I go home? I want to get out of here.'

'The paramedics gave you a sedative to calm you down.' The superintendent patted his arm. 'You've had one hell of a shock, Sergeant. They won't let you leave until the doctors are happy that you're safe to be on your own.'

'I'm okay, sir. I just feel a bit woozy, that's all.'

'He can come back to my place, sir. I can keep an eye on him,' said Nikki, trying to keep her tone as matter of fact as possible.

'If it's not too much trouble, ma'am,' Joseph gnawed on his bottom lip, then looked across to the super. 'Would you ask the doctor for me, sir? Understandably I don't have the best memories of hospitals, and I really need to get out.'

Rick Bainbridge nodded, said 'I'll do what I can,' then pulled back the curtain and walked across to the central nursing station.

The moment he was out of earshot, Joseph leant forward, grabbed Nikki's hand and pulled her close. 'It was him, ma'am. No question.' His voice was little more than a whisper.

'Billy Sweet? You actually saw him at the crime scene?' gasped Nikki.

'I heard him.'

Nikki saw a shudder run through Joseph, then he said, 'Please, get me discharged. I *have* to talk to you.'

'Okay, but it'll take a while, and you need fresh clothes. Give me your key, I'll go see your landlady, tell her you're not too well, and we'll pack you a bag. You can tell me everything when we're back on Cloud Fen.'

Joseph nodded, then shivered again. 'I keep hearing him.'

'He actually spoke to you?' asked Nikki.

'He called me Bunny.' He shook his head. 'No one other than my army mates ever called me that.'

'Oh Jesus, this is a mess.'

'Tell me about it.' He leant back into the pillow and closed his eyes. After a moment he opened them and said, 'Would you do me a favour, guv? I know it's cheek, but . . .'

'Don't tell me. Ring Bryony?' Nikki asked.

'They took my clothes and my mobile for forensics. I was supposed to ring her, ma'am. She'll be worried sick, especially if she gets to hear about this new murder.'

'You know her number?' Nikki took out her own mobile and listed a new contact.

'I think so.' He murmured a few numbers to himself, then thought again and finally got it right.

Nikki punched it in. 'What do you want me to tell her?'

'Just that I'm safe, and I'll talk to her soon.' He looked up at Nikki. 'There's one good thing though.' He gave her a weak smile. 'Billy was watching us from the river walk, and this time Bryony saw him too.'

'Really? But that's fantastic!' Her hopes rose. 'Could she identify him?'

'Too dark, but she saw him, and that's what counts.'

She saw *someone*, thought Nikki, fighting back the disappointment, and that's not nearly good enough.

'Uh-oh, the super's coming back,' muttered Joseph. 'Any joy, sir?'

'Half an hour, maybe.' The super eased himself into the only chair in the cubicle.

'Great.' Nikki picked up her bag from the floor. 'He needs clothes, sir. If you are going to be here, I'll dive out and get them.'

* * *

It was almost two in the morning when they arrived at Cloud Cottage Farm, and after half three when she finally closed the door on the guest bedroom.

Nikki hadn't expected to have her visitor back quite so soon, but if she were honest, and disregarded the terrible circumstances that surrounded his second visit, it was a relief to have him there.

After Joseph had settled down to sleep off the sedative, Nikki walked out into the garden. A whole skyful of stars glittered and shone in the indigo heavens, and she sat on a wooden bench that her grandfather had made, and stared up at them. Sometimes the vastness of the skies over the marshes almost scared her. They made her feel so small, that she wondered if she, or any of her petty problems, really existed. But tonight they were her friends; they simply helped her to think.

Two men had died. Executed. Two men who bore a resemblance to someone from Joseph's past. A killer from Joseph's past to be exact.

And there her thoughts came to a halt. Stars or no stars, she could see no further.

Joseph had said that he heard Billy call out to him, but had he? Someone could have been calling their dog for all she knew.

She had met the paramedics at the hospital, and they had said that Joseph had been weeping uncontrollably when they found him, saying it was all his fault. Luckily, they had no reason to think he meant anything other than he hadn't been quick enough to save the man. Not that anyone could have saved him. He had been professionally dispatched, exactly like Chris Forbes. And making such a gruesome discovery, well, falling over it to be precise, would have hardly helped Joseph's war-torn mind. He could have imagined anything, anything at all. She sighed out loud. And *she* was the one having a go at the super for suggesting that Joseph's mental state was shaky!

Nikki drew her jacket closer around her. It was a beautiful night, but there was a chill breeze coming in from the sea. She should get some sleep herself. Joseph was probably as safe with her as anywhere, and if he had to take more leave, he would be comfortable here.

With one last look up to the stars, she shivered then hurried back inside, taking more care than usual to lock and bolt the door.

* * *

As the door closed and the light in the kitchen went out, a dark figure slid silently from his hiding place. He had been so close, so close that he could smell her perfume. Although it wasn't perfume, was it? It was a combination of shower gel, shampoo and deodorant. And then there had been coffee, and the hint of aromatic food that clung to her clothes.

The mouth smiled, but the eyes stayed as they always did. The police ate such rubbish food, it was no wonder that they rarely got to enjoy retirement.

He sighed. If he had just reached out his hand, he could have touched her. And he would like to have done that. Liked it very much. But not now. There was a schedule to stick to. An operation to see through. And that was what he was good at.

Seeing things through to the end.

CHAPTER SEVENTEEN

The morning briefing had been a hurried affair. Nikki had laid out the facts for her officers, bare bones with no embellishment, then split them into teams and put them to work.

Back in her office, she was suddenly overwhelmed by a feeling of loss; which for a dyed-in-the-wool loner was something of a new experience. She had spent most of the last two years *trying* to go solo, doing everything she could to avoid having a permanent sergeant at her side, and now her wish had been granted, she hated it.

She had spent the last part of the night unable to sleep, tossing and turning and unusually edgy. Several times she had got up and stared down into the shadowy garden, unaware of why she was doing it, but somehow just trying to calm the feeling of foreboding. But that never happened, and when it was time to get up, she still felt jittery. She had taken Joseph some breakfast on a tray, and offered him the freedom of her DVD and CD collection, not that for one moment she believed that he would be relaxed enough to enjoy anything like that. And then the realisation dawned on her that he would be marooned on Cloud Fen with no transport. Which considering the things that had happened was not a smart move, so she had promised that as soon as she was able, she'd get his car out to him. Luckily, he had left it in the staff car park when he had left to meet his girlfriend.

Nikki pursed her lips. She had spoken to Bryony as directed, and had been strangely unsettled by the conversation. Not that either of them had made anything other than extremely polite comments. Although clearly upset by Joseph's experience, the woman reacted in a sensible way, not snivelling or throwing a girly wobbler. She had expressed her concern in an intelligent manner, and for some unfathomable reason, even that had managed to irritate Nikki.

She shook her head, and decided that Joseph's love life should be very low on her priority list right now. Two murders and a suicide definitely ticked more boxes for attention than beautiful Bryony-bloody-Barton.

'Ma'am?' Dave Harris looked enquiringly at her. 'Have you got a moment?'

Nikki threw him a knowing look. 'Okay, detective, what's worrying you?'

'The Sarge, ma'am.' He took the only other chair in the office, and pulled it a little closer to her desk. 'I was reading between the lines at this morning's meeting, and I'm concerned that he's not at work today. Is he alright, ma'am?'

Nikki took a deep breath. Right now she needed an ally. And as Dave was one of the few officers on the station that she would trust with her life, maybe she was being a fool to keep the whole situation to herself. She didn't want to betray Joseph in any way, but another perspective could make all the difference.

'Because I happen to think that you are the most dependable and honest copper I know . . .' she looked at him shrewdly, 'I'm going to ask for your help, Dave. But what I'm going to tell you stays right here, with you and me, okay?'

He nodded slowly. 'Absolutely, ma'am.'

'Right, well, you asked about Sergeant Easter . . .'

It didn't take long to explain a watered-down version of the situation, one that did not involve any mention of what happened in the Congo, and at the end, Dave simply said,

'It doesn't surprise me to hear about his old career, ma'am. I'd often thought that may be the case from the way he conducted himself, but he's too much of a gentleman to be a disillusioned squaddie.' He smiled. 'I like Sergeant Easter, I have a lot of time for him, ma'am, so just tell me how I can help, and I'll do it.'

'I want you to trace Billy Sweet. Start with army records. We know his original unit, and an approximate time when he left to go to this private security force, but from there on it's going to be tricky. And Dave, not a word to anyone, not even the super. If he starts asking questions, refer him to me.'

'No problem, ma'am. But the murder room is hardly the place for a discreet enquiry, is it?'

'Work from here. Use my computer and my phone. You shouldn't be disturbed.' She scribbled down the few facts that she knew about Sweet and handed them to Dave. 'I'm going to be out for about an hour. I don't like the thought of Joseph being stranded on the marsh with no vehicle, and as uniform are stretched to the limits, I'll take his Ford myself and he can drop me back. He's not an invalid, and I've got some paperwork he can do from home.' She noted Dave's surprised look and said, 'It's not this case, don't worry. And I'm not being a slave-driver, he needs something to keep him occupied. If the super hadn't pulled rank on him, he'd be here right now.'

'I'm sure he would, ma'am. Give him my best, won't you?'

Nikki picked up the pile of folders that contained the statistics that Joseph had been working on and the info that Dave had pulled up on the suicides, and pushed them under her arm. 'Of course. And Dave, try to get us a photo of Sweet. Doesn't matter if it's old, we can always get Cat to get her techie mates to age enhance it for us.' She paused at the door. 'Thanks for this. I owe you.'

'Thanks for what, ma'am?' Dave gave her an angelic look and logged in to her computer.

* * *

'Naturally I gave him the sanitised version, I just don't want you to think I've grassed you up in any way.' Nikki looked at Joseph hopefully.

'I'd never think that.' He heaved a sigh. 'Dave is a good old boy. If I had to tell anyone, it would be him. Besides, with me in dry dock, you need someone to trust.'

Nikki opened the key box on the kitchen wall, removed a spare front-door key and handed it to Joseph. 'Keep it. It's always good to have someone else hold a house key. Martin always had one when . . .' she let the rest of the sentence fade away.

'And what on earth are we going to do about *that*?' asked Joseph fretfully. 'It was going to be tough enough with two of us, but now?' He threw up his hands in frustration, 'Why the devil did the super have to do this? I'm perfectly fit to work!'

'Then work from here. Uninterrupted, and with all the free tea and coffee you can drink.' She pointed to the folders that lay on the kitchen table. 'Drop me back to the nick, then get back here and get your head into these.'

Joseph stared at them, then gave her a grudging smile. 'Ah . . . the stats. So you mean I won't be watching twenty back episodes of *The Bill* after all?'

'The stats are only there if you have the heart to look at them, but those suicides really could do with some attention.' Her face darkened. 'I'd wager a pound to a penny that you'll find something wrong if you look hard enough.' She handed him his car keys. 'The computer is all set up in the study, along with some reference books and directories that may prove useful. *The Bill* can wait, I think. Now, if you'd be kind enough to put on your chauffeur's cap, I need to get back before I'm missed.'

As they walked to the door, Joseph gently touched her arm. 'I do appreciate you letting me stay here, ma'am. I'm not sure what I would have done otherwise.'

Nikki gave him a long, searching look, then said, 'It's okay. After all, you're not just my sergeant, you're my friend. And *please* ditch all that 'ma'am' stuff while you are under my roof, it makes me feel like some aged crone!'

'I don't think so!' He gave her arm the slightest of squeezes before letting go. 'But I guess we'd better crack on. Time is hardly on our side, and we *both* have work to do now.' He picked up his wallet from the table and held the door open for her. 'Your carriage awaits.'

* * *

Joseph dropped his boss off close to the gates of the nick, then retraced his journey back to Cloud Fen. The more times he did the trip the less the winding and dangerously narrow lanes seemed to bother him, and as he reached the bottom of Buckledyke Lane, he slowed down and stared across to Knot Cottage.

Martin Durham had certainly lived in an idyllic location, as long as you could cope with solitude.

He wound the window down, turned off the engine and sat looking at the tiny cottage. He tried to imagine Martin coming home, lighting the fire, and preparing his dinner. Now that was something he could relate to. The preparation of food was almost a spiritual thing to him. And it would appear that Martin had been a fellow connoisseur of vegetable slicing and the careful filleting of sea-fresh fish.

Before he had even made a conscious decision to go back into the cottage, he found himself out of the car and walking down the lane.

The door was closed, but the blue-and-white police cordoning tape had gone. Forensics had finished and the restricted access had been lifted. He tried the door, and to his surprise, it swung open. 'Naughty! Naughty!' he murmured, and thought that someone should have their wrists slapped for that.

He stepped inside, and was shocked to see the place almost as tidy as it had been on his first visit. SOCOs and big-foot coppers did not leave the scene in this condition, that was for sure. He moved into the kitchen, glanced out of the window, and that was when he saw the bright red

MG parked around the back. A car he had seen before, in Old Bolingbroke when they had gone to interview Martin's sister, Elizabeth.

Without delay, he quietly retraced his footsteps, through the lounge and back to the front door, where he proceeded to ring the bell.

'Yes?' An upstairs window had opened and a face looked out.

He held up his warrant card for the woman to see. 'DS Joseph Easter' He squinted in the sunlight. 'Would I be right in thinking that you are Janna Hepburn-Lowe?'

The window closed with a slam, and he heard footsteps coming down the stairs.

'May I come in?' He didn't wait for an answer, but strode past her into the lounge. 'My! You've not wasted time getting the place tidied, have you?'

The woman must have been in her forties, but her white-blonde hair, cut in a short messy style made her look years younger. She wore jeans and a bright green T-shirt with the logo 'I Support Tree Love' emblazoned across the front, and much as he would have loved to make a comment, he diplomatically decided against it.

'Martin would have *hated* his cottage being left in that state. Sorry, but I thought you lot had finished?'

'*Us* lot have, miss. It was *me* that wanted another look.'

'Ms, actually, and don't let me stop you. I'm nearly finished anyway.' She threw him an accusatory look. 'This was somebody's home you know, it was left in an appalling state. And that was apart from what the burglar did.'

'It was the intruder who trashed the place, *Ms* Hepburn-Lowe. I saw what he did.' He raised an eyebrow. 'Any idea what he was looking for?'

'What do you mean?' The woman stiffened. 'It was just some thug seeing what he could find after he'd heard that Martin was dead, wasn't it?'

'Was it?' asked Joseph. 'I certainly don't think so, and nor do you. Where is Elizabeth Durham?'

'She's gone to the tip, if you must know. Taken Martin's broken and damaged belongings.' She returned his stare with a look that reflected both hostility and fear. 'And I wouldn't bother to wait for her, she'll be ages. There was rather a lot of stuff ruined.'

'So, did you find what you were looking for?' he asked amiably.

'I think you'd better go,' she said grittily.

'And I think you'd better start telling me the truth. Or maybe your Elizabeth will get a call saying that you're down at the police station helping us with our enquiries. We take a dim view of people who waste police time.'

The woman blanched, and Joseph hated himself for being so hard, but he knew that something was amiss, and pussy-footing around would get him nowhere.

Janna suddenly lost all her aggression, and she sounded exhausted when she said. 'We found nothing.'

Joseph also softened his tone. 'Was it something very important? Something that could help us discover why he died like that?'

'Whoever broke in must have thought that, that's for sure.' Janna pointed to a seat. 'Come and sit down.' She followed him in and flopped into a high-backed armchair. 'I don't know much, I'm afraid. You'll really have to speak to Elizabeth.' She leaned forward, and stared at him earnestly. 'All I can say is that we think they were looking for paper-work regarding something that happened a very long time ago. Long before he came to live here.'

'What was he involved in, do you know?'

Janna shook her head. 'Martin wasn't *involved* in any-thing, Detective Sergeant. He was a good man. I just know something happened, but neither Elizabeth or Martin would ever say what it was.' She looked at him earnestly. 'I'm not even sure if Elizabeth knows much. I suspect Martin never told her everything, but she may know more than I do. And that's all I can honestly tell you.'

'Well, I do appreciate that, but I'll have to see Elizabeth. Will she really be ages?' He smiled at her.

''Fraid so. That was actually the truth. I said I'd meet her back at home. She was going on somewhere after the dump.'

'When you see her, would you get her to ring my boss straightaway please?' He gave her the number for the station.

Janna took the card and nodded. 'Elizabeth's already had one message to ring the DI, but we needed to get out here and see for ourselves first. Sorry about that.' She walked him to the door, then said, 'He was killed, wasn't he? I don't know how they did it, but he *was* killed.'

Joseph decided not to lie. 'Unofficially, I believe his death is suspicious, and we have to get to the bottom of it.' He gave her his most sincere look. 'We really do need your help.'

'Then I'll make sure Elizabeth phones you.'

He thanked her and walked back up the lane to his car. As he walked he rang the guv'nor on his mobile and quickly filled her in on what he'd discovered. Just before he signed off he said. 'You're right, ma'am. You really do get more done by working from home.'

* * *

Nikki may have liked the thought of Joseph calling Cloud Fen 'home' but she didn't like the look on Cat Cullen's face as she approached her. 'Okay, what's the matter?'

Cat seemed reticent to speak, but finally said, 'I'm a bit concerned, guv, about these murder victims? I'm supposing that you've noticed that they are both dead ringers, pun not intended, for the bloke you asked me to find. The bloke who was hassling the sarge?'

'Not the sort of thing that's easy to miss, actually.' Nikki wondered how long it would be before she had to let *all* of her staff in on the full story. 'Have we got a name for the latest victim?'

'We think he's David Ryan, also from the Carborough Estate, ma'am. His wife reported him missing this morning. He fits the description, so we've sent a car to collect her. Poor cow, she's got two little kids.' Cat jammed her hands into her jeans pockets, then looked up directly at Nikki. 'Is the sarge involved in this in some way?'

'He may be, Cat,' said Nikki carefully. 'But until we're certain, I can't say.'

'An old case come back to haunt him?'

'Could be.'

'Then I'd like to help, ma'am. If there's anything I can do, you know me, I'd rather slit my wrists than betray a confidence.'

Nikki did know that, and hated keeping those closest to her in the dark, but she had Joseph to consider.

Cat was still speaking. 'Sergeant Easter is a pretty cool guy in my book, ma'am, and I wouldn't like to think that he was in deep shit and I'd not helped to dig him out, so to speak.'

'Then keep trying to find the man that Chris Forbes had been hanging around. Find me Snaz.' She stopped. 'But Cat, if you do, don't you dare try to apprehend him, understand? He could be the most dangerous man you'll ever meet.'

Cat pulled on her denim jacket. 'Wilco, guv. I'm onto it, and this time I'll find something.' With a determined expression, she turned and left the room.

Nikki walked back to her office, and found Dave studying a computer printout.

'Great timing, guv. We've got a picture coming through. It's about ten years old, but it's something.'

Nikki nodded. She was desperate to see what Billy Sweet really looked like. 'Is it from his old regiment?'

'No, it's an unofficial one that I sourced from an Internet site set up by ex-military personnel. An old mate of mine used it to find an old para comrade.'

'I can't think that anyone sane would want to tie up with this creep. What's he doing on a site like that?'

'He's not listed as a contact, guv. I was checking out his old unit, and he's in the background of a group shot that someone posted. There's a list of names beneath it and the computer search homed in on it.'

'Good work, Dave. Anything from official channels?'

'Plenty, I'm working through it now, but as you said, the trail goes decidedly chilly when he got himself discharged and went private. Oh, and before I forget, the super rang down a few minutes ago. Wants to see you.' A whirring sound interrupted him. 'Ah, here's the photo now. It's been cropped and enhanced to isolate your man.' He took the sheet from the printer tray, looked at it, then passed it to her.

In one fleeting glance, Nikki believed everything Joseph had ever told her about Billy Sweet.

He looked to be in his mid-twenties, with a deeply tanned face and close-cut blond hair. He was holding what Nikki thought may be a grenade launcher, and was wearing camouflage fatigues. He was smiling at the camera, but when Nikki looked closer, his eyes made her shudder. It was as if the flash had deadened them somehow, made them look cold and lifeless. But somehow she knew that if she ever had the misfortune to meet this man, this was exactly what she would see.

'That's good enough, Dave. Skip the age enhancement.'

Dave took it back and stared at it. 'Fair gives you the willies, doesn't it? He's holding that weapon like anyone else would hold a baby, like he loves it.'

'But his eyes are not exactly loving, are they?'

'Straight from the freezer, ma'am.' Dave gave a theatrical shudder. 'There's definitely something missing from that young man.'

'The human part, I think. Print off a load of these, Dave, but only give them to the team. Much as I'd like to swamp the streets with them, I need a bit more proof before I go public.' She pulled out her phone. 'And Cat will definitely need one.'

Cat let out a little whoop of delight into her mobile. 'Great! That will certainly help. On my way back up, ma'am.'

'I've got to see the super, pick it up from Dave. And for the time being this is just between us. Good hunting.' She closed her phone and turned to Dave. 'Did the super say what he wanted?'

'No, ma'am. But he sounded pretty harassed.'

'Wonderful. I'd better get up there.'

'Guv, how much does Cat actually know?'

'Not nearly as much as you, although I can't leave her in the dark for much longer.'

'Don't worry, I won't be gossiping. I'm too damned busy.'

* * *

When Nikki reached the super's office, he was not alone. Standing by the window, with a sheaf of papers in his hand was Chief Superintendent Ian Walker. Not a man who had ever endeared himself to Nikki, in fact she disliked him intensely, and the feeling was probably mutual.

'Sorry. I'll come back later.' She made to leave, but to her annoyance the super called her back.

'We both need to talk to you, Nikki. Have a seat.'

She looked from one to the other, and felt a sinking feeling in her gut. Just like the old days! 'Something wrong, sir?'

'We don't know. We have some serious concerns, and would like your opinion.'

The chief placed the papers on the desk, perched on it, just a few feet from her face, and stared directly at her. 'DS Joseph Easter. I understand he's on sick leave?'

Nikki nodded uneasily. 'That's correct, sir. Superintendent Bainbridge thought he might be stressed by his recent discovery of the body in Salmon Park Gardens.'

'And what do *you* think about him, Inspector?' The man's eyes glittered like a hawk spotting a juicy plump pigeon.

'I think he's had a rough few days, but all things considered, I believe he is handling everything exceptionally well.'

'So you don't think that he may have returned to active duty too soon?'

'Not at all. He's functioning perfectly well. In fact, as we speak he is working from home on some statistics for the superintendent, voluntarily, of course.' She smiled benignly.

'Mm.' To Nikki's relief, he stood up and returned to his eerie by the window.

'Sir?' Nikki turned to Rick Bainbridge. 'What's happened? Why the third degree?'

The super shook his head. 'It's nothing like that, Nikki. We are just worried about him. About his mental state.'

'Look at this from our point of view,' chipped in the human bird of prey. 'A man who has suffered serious trauma recently returns to work, and in three days is confronted by a broken body in the river, an execution-style slaying, and then falls over a recently butchered man in the park. Do you blame us for asking his senior officer as to whether he's holding up or not?'

Nikki gritted her teeth so tightly that her jaw ached. 'Of course not, sir, I'm just not sure that you are listening to my opinion.'

'There is another thing,' said the chief, completely ignoring her comment. 'And I'm referring to last night's murder. I have spoken personally to both the scene-of-crime officers and the pathologist, and other than blood evidence belonging to the victim, DS Easter's prints are the only others there. There is nothing to be found on the body, and the scene is free from any other contamination or evidence.'

Nikki's eyes narrowed. 'And what exactly does that mean?'

'Think about it, Inspector. But before you do, is it true that the sergeant was upset by some man leaping in front of his stationary vehicle the other day?'

'What on earth has that got to do with the murders?'

'The man in question looked very much like the two dead men, didn't he?'

Nikki heard the sound of blood rushing in her ears. She had no idea how the chief had got hold of his information, but she really didn't like where the conversation was going. 'There was a vague resemblance, I suppose.'

'I put it to you, Inspector, that there was a marked similarity! I find it very worrying to have two men murdered in this town, who both resemble a man who has upset one of my officers.' Walker slowly blinked his hooded eyelids.

'Surely you can't think that Joseph has anything to do with these deaths?'

'The killings were carried out by a military-trained assassin. Sergeant Easter, as I believe you already know, has a military background. And thinking about it, he was also in the vicinity of the first murder, in fact he is the only person identified on the railway station's CCTV around the time of death.'

'*You*, sir, are accusing Joseph of double murder?'

'No, I'm not, but I'm going to have to suspend him pending further enquiries.'

'What!' She jumped up.

'Nikki, please.' The super stood up, his eyes begging Nikki to calm down. 'Just hear us out.'

She flopped backward like a rag doll, and stared up at Rick Bainbridge. This wasn't happening. 'Suspension?' was all she could say.

He looked sadly at her. 'For his own sake, until we are satisfied that Joseph is in no way involved in all this, he must be relieved of his duties.'

'Involved?' Nikki's voice was husky.

'Joseph has to undergo a psychiatric evaluation. We have to rule out that he has not suffered more trauma than we suspected.'

'Sir, I know I'm no shrink, but Joseph is not capable of something like that, and he is perfectly well-balanced.' Her temper was rising again, and it was getting hard to hold it back. 'God! Just because he cried after he'd fallen headlong over a horribly mutilated man, you all seem to think he's a fruitcake! I'm telling you, anyone would have cried, I would and you would! It was a natural reaction. There's nothing wrong with Joseph's brain.'

'It's not his brain we are talking about, Nikki. It's his mind. And you know that.'

She did. And she knew an awful lot more than the super or the bloody chief, but for the time being, she needed to keep that very close to her chest.

A heavy silence descended over them, then the super said, 'He's still staying with you, isn't he?'

'Yes, sir,' she muttered. 'For as long as he wants.'

'Then I'll come over and see him this evening. I'll explain everything, and we are all just going to have to work doubly hard to sort this out.'

'This will devastate him, sir. After all he's been through, he's a bloody hero, and this is what happens. Great force we work for, I don't think!'

The tall, bird-like man at the window coughed loudly. 'I am still here, Inspector. And I suggest you save your vitriolic comments for the mess room.' He held her gaze fixedly. 'Or the sergeant may not be the only one in hot water.'

Nikki bit her tongue and decided that if anyone ever wanted to murder the chief, she'd probably go find them a suitable weapon. But then again, she didn't want to get thrown off the case, for Joseph's sake she had to find the killer. Which meant it was time for humble pie, no matter how sick it made her feel.

'I'm sorry, sir. It's just the shock. Sergeant Easter is a damned good officer, and all this seems surreal, but I shouldn't have lost my temper, I realise that.'

'Apology accepted.' Then he added, in a pompous tone, 'On this occasion.'

'Thank you, sir.' She looked down, trying hard not to follow it up with "You self-opinionated, arrogant git." 'May I go, sir? I need to get my head round this.'

The super nodded. 'I'll see you tonight. Around seven,' he paused, 'and Nikki, I'd appreciate it if you left it to me to break the news to Joseph. Correct procedure and all that?'

'Oh, you're welcome, sir.'

* * *

Having spoken to Janna Hepburn-Lowe and finally getting something positive out of her, Joseph felt better about his enforced sick leave. Maybe he really could put the time to good use, and perhaps it was safer for everyone else if he kept a low profile until someone got a handle on Billy Sweet.

He made himself a coffee, and as he stirred in a spoonful of sugar, admitted to himself that he was having difficulty even thinking about what had happened the night before in Salmon Park Gardens.

He took his coffee to the study, placed it on the desk and pulled a music album from Nikki's CD rack. As the melodic strains of Coldplay wafted around the small room, he tried to fathom what had caused his ridiculously over-emotional reaction to what had happened. Sure it had been a shock, but he'd seen far worse on the battlefield and not turned into a blubbering bag of jelly.

In his mind he saw again the carnage caused by a roadside bomb, then he saw his friend Gerry get ripped in two by a pressure mine. Terrible things, but things a career soldier learnt to cope with. But last night had been too weird to explain, and so had his behaviour afterwards. In truth, there were parts he didn't remember too well, but the medics had given him a sedative, so perhaps that would explain the blank bits.

He flopped down at Nikki's desk, and pulled the files towards him. Maybe he shouldn't even try to analyse his actions. Stress did funny things, and he'd sure been stressed of late.

He opened one of the statistics files, and turned to the computer. As he had uninterrupted time to kill, he'd get the stats put to bed first. That would keep the super happy, and then he would be able to throw all his energies into working on the Martin Durham case. He allowed himself a small smile, but he'd do all that, *after* he'd phoned Bryony.

He tapped her number into the desk phone and waited. Maybe it was his imagination, but he was certain that his heart rate had risen. After half a dozen rings, she answered, and her relief at hearing him for herself flooded down the phone.

'Joseph! I was worried sick! I didn't know what to think.'

'I'm so sorry. I would have contacted you if I could, you do know that, don't you?'

'Of course, that's why I was so frightened. I knew that you were not the type to just ignore me. I knew something must have happened. And thank your boss for me, would you? Her call was much appreciated, although she didn't tell me much other than you were okay and would contact me when you could.'

'I'm not surprised, Bry. She couldn't have said more, there had been another murder, and I was the one to find the body.'

He heard a soft gasp from the other end.

'I'm fine though, honestly,' he lied.

'Was it anything to do with your stalker?' Her voice was low, as if she didn't want to be overheard.

'It may have been, Bry. I think he killed the man that I found, but I have no proof. Still, at least you saw him. Up until now it's just been me, but you being there last night will make all the difference. Now I know that I'm not going mad!' He passed the receiver to the other hand and leaned back in the chair. 'The thing is, I want to see you, really I do, but until I've found out what this is about, I dare not. Do you understand what I'm saying?'

'Sadly I do.' She gave a little humourless laugh. 'Just my luck! I meet the most gorgeous bloke, and for once he's not gay or married, he doesn't work on an oil rig, and he doesn't suffer from halitosis or Saint Vitus Dance, but he's still about as inaccessible as a nun's knickers!'

Joseph laughed. And it felt good. 'Sorry. But I will make it up to you, I promise.'

'You'd better. Now, are you sure we couldn't meet somewhere? Somewhere where no one knows either of us? Just for a coffee, maybe?'

Every inch of him yearned to say yes, but there was no way he would risk Bryony crossing paths with Billy Sweet again. He shivered. 'Absolutely not.'

'Oh well, worth a try. But I can ring you, can't I?'

Joseph hadn't told her where he was, or that his blood-covered mobile was sitting in a laboratory in a sealed bag. 'Best I ring you for a day or so, Bry. My phone got damaged and I haven't had time to organise a new one. I'll ring you on a landline, until I'm up and running again.'

'Then I guess that will have to do, but if you don't ring, I may have to get myself arrested, just to get to see you.'

'I'll ring. I promise. Bryony, I can't wait to see you again. You're very special, you know.'

'So are you, Joseph. Ring me tonight?'

'Try to stop me.'

It had been hard to hang up. And he had been right about his heart rate, because his pulse was racing. With a shaky laugh at himself, he finished his coffee, and returned to the super's statistics with renewed vigour.

* * *

As the end of the day approached, Nikki was strung out like a high wire. There was no news from Cat, Dave was embroiled in his hunt for Sweet and with no Joseph to bounce ideas off, she felt completely exasperated. And she dreaded going home.

As the hours ticked by, she had felt more and more aggrieved by the fact that they were going to suspend Joseph, but at around four thirty when Dave went for a break, she sat alone in her office with a large sheet of white paper and a marker pen, and brainstormed everything she knew. After ten minutes, the paper was covered by scribbled words, and Nikki was beginning to feel decidedly uncomfortable. She may hate what the chief superintendent was doing, but she could see where he was coming from. He had to be very careful, and he was covering both his own and the Fenland Constabulary's back.

Nikki stared at the paper, and suddenly one word stood out. The name Bryony. She had *seen* the man who Joseph believed to be Billy. And Nikki needed to know exactly what kind of witness she would be.

She pulled out her phone and clicked on Contacts.

The phone answered almost immediately, and Nikki apologised if she was interrupting anything important.

'Only a coffee break, although with my workload at present, a break is like gold dust. How can I help you?'

Bryony sounded pleasant and relaxed. Far more so than the night before.

'Joseph tells me that you saw a man watching him, by the river wall at 11.10 last night, is that correct?'

The woman hesitated, before saying. 'You know that Joseph is terrified of him?'

'I do, but could you answer the question, please? What did he look like?'

Again there was a pause, and Nikki began to get both irritated and concerned.

'It was very dark, I hardly saw anything, although I think he had a hoody.'

'How tall, what build?'

'I'm not sure. I . . . well, oh damn it! No, Inspector, I never actually saw him.'

'But you told Joseph that you did!'

'Oh, I know I shouldn't have, but he was *so* distressed because he was the only one to ever spot him, that . . .' Bryony didn't sound so relaxed now. 'I'm sorry, I just couldn't bear to tell him that I hadn't seen the man for the second time.'

'You really saw no one at all?' asked Nikki, carefully enunciating every syllable.

'There was no one to see, Inspector. I turned around and the path by the river wall was empty. Even if he had jumped over and dropped down onto the towpath, I'm sure I would have seen him,' she sighed loudly. 'I'm sorry if I did wrong, but I really like Joseph, and I hated to see him so disturbed.'

'We *all* really like Joseph, Miss Barton, but lying won't help him one bit.' She knew her tone was frosty, but Bryony had just dashed her one hope of keeping Joseph out of trouble. She stared at her paper sheet, and put a thick cross through the name Bryony, her only witness to the fact that Billy Sweet even existed.

After she hung up, she stared again at the paper. One section said, *Chris Forbes, Railway station. Beale Street. No witnesses. No CCTV. Only one to see a stranger in the shadows, Joseph.*

The next section said, *Man in lane by nick. No CCTV footage. Seen only by Joseph. And she had been there then, and she saw no one other than the people on the CCTV.*

Man seen at river wall, only by Joseph.

Salmon Park Gardens. No witnesses. Only Joseph present.

Nikki's mouth had dried to a degree where it was almost impossible to swallow.

She thought hard about what she knew about him.

Joseph Easter, ex-Special Ops, suffered PTSD after a bodged operation in Africa, went on a journey of personal discovery before joining the police force. Admirable officer, makes detective sergeant then loses his DI at Fenchester and gets a temporary transfer, to a division where a bad case leaves him hospitalised.

Nikki's mind raced. Okay, so he'd had a tough life, but he had been fine until that man had appeared in the road in front of him.

That was the pivotal point. Everything that had happened, happened after that.

With a snort of disgust she grabbed the pen and looked at all the sections again.

Fact, she scribbled, *the CCTV at the nick is crap. Known black-spots, and they were exactly where Billy had stood. Fact. Joseph **could** have seen him.*

*The station. Poorly lit and poor security. Cab was not in the same line of vision. Fact. Joseph **could** have seen a man in the shadows.*

The river. Bryony was obviously totally wrapped up in the gorgeous Joseph's arms. The man could have shown himself to Joseph, then before she could stop dribbling over the sergeant and turn around, he could have vaulted the wall and run away. Not exactly fact, but possible.

And the second murder. The assassin could have been dressed in protective gear to make his kill. There was no CCTV in that part of the gardens. Fact. Joseph could have been set up.

She pushed her chair back and let out a long shuddery sigh. It didn't look good, and all right, she now understood why Walker was shitting hot bricks, but it was by no means cut and dried. And if Billy Sweet was the jungle guerrilla that Joseph said he was, then he would be easily clever enough to avoid cameras and witnesses. He'd survived war zones, Greenborough would be kid's stuff.

'Sorry, ma'am. Can I get on, or is it inconvenient?'

She had been so involved in her thoughts that she hadn't heard Dave enter. 'Come on in.' She folded up the paper, pushed it into her drawer and stood up. 'All yours.'

'Oh, before I start, the Salmon Park Gardens victim has been positively identified as David Ryan. His wife has also confirmed that he's been spending some time with some new mate, a guy who seemed to just show up one day when her husband was tinkering with his car. Dead helpful, apparently, but the wife never actually saw him.'

'Name?' asked Nikki, already knowing what she would hear.

'Just called him Snaz, guv. No name, no description. Ryan just told her that he was a wizard with engines.' Dave eased behind her desk, clicked on the emails and began printing them off. 'Ah, reams more info, I see.'

'I'll leave you to it, but don't work too late, will you? Your lovely wife needs you even more than me.' She walked towards the door, then heard a groan behind her.

'Hold up, ma'am. I think you'll want to see this.' Dave's voice was sombre. 'It's the copy of a death certificate. Billy Sweet is dead. Has been for four years.'

* * *

It had taken Nikki some time to assimilate the bombshell that Dave had delivered, and the first thing she wanted was confirmation that the certificate was kosher.

'There's little doubt, ma'am.' Dave produced several other documents. 'He was involved in something on the

Colombia/Ecuador border in South America. Containing marauding paramilitary groups, it says, and fighting with a small private force. A report states that Sweet died along with three others. Their Land Rover was ambushed.' He shrugged. 'No survivors.'

'Was he flown home for burial?'

'Doesn't look like it, guv. He was estranged from his family, and not being in the army anymore, I can't see anyone forking out a fortune to get him back, can you?'

'Probably not.' Nikki's head was still spinning. 'Who identified the body?'

Dave thumbed through several sheets of paper. 'Another ex-British army, turned soldier of fortune, by the look of it. Ah, and it says here that his personal effects were returned to England, where they were collected some while later by a relative. His body was interred in Colombia. There's a note of the location, some unpronounceable place outside Bogotá.'

'No chance of mistaken identity, then?'

'I'll dig deeper, ma'am. But there's an awful lot of official paperwork here, and it all looks pretty authentic.'

'Try to trace the man who identified the body, Dave. Several years have passed, maybe he's back here now. Get all the details you can, okay?'

'No problem, ma'am But would tomorrow be alright? I really need to get home.'

Nikki nodded. 'Of course. And thanks for what you've done today.'

'Not quite what we wanted to hear, though, ma'am.'

'You can say that again.' Nikki's brow furrowed. 'Where do we go from here?'

Dave tidied the paperwork into neat piles. 'Are you going to tell Joseph?'

'Good question, but I think not. Well, not just yet, he's got enough on his plate right now. So, Dave, keep this quiet for a bit longer, okay?'

Dave gave her a reassuring smile, and tapped the side of his nose. 'Mum's the word, guv. Give him my best.'

Alone in her office, Nikki stared at the death certificate. This changed everything. The last thing in the world that she wanted was for Chief Superintendent Walker to be right about Joseph's state of mind. If she were honest, she'd hate him to be right about anything at all. Sadly though, most of the aces that she thought she had up her sleeve were proving to be jokers, and Walker's case was becoming stronger by the minute. Nikki leaned back in her chair, and let out a long, audible sigh. She had rarely felt so confused, but no matter how bad she felt she needed to get home to Cloud Fen, and get there before the super. The least she could do was warn Joseph of what was to come. And procedure could go to hell.

CHAPTER EIGHTEEN

If she had felt bad before, now she felt like a complete shit.

Joseph had opened the door, a satisfied grin on his face, and presented her with a completed set of revised statistics for the superintendent. *And* she could smell something aromatic emanating from her kitchen.

'It's not much, hope you don't mind but I raided your frugal freezer and Spartan store cupboard and threw something together for supper.'

'Of course I don't mind. But surely nothing from my larder could smell that good?'

'Well, I did stop at that little farm shop just off the marsh lane, and picked up some fresh vegetables to bolster it up a bit.' He walked back to the kitchen and checked the stove. 'I thought we'd eat just after seven, if that's okay?'

Nikki's heart sank. At seven they would be receiving an uninvited guest. 'There's something I have to tell you, Joseph.'

'Shall we talk over a glass of wine?' He stood in front of her, a bottle of white in one hand, and a red in the other. 'You choose.'

'Whatever, just make it a large one.' There was no easy way to tell him. 'Joseph, Chief Superintendent Walker collared me this afternoon.'

'Haven't met him yet. Isn't that the guy who looks like a carrion crow wearing gold braid?'

'You got it, and he's after blood, Joseph. Yours.'

'Mine?' He handed her a glass of sparkly white wine, then stepped back and stared at her. 'Why?'

Nikki looked at him miserably. 'It seems top brass, in their infinite wisdom, are concerned about your health.' She took a slug of wine and shook her head in disgust. 'The super is coming here tonight to talk to you, and I want you to be prepared for the worst. He said they may be suspending you for a while.'

Joseph turned back to the hob, picked up a spoon and stirred whatever was in the iron pan. After a while, he said. 'I had a feeling this was going to happen.'

'Well, I didn't!' exploded Nikki. 'And I damn well told them so!'

Joseph gave a humourless chuckle, but kept his back to her. 'I'm sure you did. And I'm sure you got a bollocking for your trouble.'

'Sort of,' she muttered. 'Well, yes I did, and then I had to grovel to that beady-eyed, beak-nosed prig in order to stay on the case.'

'But it worked, didn't it?' Joseph turned quickly and she saw deep concern in his eyes. 'You are still on it?'

'Yeah, it worked. And I'm still leading. Just.' She took a slower sip of wine this time. 'And don't worry, Joseph. I promise to get to the bottom of this.'

'To be honest, everyone maybe safer with me out of the way for a while.' His voice lacked power and had a wistful tremor to it.

'I'm not sure I agree with that, but I'm going to get every available officer onto this. I want it cleared up fast. I want my sergeant back.'

He looked at her over the rim of his glass. 'Me too.'

'Do me one favour?'

'Of course.'

'Don't tell the super I warned you. You know, protocol, procedures and all that crap?'

'No problem. But how should I react? Shocked? Because I'm not. Angry? I'm disappointed, but not angry.' He shrugged. 'I don't know how I feel actually.'

'Then tell him that. Be honest.' She sat down at the kitchen table and looked up at him. 'And we need to be honest with each other too, Joseph. These killings have to stop, and you and I are going to have to explore the mind that is carrying them out. I *have* to find out what his endgame is, and stop him before he gets that far.'

'I'm not sure how you will achieve that, Nikki, but I'll help you all I can.'

'Thank you, Joseph.' Nikki gave him a long look. She had just said about being honest, and she was being far from that. If he knew that Billy Sweet was long dead, what would it do to him? Well, she wasn't about to find out. She needed a lot of answers to a lot of questions before she hit him with that little rocket.

'Do you think the super will want supper? I seem to have cooked enough for the whole team.'

'Probably not. I doubt he'll have much appetite after practising what to say to you.'

'He's got no choice, has he? If the order comes from higher up, he's just the mouthpiece, and I respect Superintendent Bainbridge.' He gave her a half-hearted smile. 'I won't give him a hard time.'

'I'll disappear when he gets here. Give you some privacy.'

'No. Stay. Please?'

'Who could resist such a plaintive plea?' Nikki smiled back. 'Sure I'll stay. I respect Rick Bainbridge too, and I like him, but I still think he deserves a bit of stick, don't you?'

'Okay, but nothing too harsh.' He sat down opposite her. 'You may need to keep him on our side.' He drew in a breath. 'At least I've done his figures, and I think he'll like the results. Now I can concentrate on Martin Durham.'

'You want to continue?' asked Nikki, trying to keep the surprise out of her voice.

'It'll have to be in an unofficial capacity, but I can follow up the other suicides using public sector info, can't I?'

'If you're okay with that, I'll get you everything you need. Well, as much as I can without dropping us both in the mire. At least it's a way to keep all our balls in the air, so to speak.'

'You nail Billy for me, Nikki, and I'll find you some answers about Martin. Deal?'

Nikki felt a shiver pass across her shoulders. Someone had already nailed Billy. So who was she chasing now? 'Deal,' she said with as much enthusiasm as she could muster, 'and the sooner the better. Now, what exactly is in that pan on the stove?'

* * *

Rick Bainbridge did eat with them, then left at around nine, with Joseph's warrant card safely in his inside pocket.

Joseph had pulled out all the stops to make the task easier for the super, too many for Nikki's liking, but then it wasn't her being suspended. Joseph had to deal with it as he saw fit.

After they had cleared up the supper dishes, Nikki poured them both a snifter of her father's cognac and they talked for another hour before she turned in. As she pulled her bedroom curtains she reflected on what a world-class shitty day it had been. She had had such high hopes for her new team, and in just a few days everything, in the immortal words of Dave Harris, had gone to rat-shit. Somehow she needed to get her finger out and find Joseph's murdering stalker.

With a sigh she sunk into her bed and pulled the duvet around her. And now thanks to her beloved chief, she was without her sergeant. 'Great, fucking great,' she whispered as she closed her eyes.

* * *

Joseph stood at the window and looked down into the shadowy garden below. A few hours back he had come a hair's breadth from going out to meet Bryony. He had phoned her as promised, and they had talked for over half an hour and although the whole thing had a teenage dream feel to it, he liked it and it relaxed him.

Now it was after one in the morning, and he was far from relaxed. Not that he should be too worried about the late hour, he had no work to get up for. The plain fact was the news of his suspension had floored him. He had done his best to cover his true feelings, but he was devastated. Going right back to his school years, he had been conscientious and hardworking, and he'd never been 'removed' from anything in his life. And now, with his movements severely restricted, he was going to have to find a way to get to Billy through Nikki.

For a while he paced the room, but the old floorboards creaked and he didn't want to disturb whatever sleep she may be lucky enough to get, so he pulled on a sweater and quietly slipped out.

Making sure that he had his door key in his pocket, Joseph left Cloud Cottage Farm and walked down the moonlit lane to the marsh. He needed to think what his next move would be.

More to the point, he needed to think what Billy's next move would be. And he needed to think fast, before someone else died.

Joseph was not the only one who could not sleep. Nikki's mind had no intentions of letting her switch off, and highest on her list of insomnia-inducing problems was Joseph and his conviction that a dead soldier was going around killing the residents of Greenborough.

She tossed around trying to get comfortable, but only succeeded in losing the duvet. She dragged it back from the floor and then pummelled her pillow angrily before flopping back into it. No matter how bad it looked, and Jesus, right now it looked sodding dreadful, she could not bring herself to believe that Joseph was involved in any way other than an involuntary one. There was obviously a connection, but what it was she could not begin to understand, and the dead of night was not the best time to be logical.

Nikki squeezed her eyes tight shut and decided it was time for the word game. She needed to slip her brain into a different gear, and the game usually worked. Take a letter of the alphabet and name all the film titles you could. She shifted to her side. Last time it was *F* so . . .

Genevieve, Gigi, The Great Escape, The Great Gatsby.

What if Joseph really were still suffering from the aftermath of his attack? What if the man who pulled a face at him through his windscreen reminded him of other horrors, African horrors?

Concentrate, Nikki. *Gallipoli, Gremlins, Guess Who's Coming to Dinner?*

And what if all that trauma came bubbling back to the surface? What if . . . ?

She yawned. *The Green Mile, Ghost, Gone With the Wind.*

First thing in the morning she'd talk it through with Dave. And maybe Cat. Dave had experience and age on his side, but Cat had intuition and an almost feral streetwise instinct about her. She had the feeling that she would be needing them both.

Gothika. Get Carter. Ghostbusters.

As sleep began to gently dull her senses, she vaguely heard footsteps on the stairs, but told herself that it was no wonder Joseph was awake. All evening he'd seemed so in control, but she was sure that deep down he was hurting. She wondered if she should go down and keep him company, but before she could make a decision, she drifted unresisting, into the arms of Morpheus.

CHAPTER NINETEEN

Her waking moment was a far less peaceful affair, with her alarm shrieking in one ear, the phone blaring in the other.

'DI Galena,' she mumbled, still trying to silence her clock with her other hand.

'Nikki, can you get in, pronto?' The superintendent sounded out of breath.

'Yeah, of course.' She scrambled from her bed, still holding the phone. 'What's happening?'

'I'll tell you when you get here. Quick as you can.' The phone clicked, then hummed softly. Damn! She flung the receiver back in its cradle then hastily pulled her duvet up in a poor semblance of tidiness. A shower would have to wait. As would breakfast. She pulled clothes swiftly from drawers and cupboards, then hoping she didn't look too much of a rag-bag, hunted for some shoes.

As she moved along the landing she saw that Joseph's door was still closed, but hearing the soft, sonorous sound of his breathing, she ran down the stairs, scribbled him a note, and dashed to her car. The super had left her in no doubt regarding urgency, but she just wished he'd told her why. Guessing, these days, was a pretty unnerving pastime, and her imagination was already on high alert.

As she swung past the lane to Knot Cottage, she felt a pang of sorrow tug at her heart. Martin was being put on the back burner again and that was not how she wanted it to be. Luckily Joseph was still game to keep delving, which was something, but it wasn't her, and she still felt horribly guilty about her promise to her old friend.

And this melancholia was getting her precisely nowhere.

With a grunt of irritation at herself, she pulled up onto the main road, and jammed her foot down. Something had happened, and she needed to know what the hell it was, and she wouldn't do that by dawdling along like a bloody tourist.

She didn't quite beat her PB for speed from Cloud Fen to the nick, but it had been an impressive ride, and most effective in concentrating her wandering thoughts. As she strode through the foyer, she had left the weak, sensitive woman wandering somewhere on the marsh, and she was now one hundred per cent tenacious detective again.

'The super?' she barked to the desk sergeant.

'Murder room, ma'am. With the chief.'

She raised a hand in acknowledgement, and cursed under her breath. Walker was rarely seen at this hour, and his presence didn't bode well.

'Nikki.' The super looked grey, and she guessed that he'd had about as much sleep as she had. 'Sorry to drag you from your bed but there's been another incident.' He glanced across to the chief, who looked irritatingly immaculate and very well rested, and said, 'Shall we take this into my office?'

After the door closed, he said, 'There was an attempted abduction in the early hours of the morning. Another young man with similar facial features and hair colour to the two dead men. But this time he survived.'

'So what went wrong?' asked Nikki urgently. 'If it was our ultra-efficient assassin, how come his victim escaped?'

'Pure luck, by the sound of it,' said the chief.

'Yes, chance,' added the super. 'One of our uniformed crews made an unofficial stop at the bakery on West Lee Road, at just before three in the morning.'

'Unofficial? That bakery practically relies on us for their doughnut sales! Our lads are there all hours of the day and night!'

'Maybe, but last night one of the bakers wanted to show off his new Kawasaki motorcycle. He took our two men out to the back car park, and that was when they disturbed something.'

'They saw him?'

'No. The footpath along the back has no street lights, and by the time our officers got there, the attacker had done a vanishing act through the back alleys.'

'And the victim? Did he see anything?'

'Too busy trying to avoid being murdered, Inspector,' said the chief sourly. 'But he did get a glimpse of what the man was wearing.'

'And?' asked Nikki.

The chief picked up a statement and read, 'Desert boots and camouflage pants.'

'Military?'

'You can buy any of that on the market or from a surplus store.'

'And is the victim badly injured?'

The super stretched. 'Thankfully not, other than a bruised neck and being scared half to death.'

'What was he doing there, sir?' asked Nikki.

'We think he was sneaking back home after an assignation with his mate's wife. His version varies slightly from that, but I don't think it's too important. It's the other man we want, and this time let's just hope that we get lucky with some DNA from the intended mark.' He leaned forward and in a confidential tone, said, 'This does make something a little easier though. Joseph wasn't involved this time,' he smiled at her, his relief plain to see, 'because he was with you, miles away on Cloud Fen.'

'And no doubt you will confirm that, Nikki?' The chief blinked his hooded eyes.

She threw him a withering look. 'Absolutely. There when I went to bed, there when I got up, and I heard him pacing the floor for half the night.' She gave him her best attempt at a smile and added, 'So can he come back to work, sir?'

'No, Inspector. His mental state is still in question. I want a full evaluation and medical report before that can happen.'

Yes, you would, wouldn't you, she thought, but just nodded and said, 'Of course.'

'We've got the man who was attacked downstairs, Nikki,' said the superintendent. 'He's been checked over at the hospital and given the all clear, so I expect you'd like a word with him.'

Nikki nodded. 'I'll brief my team, then I'll go speak to him, sir.'

'Right, well I have a meeting.' The chief picked up his hat from the table and walked to the door. 'Keep me up to date, Superintendent.'

Nikki followed him out and saw the retreating figure of Walker heading towards the lifts. She had sworn to him that Joseph had been in her home from dusk to dawn, but had he?

As she made her way along the corridor, all she could hear were footfalls on the stairs of Cloud Cottage Farm, and maybe the sound of a door closing? She'd rather stick pins in her eyes than tell the chief, but in truth, she had no idea where Joseph had been at three that morning.

* * *

Dave and Cat arrived early, both carrying paper bags and polystyrene beakers. By that time Nikki had put together a pretty concise overview of the whole murder case, and after instructing them to bring their breakfast into her office, she closed the door and proceeded to tell them everything she knew. She left nothing out, except the details of the massacre in the Congo and Joseph's unfortunate involvement. She did tell them however that Billy Sweet had been suspected of killing both his own mates and innocent women.

'And Joseph believes this lunatic is here in Greenborough?' asked Cat incredulously.

'He's certain of it.' Nikki drummed her fingers on the desk. 'But as Dave will explain, this can't be true.'

Dave detached the death certificate from a sheaf of papers and handed it to Cat.

'Oh dear. So *who* is running around town trying to eradicate corn-dolly haircuts and pale blue eyes?' Cat nibbled on her lip. 'And we mustn't forget that all the victims are Billy Sweet lookalikes.' She scratched her head. 'I don't get it.'

'Well, I've been up half the night thinking about it, and this is my only conclusion.' Dave stared at his Danish as if he hoped that it would give him inspiration. 'It's got to be an old case, something from Fenchester. We have to get him to think about anyone who has threatened him or bears him a serious grudge.'

'But where does Billy Sweet come into it?' asked Cat.

'Hate is a powerful emotion. It can make a man very patient.' Dave took a small bite of his pastry. 'Someone has taken a lot of time to go back into the past, and they found a nasty rotten apple called Sweet. The very reason that Joseph threw up his glowing career in the army.'

'But we've established that Sweet is dead,' added Nikki impatiently.

'But Joseph doesn't know that, does he?' said Dave patiently. 'So you find someone who looks like him, then you make sure that Joseph believes it *is* him.'

'Mm, that's possible,' said Cat hopefully. 'And what a perfect time to hassle the sarge. When he's just returned from sick leave and is still pretty shaky.'

'Sorry . . .' Nikki rubbed her forehead. 'Surely you're missing something. Why would this Pseudo-Sweet kill people? Why not just haunt Joseph, and send him quietly batty?'

'Because,' said Dave. 'The real Sweet was a killer. It's part of the package if he's to convince Joseph.'

Nikki considered his point. 'Okay, I'll run with that, but where does all this finish? What is his endgame?'

'To ruin the sarge, I'd reckon,' muttered Dave grimly.

'And it looks like it's working, wouldn't you say, ma'am?' added Cat. 'He's already been relegated to knitting socks and watching *Loose Women*.'

'He's not quite that bad yet,' said Nikki ruefully. 'But I get your point.'

'Let's just hope it's not going to go one step further,' said Dave ominously. 'And the sarge becomes the final victim.'

'Oh shit,' whispered Cat. 'The assassin is clearly being paid very well by someone, so that could be the logical finale for total revenge. Put the frighteners on him, then kill him.'

At that, the office fell silent, and several things ran through Nikki's brain simultaneously. If that were the case, then Joseph was not safe out on the fen. He was actually very vulnerable. And something Cat had just said jarred off an even worse scenario. One that she didn't even dare to voice out loud.

Cat had mentioned Joseph's recent trauma. So what if there was no revenge plot? What if there was no Billy Sweet? Real or otherwise. What if the face in the windscreen had just been some brainless yob, one who closely resembled the worst person Joseph had ever met? And it had sent his mind into freefall. Could Joseph be hunting this mythical being down and killing men who were unfortunate enough to look like Sweet?

Nikki physically shook her head to rid herself of those terrible thoughts. Of course he wasn't a killer! He was her sergeant and her friend! He was living under her roof, and she cared about him. A lot, actually. The idea that she had just considered belonged to people like Walker, or the gutter press, not to Nikki Galena. 'Okay, any other thoughts?' she snapped.

'I think I'm with Dave, ma'am,' said Cat, 'But, if you don't mind me saying, Joseph is only a sergeant. I can understand him being threatened with a damn good thumping, or getting his car vandalised, but surely death threats are more suited to the higher ranks, the ones who actually head up the investigations. Joseph is a worker, not a big cheese. If some villain got slammed up forever, wouldn't he or his loved ones, go for someone like you, or the super, maybe?'

'You can still piss someone off, no matter what your rank, Cat. And who's to say we are dealing with someone sane?'

'That's right,' Dave nodded vigorously. 'If you're short on your quota of marbles, rational thinking doesn't apply.'

'So we check his old cases?' asked Cat.

Nikki nodded. 'I'll ring him and ask him to get us a list of 'possibles' together. And until then, you Dave, follow up those enquiries on Sweet, and Cat, keep busy until I've made my call, then come with me and we'll talk to the one that got away.'

'Ah yes, the third lookalike? Will do.' Cat stood up, and gave a small laugh. 'Shame they're not all still alive, we could start a Billy Sweet tribute band.'

As Cat left, a civilian messenger knocked on the door. 'Sorry to interrupt, ma'am, but there's someone to see you downstairs.'

'A name would be helpful.'

'Sorry.' The woman glanced at a memo held firmly in her hand. 'Bryony Barton, ma'am.'

Nikki felt her lips purse together, then she forcibly relaxed them and said, 'I'll be right down.'

'Ah,' said Dave knowingly, and then shut up as she lobbed a few imaginary daggers in his direction.

'Ah nothing.'

'Whatever you say, guv.' Dave grinned. 'But I was only going to offer to see her for you, as you're so busy?'

'Drooling is not gentlemanly, Dave. Please slip a bromide in your tea and get on with your work. I can manage, thank you.'

Nikki hurried down the corridor, and silently cursed the super for interrupting her morning ablutions. Her outfit didn't even qualify as bag-lady chic. It was more like she had dressed herself entirely from Help the Aged, and now she was to meet Joseph's stunning new girlfriend. O deep joy!

Nikki stared at her surreptitiously from the office behind the front desk, and felt her heart sink.

Joseph had been right. Bryony was beautiful. But not in a glamorous way, she was not fashion magazine, size zero and brainlessly sort of gorgeous, she had more the beauty of the panther. She was one of those incredibly lucky people who seemed to be perfectly proportioned, and knew exactly how to dress to make the best of everything.

And she looked intelligent, which made Nikki definitely wish she had allowed Dave to take her place.

A low babble of voices pulled her from her reverie, and she realised that breathing was becoming difficult due to the office rapidly filling up with testosterone. At least ten male officers had magically appeared from nowhere and were collectively staring towards the waiting area.

'For goodness sake! Haven't you lot got something better to do?' she exclaimed. The expected chorus of 'No!' followed her as she left.

'Bryony?' She stretched out a hand. 'Nikki Galena. You wanted to see me?'

The handshake was surprisingly firm. 'Thank you. I'm sorry to bother you. I'll only take a few moments of your time.'

Nikki glanced across to the sergeant. 'Is there a free interview room, Jack?'

'Number three, ma'am. All yours.'

'This way.' Nikki made herself walk confidently, but still felt like one of the ugly sisters escorting Cinderella.

She held back the door and indicated towards a chair. 'Sorry it's not more comfortable, but most of our guests aren't here for the fine facilities.' She managed to install a smile for the occasion. 'What can I do for you, Bryony?'

The woman looked up at her, her expression concerned and intense. 'Joseph rang me last night, Inspector. He told me that he'd been suspended. Is that true?'

'Joseph's not in the habit of lying.' She kept her own gaze impassive. 'It's true.'

'Oh no.' The woman seemed to visibly crumple. 'This is my fault, isn't it?'

Nikki felt confused, but didn't show it.

'You suspended him because of what I told you, didn't you? But the thing is, I don't think I put it very well, Inspector.'

Nikki sat down opposite her. 'First, *I* did not suspend him, and second, your failing to identify the mystery man had no bearing on why Joseph was asked to rest up for a while.' She was not known for her tact, but she thought that sounded fairly acceptable.

'But I still let him down.'

'You finally told the truth, and believe me, that's a far better bet than lying.' She stared at the fine-boned face and porcelain skin, and said. 'Have you told Joseph that you didn't actually see anyone?'

Bryony shifted around in the uncomfortable chair, and stared at the table in front of her. 'Not yet. I've been going over and over it. Now I honestly don't know if someone was there or not. It was dark, and I admit, my attention was rather more on Joseph than what was happening on the other side of the road.' She hung her head. 'All I know is, Joseph truly thought someone was watching us. His face changed from a smiling, relaxed man, to some kind of awful mask. He was terrified, Inspector. And when I made to run over to the river path, he *screamed* at me to let the man go.'

Nikki watched the other woman carefully. Bryony was not finding this easy, and it was obvious to Nikki that she really did care about Joseph, which was not exactly what she wanted to know right now.

'I know that you won't be able to tell me where he is, Inspector, but is he all right? I feel dreadful that I can't see him, but he says it's too dangerous.'

'He's only thinking of you, Bryony. And I know you wouldn't want to add to his present worries, he has a lot to deal with right now,' she paused, 'but yes, he's taken everything very well, all things considered.'

'Well, that's something. I'll just have to be satisfied with his calls until this is all over.' She straightened her skirt, even though it didn't need it, and looked almost coyly at Nikki. 'I've never met a man like Joseph before. He's so . . .'

Special? Different? Caring? Honest? Nikki automatically filled in the gap.

'. . . so selfless, and gentlemanly. And that's rare in a good-looking man.'

Nikki nodded. Yes, that was two pretty good adjectives, but at this point in time Joseph's love life was not what she wanted to be talking about. 'I'm sorry, I have to get on. I hope I've put your mind at rest?' She stood up.

'You have, and thank you for your time.' Bryony said, picking up her handbag. 'And, Inspector, if you see him or speak to him, please don't tell him I was here, or what I said to you. I think it's down to me to explain to him, don't you?'

'I think you *should* explain things.'

'I will. I promise. And maybe I should come clean about a few other things as well.'

Nikki tensed. 'Like what?'

Bryony gave a small conspiratorial laugh. 'It's okay. It's nothing serious, and nothing to do with what is going on, but I've liked him for ages. I saw him months ago at Greenborough Hospital, and I tried to find out about him.' She halted as she approached the door. 'I thought a gorgeous man like that would be bound to have either a wife or a significant other, so I kind of engineered an 'accidental' meeting.'

'The fitness club?' asked Nikki, trying to keep the surprise out of her voice.

'Mm. I do swim and I do exercise, but I'm a strong swimmer, so I've always used the big pool out at Carness. I was dropping off a friend at the Greenborough club one day, and couldn't believe that he was there, in the pool! I immediately bought a membership, and the rest is history.'

'And the meeting in the Hammer?'

'Oh God! You make me sound like a stalker. No, that was for real. My boss truly was organising a charity scavenger hunt.'

'You really like him, don't you?' said Nikki almost sadly.

Bryony looked at her for a minute, apparently weighing something up, then said, 'I've had some seriously shitty experiences in the past, Inspector. My opinion regarding men is not high, but Joseph is different. Very different.'

'Then I strongly urge you to tell him everything. Policemen don't like being lied to, Bryony, no matter how well-meaning your intentions. We get lies every day from the bad guys, so we don't expect it from the good ones.'

'I've been a complete fool, haven't I?' Bryony drew in a breath. 'But I do hear what you say, and thanks.'

Nikki escorted her back to the foyer, and as she turned to leave, Bryony said. 'Take care of him for me, Inspector. I think he's very lucky to have you for a friend.'

Nikki moved closer to her and spoke in a soft but urgent voice. 'I'll do my best. Just don't be tempted to see him, Bryony. Considering how you feel, it could be very dangerous, for both of you, understand?'

Bryony nodded slowly, then moved towards the automatic doors. 'I understand.'

Nikki listened to the whoosh of the doors, and made her way thoughtfully back to her office.

* * *

As Bryony Barton crossed the street, and walked down the narrow side road to where her car was parked, a man watched her with great interest.

He did not attract attention to himself. He realised a long while ago that Good Ordinary People preferred to avert their eyes from his kind. And he had a lot of things about him that those Good Ordinary People would rather not associate with. He was dirty for one thing. His clothes told of neglect and abuse, ergo, he would smell. GOP's didn't like bad smells at all. He had strange eyes, which probably meant drugs, and oh my! How GOP's hated drugs! And he was pretty big, which meant don't pick on him. A fight would definitely see a GOP coming second. Oh yes, and he was begging. Which was the only risky thing in his beautifully practised repertoire for blending in perfectly with the pavements, the trodden-in chewing gum and the dog shit. The paper cup with Please Give scribbled on it could be the weak link, because some of the GOPs were actually Do-Gooders, and DGs looked upon beggars as a large part of their insurance to travel on the road to heaven. Beggars were to be fed, nurtured and cosseted, at arm's length of course, but that could be dangerous.

Today however he was having an invisible day, which suited him perfectly.

That meant that no one saw him stand up, slip catlike across the road, and as Bryony opened her car-door, he was behind her. Breathing in her perfume.

Escada. Magnetism.

My God, the woman had good taste.

But sadly there wasn't time right now to extol her virtues, because there was work to be done and an exacting schedule to keep to.

In less than a minute, the car had pulled away, and the side road was once again empty, with no trace of either Bryony Barton, or her invisible follower.

CHAPTER TWENTY

Joseph looked up from the computer screen and rubbed his eyes. He could hardly believe that it was after one o'clock and somehow he had finally calmed down enough to concentrate on Martin Durham.

Nikki had called earlier and told him that Sweet had attempted to kill again. The news had almost sent him to the wire, but somehow he'd managed to drag himself back. Deep down he knew that the only way he was going to come through this with his sanity intact was to throw his whole self into working. Which sounded great, but without his warrant card he was stuffed! Even with the Durham case, he had taken his search about as far as it could go without using official channels. He needed Nikki to get him some more information, but with the world going crazy at Greenborough nick, he didn't have the heart to bother her. Then on the other hand, perhaps he should, because there were things about those two odd deaths, Amelia Reed and Paul Cousins, that were starting to bug him.

He pushed his chair back and stretched his cramped legs. On the desk in front of him was a rough list of known villains who might carry a grudge against him. Nikki had wanted him to think about old cases, but although there were a lot of them, and some where vague threats had been made, no one stood out as being flaky enough to want to destroy him. He pushed the list to one side. It was a total waste of time. No crook he had ever banged up would organise a vendetta like this. And right now he needed a break. He wanted to think objectively about Reed and Cousins and everything else was getting in the way. Maybe he should go out for a while. Go get some food in. Some proper food, not makeshift junk. Something he could use as therapy to help him think.

He stretched again, stood up and tried to remember what was the most labour intensive dish he had ever cooked. And what would Nikki like? Frankly, she seemed to enjoy anything that was put in front of her. He smiled. It was nice to cook for someone else. And that made him think about Bryony, and he couldn't wait to prepare a meal for her. He was sure she'd appreciate it. Not that Nikki didn't, but it would be different cooking for a . . .

He stopped himself. A what? What would Bry become? A lover? A partner? He wasn't sure, and dreaded to let himself get too far ahead. And where exactly did he intend to do this fancy cooking? His digs had very limited facilities and certainly didn't include a *Master Chef* kitchen.

Again his mind wandered. He had said he'd sit on the money from his Fenchester home after he'd sold it, but maybe he should be looking for somewhere in or around Greenborough.

And maybe he should damn well keep his mind firmly on his work. He had no right to make plans for anything or anybody until Billy Sweet had been caught. Even thinking of that name made him angry. Sweet had no right to walk back into his life and bring his whole world crashing down around his feet.

With a muttered curse, Joseph picked up the phone, dialled Nikki's landline and asked her if there was any new developments.

'Nothing yet, Joseph.'

The boss sounded preoccupied, and why shouldn't she? 'I was wondering if you'd heard from Elizabeth Durham?' he asked.

'She rang earlier, but with all of this going on, I can't get out to see her.'

'Could I go, ma'am? I'm well and truly stuck here. There are things I need to know about Martin and I'm sure she could help.'

There had been a long wait, then in a low voice, she said, 'I'd rather you didn't, Joseph. I don't want the chief on my back. But then again, it has nothing to do with the main murder enquiry and I'm not your jailer, so if you did take upon yourself to go out for an afternoon ride, I would know nothing about it, would I? Just don't breathe a word about your suspension to anyone. We could both finish up down the Job Centre.'

'I have to go out anyway, unless you want us to starve. I thought I'd try the big supermarket on the Old Bolingbroke Road?'

'How convenient. But Joseph?'

'Yes, ma'am?'

'Take care, won't you? We haven't caught this killer yet, and I'm really not sure that it's wise for you to be trailing round the countryside alone.'

* * *

He had rung Elizabeth before he set out, and she had seemed pleased that he was able to see her. When he arrived, the door was opened by Janna.

'I'm surprised that you could spare the time, with these awful murders to investigate.' Her comment was not sarcastic, just a genuine observation, then she led him through to the garden room and flopped into one of the deep comfortable chairs. 'Have a seat, Sergeant.'

'Thanks. It's true we're busy, but the boss doesn't want you to feel that we are doing nothing about Martin's death.'

'Elizabeth will be grateful for that. She's starting to get very jumpy about everything, especially the break-in.'

'Wouldn't anyone feel jumpy?' Elizabeth had just done one of her famous silent entrances.

'I think you have every right,' said Joseph seriously and took out his notebook and a pen. 'Now I wonder if you would help me out with the answers to some questions?'

Elizabeth sat down. 'Anything I can tell you, I will.'

'Janna mentioned that something happened to your brother, a very long time ago. What was it?'

'Sadly, he never told me much, but it concerned his health and some treatment that he received. He was very poorly, he nearly died, but when he recovered, he had changed.'

'How so?'

'It's hard to say, but he was different.' A perplexed expression clouded her features. 'Maybe these will help you to understand.' She leant down and picked up a box that sat on the floor beside her chair. 'You are welcome to take them as long as I get them back.'

Joseph took the box and opened it. Inside were two large envelopes, one marked BEFORE, and the other, AFTER. Inside were press cuttings and dozens of photographs. Some coloured, others black-and-white. Most had names, dates and locations carefully written on the back.

'I couldn't remember all the names or places. But you'll see when you look through, he has gone from being outgoing and gregarious, to becoming a loner.'

'Oh, he was not that bad,' chipped in Janna. 'He just liked the marshes and his work. Everyone on Cloud Fen loved him, he was hardly some Fenland Howard Hughes, now was he?'

'You never knew him before, sweetheart.'

'A brush with death does alter people,' said Joseph gravely.

'I'm sure. But there were other things. We'd always been so close, but he just stopped confiding in me, Sergeant. He had been practically penniless, then he came home and he had money in his pocket, and he would never say where it came from.'

Joseph thought quickly. It sounded like a bungled operation, or some medical blunder that had ended up in an out-of-court payout. 'Where was he treated?'

'The Gordon Peace Memorial Hospital. It closed when they built Greenborough General.'

'I recall hearing the name somewhere.' Joseph racked his brain for a connection, but nothing materialised. 'I'll try to look into that, but the length of time that had passed won't make it easy, neither will the fact that all their notes will have been transferred, maybe even destroyed, years ago.'

'Martin was adamant that there had been no blunders, if that's what you're thinking. He said they had done all they could, and he was indebted to them.'

Maybe he was, but maybe he had accepted a hefty bung, and was happy with his lot. Joseph scribbled a few notes, then asked. 'About his medication? Am I right in thinking that you were upset when we asked about them before?'

Elizabeth Durham sighed. 'I'm sorry. It was all rather too much to handle at the time.' She sat back. 'His ongoing medication had been something of a *bête noire* for me. They gave him some quite awful side effects, and no matter what I told him about medical advances, he refused to have them reviewed. He said that the clinic who looked after him knew exactly what they were doing and that I wasn't to interfere.'

'It was the only thing they ever argued about,' added Janna.

'Would that be the oncology clinic?'

'I think so.' Elizabeth frowned. 'It must have been. He didn't go anywhere else.'

'Did you ever go with him?'

She gave a cheerless shake of her head. 'Never. He never allowed me to.'

Now, there's a surprise, thought Joseph. 'So, when you two decided to turn sleuth, you were checking Knot Cottage for anything that could relate to his time in hospital?'

They both nodded glumly. 'Sorry about that, Sergeant. We weren't trying to hamper your investigation, we just thought we might recognise something that would mean little or nothing to you.'

'But there was nothing at all.'

'Nothing. Either the intruder took them, or they were never there.'

'One last question, Ms Durham. Did Martin ever mention, or do you know of Paul Cousins, or Amelia Reed?'

'Amelia! We all knew her, Sergeant. St Francis was a positive philistine compared to Amelia! She was an animal angel, poor soul, until that terrible accident.'

'Or was it suicide?' added Janna quietly. 'They never gave a verdict, remember?' She stared at Joseph. 'You surely don't think there's a connection, do you?'

'No, I'm just trying to make comparisons, and as they were both local, I wondered if you or your brother may have known them.'

'The name Cousins means nothing, but Amelia was an institution around here. We went to the same school, were quite friendly at one point, although that seems a very long time ago.' Elizabeth Durham pointed to the box of photographs. 'I think there's a snap of all of us in there.'

'Sergeant?' Janna leaned forward. 'When I saw you last you indicated a possibility of foul play? Do you still feel that way?'

'I can't comment officially,' said Joseph cautiously. 'But I am very disturbed by the whole scenario, it just doesn't ring true, and there are too many unanswered questions regarding his medication.'

'Like what?' asked Janna.

'He received tablets from his GP, a controlled regime that she was hoping to revise in the near future, but he also had other medication, in plain white boxes.'

'They would be the ones that he received direct from the clinic,' responded Elizabeth. 'They were sent either by courier, or Martin would collect them from the post office in the next village.'

A prickle of discomfort jabbed away in Joseph's head. Clever, considering the clinic said they had never heard of Martin Durham. Still, now was not the time to share this knowledge. 'And that was a long-term thing, was it?'

'Oh yes, for years.'

'I think I'd better go see this clinic,' said Joseph, almost to himself.

'Then perhaps you would be kind enough to notify them of my brother's death, and tell them to stop sending the medication?'

'Of course. Happy to.' Best that way, mused Joseph. We don't want too many people getting involved in that place. Not until we've found out why they are denying all knowledge of Martin. 'Now I should be getting back. But thank you for your assistance.'

'Any time, Sergeant Easter. And if I find anything else that may be helpful to you, I'll ring the station, shall I?'

'Ring DI Galena direct. I'm out and about rather a lot at present. She'll pass anything on, I can assure you.'

* * *

It took Joseph two hours to shop and find his way back to Nikki's place. And when he finally arrived on the fen, ominous dark clouds were moving in from the east, and the marsh was beginning to lose its magic. In fact, to the town-boy even the air seemed charged and threatening.

'Too much sky,' he muttered as he pulled bulging bags of shopping from the boot.

Once inside he felt better, especially when he entered the kitchen. He had thought it before, but there was such a good feel to that particular room that if he had lived there permanently, it would have been the hub of his universe.

He unpacked the provisions and put them away, then pulled out a sealed package from the last of the bags and unwrapped a new pay-as-you-go mobile phone. He had felt naked without any form of contact while driving, and this would suffice until he got his own all-singing, all-dancing version back from the lab.

He inserted the SIM card, set it up and activated it. As he waited for it to charge, he rang Bryony on the landline. After a while he hung up. She would probably be busy. Maybe he shouldn't phone her at work anyway, a lot of companies didn't appreciate their staff taking personal calls. Still, it was strange that her voicemail didn't pick up.

Not to worry, he told himself, they'd have a long talk later that night, right now it was time for his therapeutic hobby.

Joseph chopped, sliced and diced for half an hour, then with a contented sigh, covered all his preparations with cling-film and stored them in the fridge. He then cleaned the table down, and went to get the Durham family picture archive and all his previous notes, photos and files on Reed and Cousins.

He looked at the photos first, laying them out over the table, and quietly scanning them. It didn't take long to understand what Elizabeth had meant. His early pictures showed a true live wire, a Jack the Lad, surrounded by friends, grinning, pulling faces and acting the fool. The later ones were far more subdued, and generally they featured only Martin, although one or two were taken with Elizabeth. A close brush with death? Joseph shivered, then replaced the recent ones in their sleeve, and concentrated on the early years. If he were to find something, he was sure it came from a long time ago.

He then looked at the notes and files pertaining to Amelia, Paul and Martin, scribbling down anything that might be relevant, then cross-checking them. Dates of birth, addresses, schools, religion, hobbies, early jobs, family history. Nothing particularly linked them, except the fact that Martin's sister had gone to school with Amelia, and that wasn't enough.

Joseph returned to the photographs, but after thirty minutes still had found nothing. With a grunt of disapproval, he got up to stretch his legs, but as he did so he clipped the folder on Amelia Reed with his elbow, and sent pictures and reports flying across the quarry tiles.

Grabbing them back up, and trying to replace them in some semblance of order, he was struck by something he hadn't noticed before. A forensic photograph of Amelia's body. But it wasn't the pale corpse that drew his eye, like iron-filings to a magnet. To one side of her, on a shelf close to the bath, was a tablet box. A plain white tablet box.

Joseph raced through to the study and scanned the picture. As soon as he had it on the screen, he zoomed in on the packet, and let out a low whistle. The enhanced picture showed a box of the same dimensions as the ones found at Knot Cottage, and the only thing on it was a small rectangular label. It was exactly the same as Martin's.

He printed off the picture and picked up the phone. 'Ma'am, I need a favour.'

Nikki had sounded horribly distracted, but scribbled down his request. 'I'll get Yvonne or Niall to go down and see what they can find, but it'll take a while, you know what the evidence store is like.'

'At least the store is on the premises. At Fenchester our store was twenty miles away in a secure unit.'

'And you realise there may be nothing there. It's not as if Paul Cousin's death was considered a murder.'

'I know that, ma'am. But it's on record that there was such a furore when it happened that a lot of questions were asked, and serious enquiries were made, to cover ourselves I guess, but his medication was definitely sent for analysis.'

'Okay, well, I'll ring you if they find anything.' He heard her yawn, then she said, 'Is everything alright there?'

'Apart from looking like Armageddon outside.' He glanced at the window and saw diagonal splashes of rain across the glass. 'I think we're in for a summer storm.'

'They can be quite spectacular out on the marsh. I'd batten down the hatches if I were you.'

'Will do. Any idea what time you'll be back? I have a small banquet planned, and a nice Sancerre chilling in the fridge.'

'I can't say, Joseph, and I'm not sure I'm that hungry, so please don't go to a lot of trouble.'

He frowned down the phone. Generally, when you mentioned food or wine, Nikki showed considerable enthusiasm.

'Hey! It's no trouble,' he said sincerely. 'You are being good enough to put me up, the least I can do is look after you, and maybe even rekindle your culinary spirit?'

'*Re*-kindle?' she asked. 'I don't think that spark ever got ignited in the first place.'

There was at least a slight hint of amusement. 'I'll try to get back by seven, okay?'

'Then go careful on the roads. This is the first rain we've had for weeks, so it could be slippery.'

'Thank you, Grandmother. I'll be sure to heed your sage advice.' She hung up abruptly and left him wondering what was going on at the nick, and whether anyone would find what he was looking for in the evidence store.

He walked slowly back to the kitchen and began to gather up the pictures. Elizabeth had said that there was one of Amelia. From the press cuttings she had appeared tall and willowy, with a wiry strength, strong jutting jaw-line and piercing intelligent eyes. He wondered what she had looked like as a young woman. He skimmed through the names on the back, then saw *Martin, Barry, Mel, Lewis and me. Home after second term at uni.* Mel? Amelia? He looked closer.

The picture showed five friends fooling around beside a rust-bucket of a Ford Anglia. Elizabeth was easy to spot, so as Amelia was the only other girl, he quickly identified her, and even back then her appearance was striking. Joseph stared at the photograph and memories of his own uni days washed over him. This was considerably earlier of course, Martin had been fifty when he died, almost fifteen years older than him, but the dynamic of the group looked very similar.

He wondered where they were, but as he was not a local, he wasn't sure. Then he made out a lot of other cars in the background, and saw part of a large sign, in particular the word, *Gordon*. Maybe the Gordon Peace Memorial Hospital? Joseph stared again. Funny place for kids to hang out.

Suddenly his thoughts started to crank up again. He'd seen mention of this hospital somewhere in Paul Cousin's notes. That was why it had rung a bell when Elizabeth had mentioned it earlier! That, and something else. But to his annoyance, the something else was still lying dormant in some closed compartment of his brain.

Whatever, it actually linked all three. Not that he should get too hopeful. The hospital served a wide area, and Martin, Paul and Amelia were locals, it stood to reason they would have attended at some point in their lives.

He turned the photo over again. There was no date on it, but that could easily be checked with Elizabeth. He sat back and smiled at the table full of old pictures. It all starts here. I'm certain of it. And if the evidence store came up trumps too, we've finally got a lead.

At four p.m. the phone rang.

'You are one jammy sod, Joseph Easter! Yvonne has located a box marked Cousins in the evidence store. And guess what's in it?'

'Medication?'

'Too right. And one lot of tablets is in a very familiar plain white box.'

'Yes!' Joseph punched the air. 'That's it! Now we've got a place to start!'

CHAPTER TWENTY-ONE

Nikki arrived home just as the storm hit. Winds gusted straight in from the North Sea and battered against the old house, and it was all she could do to keep upright as she fought her way from the car.

She practically fell inside and slammed the door behind her, then was greeted by the most delicious smell of cooking.

'I thought I said no trouble!' she said, pulling off her soaking wet jacket.

'Eat what you want, and the rest will freeze.' Joseph grinned at her. 'It's the Easter version of a bloody good takeaway!'

'You can cook Indian?' said Nikki, half believing that if it didn't come from the Taj takeaway, it didn't exist.

'Very relaxing, preparing Eastern food, all those lovely spices to grind and blend.'

'You're something else, you know that? Most people do a crossword, or play Sudoku to unwind; you grind spices and chop chillies.' Nikki shook her head in amazement, and stepped out of her sodden shoes. 'It's certainly wild out there tonight, but it should subside when the tide turns.'

'I've taken the liberty of running you a bath. I thought you'd probably get drenched.' He turned back to the stove. 'When you're through, this should be just about ready.'

Nikki went upstairs and took off her wet clothes then slipped on her dressing gown. She pulled some casual slacks and a soft fleecy top from her wardrobe and went to the bathroom.

As he had said, her bath was run, and a glass of wine stood close to the taps. Standing against it was a note. It just said, 'Relax.'

Nikki eased herself down into the silky hot water and found herself fighting back tears. She couldn't recall anyone ever doing this for her before. Robert, her ex-husband could be called a lot of things, but thoughtful wasn't one of them, and her few other fleeting affairs had been just that, fleeting. No time for niceties.

For a moment she hated herself for ever even dreaming that this attentive and gentle man could be so psychologically damaged that he could systematically hunt down and kill people.

She sipped the chilled wine, savoured it, and decided that Bryony was a lucky woman, a very lucky woman. She would miss Joseph when he left, and not just for his culinary skills. The old place felt like a home while he was there.

She soaked for a while, going over what the day had produced, which wasn't much, then she allowed herself to think about Martin Durham. She couldn't believe that Joseph had made such headway. She just wished that she could do the same with the Greenborough assassin.

Nikki stood up and wrapped herself in a thick fluffy towel before stepping out of the bath.

'Five minutes!' echoed up from downstairs.

'Coming,' she called back. She pulled on her clothes and carefully holding her wine, ran downstairs.

* * *

'For a woman with no appetite, there's precious left for the freezer,' commented Joseph. 'I'd hate to see you when you are really hungry!'

'Not a pretty sight, believe me. But that was too good to leave, thank you.' She paused. 'Tell me what else you've found out about our suspicious deaths.'

'Very little, I'm afraid, apart from a tenuous connection to the Gordon Peace Memorial Hospital, but even the Internet doesn't give much info on it.'

'There was uproar when they built the Greenborough General and forced its closure. Protest marches and everything.'

'I keep thinking that I know something else about it, but it escapes me.'

Nikki took a mouthful of wine. 'Can't help you there, I'm afraid. I never needed to go there as a child, and I've kind of grown up with Greenborough General.'

'It'll come to me, no doubt. So? Was it really as bad as it sounded at work today? You seemed hairspring taut, when I spoke to you.'

Nikki sat back and held out her glass for a top-up. 'It was about as shitty as it gets. Victim number three was so freaked out about what had nearly happened that he was all but useless. He'd spent time with sodding Snaz, but his description was rubbish. Then he begged us to let him stay in the cells, just in case his attacker was waiting to finish him off.'

'I bet the custody sergeant liked that.'

'We found an out of town relative that was prepared to take him, until it's safe to go home.'

'And I wonder when that will be?' muttered Joseph morosely.

For a moment Nikki felt angry, then sadness took over. For all his brave front, his fancy cooking, and his commitment to finding out what had happened to Martin, Joseph was hurting. Hurting and scared about what was going to happen next.

'I'm doing my best, honestly, Joseph.'

'I know. And don't think I don't appreciate it,' he said miserably. He ran his hand through his hair. 'It's just that

I've never felt so frustrated, so totally helpless.' He gave her a dark look. 'Well, actually I have, just once, and that was all to do with Billy Sweet. He really does have a knack for screwing up my life.'

Nikki didn't like his sombre mood and decided to change the subject. 'Have you spoken to Bryony today?'

'Not yet.' He drank his wine and stared into the glass. 'I tried earlier but her phone was switched off. Busy at work I guess. I'll ring her later.'

Nikki hoped that Bryony would do as she'd said and tell Joseph that she hadn't seen his stalker. She frowned to herself when she considered how Joseph would take that news. He was hanging onto Bryony's status as an eyewitness to keep himself sane. She sipped her drink and thought it best not to predict his reaction but just to deal with it when it happened. 'So, I guess it's time to discuss where we go next with Martin Durham.' She looked across at Joseph and raised her glass. 'Well done, by the way. That was astute of you to spot that medication box in the forensic photo of Amelia.' 'Thanks. Oh, but you must look at this.' Joseph got up and left the room, returning a few moments later with a photograph.

Nikki stared at it, then smiled when she saw a grinning and happy young Martin Durham. 'Just look at you, not a care in the world,' she whispered.

Joseph leaned over her shoulder and pointed to the sign. 'And this *has* to be what links them, Nikki. The hospital. Those tablets must have originated from there.'

'But the hospital has long gone, so who is sending them out now?'

'That is going to be my next line of enquiry. There has to be a paper chain, and if I can trace it back, I'll find the source.' Joseph bit his lip anxiously. 'As long as my recently imposed civilian capacity allows me to.'

Nikki stared at him. 'So what if I allocated you some help? In the form of either Niall or Yvonne?'

Joseph straightened up. 'Would you? That would be great!'

'Well, let's face it, if we weren't hunting down our killer, Martin's case would be active. It would have a whole team of officers asking questions, not just one constable.' She smiled at him. 'Yes, I'll sort that. We just have to keep shtum over precisely what they are doing, okay?'

Joseph grinned. 'Well, I'd be the last one to argue with that.' His face grew serious. 'But please don't put your neck too far onto the block for me, Nikki. I know how close to the wind you're sailing by even letting me proceed with this investigation, no matter how covertly.'

'Oh, don't worry too much on that score. I'll be discreet, but with my reputation, it's pretty well expected of me!' She leaned back in her chair and stared at the photograph. 'Are there any more like this?'

Joseph shrugged. 'I'll get the box. Some of them may mean more to you than me.'

For half an hour they sorted through the old pictures. Some of the ones taken on Cloud Fen made Nikki feel quite nostalgic.

'Look at this.' Joseph brought her back to the present. 'Tell me what you see.'

Nikki stared at the dog-eared picture. Once again the five friends hung around the old car, and initially Nikki thought they were consecutive shots, then she noticed subtle differences.

'There are fewer leaves on that tree, and the girls have light jackets on. This was taken at the same spot, close to the hospital, but at a different time of year.'

'So they met there, or drove there on a regular basis.' Joseph frowned. 'But why?'

'A sick friend?' Nikki ventured. 'When Hannah was first ill, I practically lived at the hospital.'

'Maybe.' Joseph didn't look convinced. 'Would you have any objections if I gave Martin's sister a ring?'

'None at all. She's bound to recall what they were doing.'

While Joseph was in the study, Nikki piled up the plates and began to load the dishwasher. Thunder was rumbling ominously over the marsh, and the lights suddenly flickered a few times.

'Oh great,' she muttered, and began to rummage around in the cupboard beneath the sink. Power cuts were not unusual on the fen and she always kept a couple of battery-powered storm lanterns at the ready. 'The perfect end to a sodding awful day.'

Nikki checked the lanterns were working, then went through to the study to close the computer down. Joseph sat at her desk, staring thoughtfully at the photo. 'Any joy?'

'Oh, I think so,' said Joseph softly. 'In fact we may have just stumbled on a real lead.' He looked up at her. 'Elizabeth said that as students they were all feeling the pinch financially.'

'Nothing new there then.'

Joseph raised his eyebrows. 'Just remember the timescale. We are talking about the early seventies. To get some extra cash, Martin, Elizabeth and their friends signed up with a clinic run by the hospital.'

'What sort of clinic?'

'Common cold cure trials and sleep studies, apparently.' Nikki let out a low whistle.

'And *that* is why the Gordon Peace Memorial rang bells. Do you ever recall reading about the Porton Down experiments?'

Nikki frowned and tried to think. All she could recall was that Porton Down had been, and probably still was, a government and military research centre testing biological and chemical weapons. 'Nerve gas, wasn't it? Sarin and CS gas were developed there, weren't they?'

'They certainly were, but I was thinking about the allegations made about unethical human experimentation.' Joseph's voice had taken on a very different timbre, and it was one that Nikki recognised from when they first met. He sounded enthusiastic and eager to get to the truth. 'The thing was, Porton Down worked loosely in collaboration with a CCU that was located at Harvard Hospital to the west of Salisbury. But they weren't the only ones experimenting. There was another centre in the east of England. Here to be precise, at the Gordon Peace Common Cold Unit!' He looked at her intently. 'That's why the name rang a bell! They were investigated way back in the 50s, but whatever went wrong was overshadowed by the more documented one about Porton Down and the national servicemen who had been conned into taking part in something that they didn't understand. You remember? They were given extra pay and extra days leave if they volunteered for testing drugs for the common cold, except some of them were tested with nerve agents.'

'And one died, didn't he?' Vague memories were returning to Nikki. Her face screwed up in confusion. 'But surely you're not suggesting that those kids were caught up in some dreadful experiment right here in Greenborough? This was years later.'

'The trials didn't stop. Elizabeth Durham has just told me that lots of the students went through them in the 70s, but some, Martin and Amelia included, volunteered for several, and whatever tests they were, they had nothing to do with colds.'

'And she didn't?'

'No, she said that some of her friends felt quite strongly about doing their bit for medical science, but she wasn't comfortable in the role of a guinea-pig.'

'Did she say what the other trials were about?'

'She has no idea. Apparently Martin and Amelia were really cagey about what it involved. Then her brother was diagnosed with cancer and they forgot all about the trials.'

Nikki took a long shaky breath. 'I don't like where this is going.'

'Nor do I if we find ourselves up against the MOD.' Joseph set his jaw. 'We just have to hope there's no connection to the military and whatever was going on in that unit was a privately funded trial.'

An ominous rumble of thunder added gravity to his words, and Nikki shivered. Martin Durham, Amelia Reed, Paul Cousins, and who else? Three known deaths, all fairly recent, and connected by sinister medication and an experiment that took place decades ago. She struggled to get her head around it. 'We need to know everything we can about those trials. We should go see Elizabeth Durham.' Nikki regarded Joseph seriously. 'Tonight.'

'In this?' Joseph's eyes were wide. 'We'll be lucky to get as far as the main road without calling the coastguard!'

Lightning flickered around the room and a deafening crack of thunder made Nikki jump. 'Jesus! It's right overhead.' She leaned across the desk and pulled one of the storm lanterns closer. 'If this keeps up, ten to one we lose the bloody power.' She thumped her fist down and cursed. 'Damn it! I really need to talk to Martin's sister. She's our only link to what happened to him.'

'Talk to her on the phone.' Joseph lifted the handset and offered it to her. 'Ask her to dig out everything she can about the CCU, and I'll go out there first thing in the morning and see her.'

'I suppose.' Nikki sighed and took the phone from him. She tapped the button a couple of times, then rolled her eyes and slammed it back in its cradle. 'Great! Now the lines are down.'

'Mobile?'

Nikki shook her head. 'And get a signal out here in the middle of a bloody storm? I don't think so.'

'How long do these summer storms last?' asked Joseph.

Nikki glanced at the clock. 'It should move away when the tide turns, which is in about an hour, or it could rumble around all night long.'

'Well, if you are really worried, I'll wait until it subsides a bit then I'll drive up to Old Bolingbroke and talk to her tonight.'

'I'll come with you.'

'No.' Joseph stared at her. Concern played across his face. 'You need some rest. You've got a murder enquiry hanging over you, and Billy Sweet is still out there somewhere.' He leaned across and squeezed her shoulder gently. 'Listen, I know Martin Durham is important to you, but catching

Billy is important to me, and to anyone else who accidentally crosses his murdering path, and there's sod all I can do about him right now. It's all down to you and the team, Nikki.' He let his arm fall but still looked her full in the face. 'I'll do this for you, if you keep focussed on catching that murdering bastard for me.'

Nikki swallowed. Billy Sweet was dead, but how could she tell Joseph? And even if his name was not Sweet, there was still a killer wandering the streets of Greenborough.

'Okay. But go careful, these lanes are treacherous at the best of times.'

'I'll be back before you know it.' He paused just long enough to pick up the two old photos and push them into his pocket. 'Just get some sleep. And don't you dare wait up. You look shattered. I'll fill you in on everything tomorrow.'

Maybe it was the wine, or the weight of so many deaths draped around her shoulders, but Nikki suddenly felt mind-numbingly tired. Exhaustion swept over her, and she felt herself nodding. 'Okay, okay. I get the message. Just watch those bloody roads, you hear?'

'Loud and clear, ma'am.'

As Nikki forced herself to stand, she heard him pulling a waterproof jacket from the coat cupboard, and then the front door clicked shut. She yawned. He hadn't even waited for the rain to ease. For a moment she felt guilty. Elizabeth may know nothing more than she'd already told him, and frankly, whatever she did know could have waited until the morning. Hell, he was going to have one awful drive, and maybe a fruitless one, but for some reason Martin seemed to be calling out to her, and she had no wish to ignore him. They were onto something; she felt that in her heart. And because of everything else she had on her plate right now, it would have to be down to Joseph to prove it.

CHAPTER TWENTY-TWO

As Joseph drove away from the coast, the rain slackened. He could still hear the thunder rumbling in the distance but he could tell from the condition of the roads that the worst of the storm had been confined to the marshes. By the time he reached Elizabeth's home he could see clear dark skies and twinkling stars.

The downstairs lights in the big lodge house were still on and he felt a rush of relief that the two women had not turned in for the night.

Janna opened the door and beckoned him inside. She smiled wanly at him. 'We had a feeling we might see you tonight. It's about the clinical trials, isn't it? You think Martin's death is connected?' She suddenly gathered herself. 'I'm sorry. Look at you, you're soaked! Let me take your jacket.'

Joseph took off his wet coat and handed it to her. 'I should have phoned ahead, but the storm on the coast took out the phone lines. I hope this isn't an imposition?'

'Not at all. Go on down to the garden room. Elizabeth is there. I'll go make us all hot drinks.'

Elizabeth Durham was standing staring out of the great picture window into the night. On hearing him enter she turned, and he thought that she might have been crying.

'Am I intruding, Ms Durham?' he asked softly.

'Ah, Detective Sergeant Easter. No, of course not. Please, have a seat, I was just being silly and selfish, and feeling horribly sorry for myself.' She gave him a rueful look. '*And* I was wondering how much I really knew about my beloved brother.'

'When something like this happens, I think we are made very much aware of just how much we humans hold back from sharing what is going on deep inside. Even from those closest to us.'

'I need to know what happened, Sergeant. If I don't, it'll eat and eat away and drive me mad.'

Joseph nodded. He thought about Billy Sweet and knew exactly how she felt. 'We'll find your answers, I promise.' He took the two photos from his pocket, stood up and walked across to Elizabeth. 'I know it was a very long while ago but I really need you to tell me everything you can remember about those trials and the people in the pictures.'

Elizabeth stared at each photo in turn. 'From the moment we spoke, I've thought about nothing else.' She blinked slowly. 'I'm just not sure what I can tell.'

'Did you know who actually ran the Common Cold Unit?'

'Not at the time. We believed it was just a research side to the hospital itself, but then rumour had it that it may be a government run organisation.'

Joseph's heart sank. That was not the kind of thing he wanted to hear.

'But later still Martin told me that it was privately funded by a pharmaceutical organisation.'

His spirit lifted. 'Did he mention a name?'

Elizabeth shook her head. 'He just said it was massive, based abroad and encompassed a lot of smaller companies. I don't think he knew any more than that.'

'So you and your friends in those photos all took part in the same studies?'

'Initially, yes. It was Martin, Amelia, Barry Smith, John Goring and myself, we were part of a larger group that was split in two. The procedure was nasal drops of cold virus, then half the group given placebos and the other half cold cures.'

'Were you ill afterwards?'

'Not really. A few developed assorted cold-like symptoms. Just coughs, sneezes, raised temperatures. One girl I remember was rather poorly, but nothing major.'

Joseph frowned. 'And this Barry Smith and John Goring? Are you still in touch with them?'

'Barry died young. Killed in a car smash not long after he left university, and I lost contact with John. He went abroad to work years ago.'

Janna appeared with a tray of hot drinks and placed them on a low table. As she handed them around, she paused and took the picture from her partner. 'I've been wondering something, Liz? If your little group of the famous five were all grinning happily here, who took the photograph?'

It was Elizabeth's turn to frown. 'I can't remember.'

'And the second one was taken at a different time of the year,' added Joseph, 'but it's still the five of you. Maybe the same person took that one too?'

Elizabeth rubbed her temples as if trying to coax back an old memory. 'I can see him, just vaguely. A friend of Martin's. He had long wavy untidy hair and shabby clothes. But what the hell was his name?'

'Was he in your group?'

'No. He was one of the few kids who did the sleep studies. He was with us because Martin used to give him a lift into the hospital from the village. Davey! That's it! Davey Kowalski! Lord, I haven't thought about him in years.'

Joseph checked the spelling and wrote the name in his notebook. He'd get a check run on both Goring and Kowalski first thing in the morning. He drew in a long breath. 'I hate to ask this, but did you ever think the trials and Martin's illness might have been connected?'

'No, never.' She shook her head emphatically. 'He assured me that he had the medical team at the trials to thank for his life. He would have died had they not made the diagnosis and acted so swiftly in getting him the right treatment. I know it *sounds* like a medical disaster. You do hear of terrible cases where clinical trials go badly wrong, but I'm certain that wasn't it. My brother wasn't a very good actor, and he really wouldn't have a word said against the team of researchers. If something had gone wrong, I think I'd have known, Detective Easter, really I do.'

'But he did change, didn't he? You said he lost his spark.'

'Maybe I read too much into that. Cancer changes people, and Martin was a vibrant young man. A young man forced to spend the rest of his life on a crushing drug regime and following a much restricted lifestyle to the one he probably had seen for himself. Surely anyone would change?'

'Of course, you're right,' said Joseph softly, but inside he felt that Martin's sister's beliefs were a long way from correct.

The little group fell silent, then Janna suddenly stood up. 'Liz? Did you say Kowalski?'

The other woman nodded, then watched as Janna retrieved a briefcase from behind one of the chairs and began to strew its contents across the marble-tiled floor.

'It's here somewhere, damn it.' Janna rummaged impatiently through reams of paperwork.

'What on earth are you looking for?' asked Elizabeth.

'This!' Janna jumped up triumphantly. 'It has to be the same man!' She waved a typed sheet at him. 'Listen to this, it's a letter of resignation from one of my staff. Linda Kowalski.' She scanned the sheet quickly then read out the relevant part. '*Really sorry*, etc, etc, *been so happy in my job*, blah, blah, but, yes, this is it! *But due to my brother David's illness and I have decided to give up work to look after him. Please God he recovers and is allowed home.*' She handed him the letter and said, 'So how many David Kowalskis do you know?'

'It could be the same man,' said Joseph. 'If his age corresponds?'

'Linda is in her fifties. She told me they are true yellow-bellies, born and bred here in the Fens. The name comes via their grandfather who was a Polish immigrant.'

'Well, the age may fit.' He looked across to Elizabeth. 'Did Martin's friend Davey have a sister?'

'Two, I think.' She nodded slowly. 'And another thing, I'm pretty sure he was on the last trial with Martin.'

Joseph drew in a long breath. Then that was the man he needed to speak to, and the sooner the better. He turned to Janna. 'Do you know why David is so ill?'

'No idea, but I know he's in intensive care at Greenborough General.'

Joseph's mind raced. A failed suicide maybe? He needed to get onto the hospital. 'Could I borrow your phone book, please?'

'Use the phone in the kitchen, Sergeant,' said Janna. 'Greenborough General's number is on the chalk board. It's listed between the doctor and the vet.'

He returned to the garden room a few minutes later. 'I need to go see them, but it could well be the same man.' He quickly drained his coffee cup. 'Thank you both for all this and I promise to keep you updated in what we uncover.'

Outside in the car Joseph checked the time. Almost midnight, and without his warrant card it was useless going to the hospital. There was nothing left but to go home. He pulled his new phone from his pocket and smiled in the darkness, *after* he'd phoned Bryony.

He began to punch in her number, then closed the phone again. Was this fair? They were not even what you might call an item. Yes, they were on the brink of an affair, there was no denying that, but did he have the right to start ringing her at any godforsaken hour just because it suited him?

He slumped back in his seat and wondered what to do. Bryony had given him every indication that she wanted to take their relationship further. She would probably appreciate a call, knowing how scary everything had been of late. Joseph took a deep breath and re-dialled her number. After a moment or two he heard the voicemail cut in. Well, that settled that.

'Eh, hello Bry, it's me, Joseph. Um, well, it's really late I know, but I just wanted you to know that I'm fine and I'm looking forward to catching up with you. I'll ring you in the morning before you go to work.' He paused. 'I miss you, Bry, and I can't wait to get all this sorted out so that we will have some time to get to know each other better. You take care. Speak soon. Bye.'

He closed the phone and sighed. He had hoped that she would have picked up his call. She was the one bright star in all this mess right now. The one sane and solid thing for him to hold on to.

Joseph turned the key in the ignition and prayed that Nikki Galena would find a way to stop Billy Sweet, before he destroyed everything beautiful in his life.

CHAPTER TWENTY-THREE

Nikki must have left very early, because when Joseph emerged at around six thirty, he found a short note propped against the toaster. It simply said that she hadn't forgotten that she had promised to send him some help. He could expect someone as soon as she could arrange it, hopefully just after nine o'clock.

He showered and dressed, then unenthusiastically ate a couple of slices of toast and marmalade. Beside his plate sat an A4 writing pad. If he were to have some help, he couldn't afford to waste time. He should sort out his enquiries into those that could be tackled by a civilian, in this case himself, and those that needed an official warrant card to obtain answers.

He sipped at his mug of tea and began to get his thoughts into some sort of order. And that wasn't easy when all he could think about was a dark-haired, elfin-faced woman; a woman who wasn't answering her phone.

Joseph rinsed his plate and wished vehemently that he had not stopped Bryony from ringing him. It really would do no harm for her to have his new mobile number. She was hardly likely to plague him with calls. Yes, he'd leave it on her voicemail, that would stop him worrying himself sick every time she left her phone switched off. Joseph quickly recorded his second message, then opened his notebook and began to write.

David Kowalski was top of his list. First and foremost they must ascertain that he was the same man who had been a friend of Martin. And if he was, then why was he in hospital, and would he be in any state to talk to them.

Next he wrote: Cold Cure Unit. Somehow they had to find out if it had been originally run by a pharmaceutical company, then see if it was still operational.

Under that he scribbled oncology unit. Now that was really bugging him. Joseph placed the pen carefully on the pad, and hoping someone would be in early, went to find their number.

The manager had not arrived, but the receptionist seemed eager to help. 'There is only one other possibility, Sergeant.' The accent was heavily Geordie. 'Some private referrals aren't always listed in our records. Dr Muller's patients for example, his secretary kept a separate appointment diary.'

Joseph felt a glimmer of hope. 'Could I speak to Dr Muller or his secretary?'

'I'm sorry, Dr Muller left six months ago. Went back to Europe, I believe, although I have no idea where.'

The glimmer faded and went out. Joseph thanked him and hung up; he knew a dead end when he was down one.

He sighed and found his concentration wandering from the all-important work sheet to the phone that lay on the table tantalisingly close to his right hand. He'd have thought that Bryony would have checked her mail by now, and part of him had been expecting a call. He hoped that there was nothing wrong. Maybe his dangerous situation had scared her off. It was an awful lot to ask of anyone, let alone a new girlfriend. She didn't seem like the type to get cold feet, but having a murderer stalking your date could send the toughest Amazon heading for the hills.

He stared at the clock. If he hadn't promised Nikki that he would do all he could to find out what had happened to

Martin, he would have driven over to Bryony's home, and spoken to her before she left for work. As it was, the best he could do was to ring her office. He was probably being stupid and over protective, but with Billy Sweet still out there, Bryony's lack of communication was giving him the jitters. All he wanted was a few words to say that she was safe.

As if on cue, his phone burst into a loud, tinny discordant tune, and he grabbed at it, his heart thumping in his throat.

'Joseph? You sound weird? Something wrong?'

His heart sank. 'Nikki, eh, no nothing's wrong. I just need to change the ringtone on this new phone, it scares the pants off you when it rings.'

'Oh, right. Well, just to say that Niall Farrow is on his way to you. Yvonne was my first choice, she's more experienced, but she's also cleverer at fending off questions as to where her crewmate is, so you have Niall, okay?'

'Great. We'll get stuck in as soon as he arrives. How are things there?'

'About as busy as Christmas Eve in Tesco's car park. It's bedlam. Anything more from Elizabeth last night?'

'Maybe. I'll check them out and report my findings, but I was just wondering . . .'

'I'm not sure I like the tone of your voice, Joseph. Don't tell me you want more help?'

'Not help exactly, just a small favour.'

'And that is?'

'It's Bryony. I haven't been able to get an answer on her phone. We agreed to talk last night but she never answered. Same thing this morning.'

There was a silence, and Joseph wondered what Nikki was going to say. When she did finally speak he noted concern in her voice. 'And what are you thinking exactly?'

'I'm not sure. I may be panicking unnecessarily, but he did see her. Billy Sweet saw her. Down at the river walk. And he knows that she saw him too, which could put her in grave danger, couldn't it?'

Another silence. This time longer.

'Joseph.' Nikki sounded tense.

'What?' He frowned at the phone. 'Nikki, has something happened?'

'Not what you're thinking, Joseph, so don't jump to conclusions, but there may be a good reason why Bryony hasn't answered your calls.'

His discomfort increased. 'And?'

'Oh shit! I'm not sure I should tell you this, but hell, you need to know. Just don't bite my head off, okay?'

Joseph began to feel a heady mix of concern and anger fill his mind. 'For God's sake, just tell me!'

'I spoke to Bryony yesterday, Joseph. I needed her to give me something more of a description of your stalker.'

Confusion blunted the growing anger. 'But I told you, she said that she only saw a shadowy figure jump over the wall and down onto the towpath.'

'I needed to hear her account, not yours, do you understand?'

Joseph swallowed. 'Yes, I suppose, but what did she say?'

'That she never saw anything, or anybody.'

'No! No, that's wrong!' His voice rose to almost a shout. 'She said . . .'

'I *know* what she said to you, but she saw how upset you were, and she wanted to give you some sort of support. She lied, Joseph. For your sake. She thought she was helping you.'

'And you knew this? So why the hell didn't you tell me last night?' He knew he should never speak to Nikki in that way, but the anger made his head ache with its burning intensity.

'Because she wanted to tell you herself. She made me promise not to mention it. And I thought that was only right.' Nikki's voice had softened. 'And I believed she would, Joseph. She cares about you, I'm sure of that, and I thought that she deserved the chance to explain.'

'Well, she's obviously thought better of it,' he muttered. 'Probably thought better of the whole damn thing and she's dumped me. She just hasn't found the courage to actually tell me yet.'

'Don't get ahead of yourself, Sergeant!' barked Nikki, her voice now back to normal. 'We know nothing for sure, and I only told you that because I thought it would help you. Think about it! If she didn't see your killer, then he didn't see her either. So the chances of him going after her are negligible, yes?'

Joseph's head was spinning. 'I suppose, but . . .'

'Look, give me her address. I'll get someone to knock on her door. What time does she leave for work?'

Joseph checked his watch. 'In about fifteen minutes.'

'Damn it! Oh, if it makes you happy, I'll go myself, it'll be quicker than trying to organise someone else.'

He heard her chair squeak as she jumped up. He rattled off the address, then said, 'Thank you.'

'Yeah, and you really owe me, Joseph Easter. I'll ring you when I get there.'

Joseph stared at the phone. His hopes had been dashed. Once again, he was the only witness. No one else had ever seen that murdering bastard Sweet, unless they were being killed by him, and then they would have had the dubious pleasure of seeing those dead eyes staring through them. He shivered. The thought of Billy Sweet being the last thing you ever saw was terrifying.

He placed the phone back on the table, then almost yelped with shock as it rang again. He grabbed it, but saw it was a message rather than a call.

Joseph. Sorry 2 miss your calls. Mobile on the blink. Will sort it and ring tonight. Miss you 2. CU soon. Bryony xx

His breath caught in his throat. Thank God! He saved the message then pushed the button for dial. Shit! He'd just sent Nikki flying off on a wild goose chase! He punched in her name, and heard it ring only once before she answered it.

'This had better be good!'

'Ma'am! It's me! Cancel my last! I've just heard from her!'

'You are *so* lucky that I'd only got as far as the car! Is she okay?'

'I had a text, said her phone was malfunctioning. She sounds fine.'

'Are you happy with that?'

'Yeah, I'm sure it's kosher,' he sighed with relief. 'Thanks anyway, Nikki. I still owe you.'

'You're so right, sunshine! Now go get your fuzzy little head around Martin Durham's death, okay?'

'Roger! Over and out.'

* * *

Niall arrived ten minutes later, placed his car keys inside his hat and laid it on the kitchen table.

'Before we get to work, Sarge, the team asked me to tell you how sorry we all are, and that we are all right behind you. The chief must need his head read to be standing you down like this.' Niall flopped into one of the old pine chairs and gave Joseph a boyish grin. 'So, whatever I can do to help, bring it on.'

Joseph made more tea, and as he did, he carefully filled the young officer in on everything he knew about Martin Durham and the suspect 'suicides.'

'Phew.' Niall let out a low whistle. 'This all has a very bad feel to it, doesn't it?' He scratched his head. 'One thing I can tell you is that forensics say there is no more to be gleaned from Knot Cottage. It was the work of a highly trained pro, and no evidence was obtained that would help to identify the intruder. And sorry, but the guv'nor asked me to mention that the DNA that she extracted from him during their fight came up with no match on our database.'

'Damn it! We were kind of relying on that.'

'That's approximately what the DI said, only her version was more colourful.'

Joseph shrugged. 'Okay, so let's adjourn to the study and see what we can find out about David Kowalski. You ring the hospital, and I'll try to contact his sister.'

Linda Kowalski sounded nervous on answering the phone. 'Every time it rings I dread bad news,' she explained.

Joseph carefully told her why he was ringing, then waited for the woman to say that she had no idea what he was talking about. Instead, after a short pause, she simply said. 'We need to talk, Sergeant, and the sooner the better.'

Joseph took a sharp breath. 'When and where?'

'I'll be leaving for the hospital soon, but we need to talk privately. Do you know the playing field next to the hospital? I'll be in a red Ford Ka. I'll meet you in the car park.'

Joseph lowered the phone, and looked across at Niall. 'What have you got?'

'David is critical. No chance of talking to him,' he pulled a face. 'Doesn't sound good, I'm afraid.'

'Then everything depends on his sister.' He stood up. 'We want the park next to the hospital, and separate cars may be sensible. I'll follow you.'

* * *

Linda Kowalski had grey hair and the look of a woman who had spent most of her years exposed to the elements. She smiled wanly at Joseph and he prayed that Niall's uniform and the fact that they were sitting in a Fenland Constabulary squad car would deter her from asking to see his warrant card. 'Why is David in hospital?' he asked gently.

'He had an allergic reaction to his medication.' She stared at him almost angrily. 'Although why? He's been on the same drugs for years.'

Joseph exhaled sharply. 'And were they as a result of clinical trials in his youth?'

Linda nodded grimly. 'I was on them too; all young and fired up to do our bit. But I opted out early, and Davey, passionate to this day, continued for years.'

'I hate to tell you this, but we have reason to believe that your brother's medication was tampered with.'

Linda suddenly grasped his wrist. 'So do I!'

'How much do you know about what went on?' asked Joseph urgently.

'Pretty well everything. And although David swore never to speak, I didn't.'

Joseph swung round to face Niall. 'You have to take Miss Kowalski to the station. Directly to DI Galena, understand?'

'Not before I've seen my brother,' she added firmly.

'You could be in serious danger, Linda. I need to get you to a place of safety.'

'Fine. After I've seen David.'

'I'll call for another crew, Sarge,' interjected Niall. 'We'll stick with Miss Kowalski, then they can keep watch on her brother while I take her back to the nick.'

'Yes, do it.'

As Niall radioed in, Joseph looked carefully at Linda Kowalski, 'What was the last trial about? It wasn't cold cures, was it?'

'Very few of the trials were,' she snorted distastefully. 'Mainly they were for rheumatoid treatments, testing with gold, or sulphasalazine. The last one however . . .' her voice dropped to a whisper, '. . . was for drugs that were being used to interrogate prisoners, well, foreign spies and traitors, more like. We are talking the Cold War, Sergeant.'

'So this *is* MOD stuff?'

'No, I don't think so. It was a big pharmaceutical corporation. We were told it was British and we truly believed that we were helping our country, now I'm not so sure.'

'And what was this drug? A truth serum?'

'No, a special kind of hallucinogen. It didn't make the user tell the truth, it altered their perceptions of reality, so things that normally would have been of paramount importance meant absolutely nothing.'

Joseph shivered. 'And did David know what he was being tested with?'

'Oh yes, they all did. The group was totally committed to the trials. They believed they were pioneers.'

Joseph thought about Martin, Amelia and Paul, and the terrible deception made him feel nauseous. 'So what happened?'

'They signed waivers. They were well paid, and when the drug proved to be a devastating mistake, they were offered a very large one-off payment and private medical care for the rest of their lives. Then they willingly signed more legal disclaimers that bound them from ever talking about the tests and everything and everyone involved. And why not? They believed the doctors were the good guys.'

'And *were* they looked after?'

'Absolutely. And with great care. Medication, regular check-ups and even highly qualified personal liaison managers to help with any problems.'

'Can you get hold of one of them for me?' asked Joseph quickly.

The woman's face darkened. 'Funny that. Their numbers are suddenly unobtainable.'

Joseph cursed silently, then murmured, 'So what's gone wrong?'

Linda shook her head. 'I really don't know. After all these years of support, why abandon them now?'

Not abandonment, thought Joseph, this is termination.

'There is one thing.' Linda stared at him. 'About a year ago a woman came sniffing round asking questions. David was sure that she was a reporter. He told her nothing and reported it to his liaison officer. He was pretty certain that he was the only member of the trials group that she'd managed to trace, but it was just after that that Amelia died.' She shrugged. 'Maybe nothing to do with the journalist, but . . . ?'

Joseph's mind raced. A reporter onto something? Can't kill the reporter, too high profile, so damage limitation? Quietly dispose of the 'loyal pioneers' so that there was nothing left to uncover.

'The other crew is pulling in, Sarge. We'll take it from here.' Niall pulled on his hat. 'You'll be safe with me. I'll escort you all the way, Miss Kowalski.'

'Take great care of her, Constable.' Joseph turned to Linda. 'And humour me here, will you? Please don't eat or drink anything until you are safe at the police station. Nothing at all, is that clear?'

Linda nodded, and as Joseph stepped from the car he knew that she totally understood the implications of his request. He watched the two vehicles pull away, then raced back to his Ford and rang Nikki.

'Then it's almost a given thing that they were murdered, isn't it, Joseph?' There was a tremor in his boss's voice. 'I really do have to thank you for that, and Martin would thank you too.'

'It's nothing, Nikki, but I suggest it's going to get even more difficult from here on in, finding those responsible. If we ever do,' he sighed. 'But still, if you can do as much for me with Billy Sweet, I'd be eternally grateful.'

'I will get you answers, Joseph. I will take this killer off the streets, I promise you.'

'I know you will. And no matter how painful this is for me, Nikki, you have to do whatever it takes, you know that, don't you?'

He hardly heard her reply. It was little more than an under breath. 'Whatever it takes, Joseph, I'll do it.'

As he drove back towards Cloud Fen, he prayed that she meant it.

CHAPTER TWENTY-FOUR

Nikki picked up the photograph of Martin, Hannah and herself and gave it a light kiss. 'I never believed for one moment that you could have voluntarily jumped from that tower, my friend, and certainly not in front of those little kids.'

She felt a surge of optimism. As Joseph had said, it wouldn't be easy, but they were on their way to clearing the stigma from her old friend's name.

Then she thought about Joseph. As she had replaced the handset, she felt his frustration pouring out across the ether. She'd come very close to being suspended herself on more than one occasion. She'd sailed too close to the wind and ruffled an awful lot of gold braid as she did, but somehow she had always managed to hang on to her position. Which made it all the tougher on Joseph. If they'd thrown the book at her, she would have deserved it. In the past she had crossed lines, cheated, bullied and flaunted the rulebook to get the drug dealers sent down. Joseph on the other hand had been an exemplary officer, honest, full of integrity and moral fibre, and it was *his* warrant card that was sitting in the super's filing cabinet along with a half-bottle of malt whisky.

Nikki shook her head. It wasn't fair, but at least his enforced absence had brought them closer to unravelling the sinister cover-up and ruthless killing of innocent people.

She took a long look at the old picture, then placed it back on her desk. As she did, she noticed the scrap of paper on which she had written Bryony Barton's address. She picked it up and stared at it. Joseph had seemed quite happy at receiving the text, but had Bryony actually sent it? It had come from her number, but anyone could have tapped it in. She stared at her own cell phone. How many times had she left it unattended on the desk?

Allowing herself to forget Martin Durham for the first time in days, she looked again at the address. If she had been Joseph, knowing there was a killer on the loose, she wouldn't have been content with a text message. No way. And Bryony had been out of contact for quite a while now. Perhaps too long for comfort.

Nikki pushed back her chair and looked around her small office. Something wasn't right. With a determined snort, she pulled a contact file from her drawer. Joseph had told her that Bryony worked at the Public Analysts Laboratory, and that number would be listed. She ran a finger down the page, then stopped and grunted with satisfaction.

Nikki dialled the number and waited.

'I'm sorry but Miss Barton called in sick today. If it's regarding a sample for analysis, I can put you through to the technician who is covering her workload?'

Nikki paused, then said, 'No, it's nothing like that. I am DI Galena, Greenborough CID, and I need to speak to whoever is in charge.'

'I'll put you through to the lab manager.'

There was a period filled with clicking sounds and a melee of tinny music, then a deep voice said, 'Simon Lewis, how can I help you?'

Nikki introduced herself and told him that she needed to contact Bryony Barton on a matter of some importance.

The man was naturally hesitant, so Nikki gave him the station number and after a few moments, he was back on the line.

'I understand her mobile is down so I need to check her home address with you, if that's okay?' Nikki quoted the street number that she had, and Lewis confirmed that it was correct.

'I'm not sure about her mobile being down though. I'm sure it was her number that showed up on the display when she rang in sick,' the man paused then added, '. . . even though it was her friend that spoke to me.'

Nikki felt a hard jolt of concern. 'Friend?'

'Yes, a man. But I didn't like to pry. I know very little about her private life so I rather assumed it was a partner.'

Nikki's mouth felt dry as she asked. 'How long has Bryony worked for you?'

'Around eighteen months now, I suppose.'

'And is she popular?'

'Very. She's an asset to our little team.' Lewis gave a short chuckle. 'Although I'm sure she won't be here long term. She is far too highly qualified to waste her life doing lab checks on dodgy kebabs.'

'Qualified in what way?' asked Nikki suspiciously.

'She is a biomedical scientist, Inspector. She specialised in pharmokinetics.'

'Is that as complex as it sounds?'

'Complicated is correct, and Bryony is top-notch.'

'So what's she doing with you?'

'It's nothing unusual, Inspector. When kids with PhD's are stacking supermarket shelves, this could be classed as a good job to have. And she's very happy here.'

Nikki thanked the man, but before she hung up she added. 'Sorry to ask, but is she helping you to arrange a charity event of some kind?'

'The scavenger hunt? Oh yes, it's for the Butterfly Hospice. Can we put you down for a donation?' he asked hopefully.

An image of her ailing father flashed across her mind. 'Sure. Put me down for twenty quid.'

Something was terribly wrong. She knew it as clearly as when a musician hit a bum note. It jangled like a cacophony of lies in her head. Nikki had a built-in warning system. A heightened sense of wrongness.

And right now it was smothering her. She was pretty certain that there was more to Bryony than Joseph knew about, but whatever that was, she may be in terrible danger.

She jumped up and opened her office door. 'Yvonne! Quickly, take a couple more uniforms and get yourself around to 176 Blackfen Road. Ring me directly you're on scene and let me know whether Bryony Barton is there and safe, okay?'

* * *

The answer was back in ten minutes.

'There's no response, ma'am. The next door neighbour says she hasn't seen her since early yesterday morning.' Yvonne sounded worried. 'Shall we force an entry?'

Nikki thought about the fall-out if she happened to be wrong. 'Yes. Do it now.'

A few seconds later she heard the sound of several crashes, then hurried footsteps.

'Place is clear, ma'am,' said Yvonne. 'There's no sign of a struggle, but we'll do a thorough check and report back in a few minutes.' The line went dead and Nikki was forced to wait for what seemed like an eternity before Yvonne got back to her.

'There's nothing to indicate that she was planning on doing a runner, ma'am. Her laptop is still on standby, Sky+ is set to record an OU lecture, and there's fresh milk and food in the fridge. And importantly, her clothes are still hanging in the wardrobe.'

'Is there a diary or a calendar? We need to know if she had any meetings planned.'

'Nothing, ma'am. I'd thought of that.'

Nikki thanked her and asked her to hurry back to the station, and bring the computer with her. It sounded to her

225

like Bryony had had every intention of returning home but something or someone had prevented her.

'You look like you could do with this, guv.' Cat Cullen placed a mug of coffee in front of her.

'You are so right.' Nikki rubbed her forehead.

Cat perched on the edge of her desk. 'What's worrying you?'

'Bryony Barton,' murmured Nikki. 'She should be at work. She isn't. Work thinks she is at home sick. She isn't. No one has been able to contact her to actually talk to her since yesterday. All her belongings are untouched. Ergo, she isn't on her toes. Plus . . .' she stared at Cat uncomfortably, 'an unknown male rang her office this morning using *her* cell phone. And that makes me feel very uneasy indeed.'

'So where the hell is she?'

'I wish I knew, and weirdly it seems that I may have been the last one to see her.'

'You're worried about her connection with Joseph, and *his* connection with the psycho-assassin, aren't you?'

'That woman has been out of touch for around twenty-four hours,' Nikki shivered, 'that's far too long.'

'Does Joseph know?'

'No. He had a reassuring text from her, but I'm not so sure that *she* sent it.'

'Shouldn't we tell him?' asked Cat.

'Joseph's in a very dark place right now, Cat. He'll have to be told of course, but I have no way of even guessing how he will react. Not only that . . .'

Before she could continue, her desk phone rang.

'Ma'am? Sergeant Conway here. A couple of my officers have just attended a shout at 3 Granary Close, off Fishguard Avenue. We were called regarding a suspected break-in, but they've found the body of an IC1 male.'

Nikki stiffened. Not now. 'Please don't tell me he has blond hair and blue eyes?'

''Fraid so, ma'am. Forensics have been notified and are already on their way, but will you attend?'

'Damn right I will!' Nikki threw down the phone. 'Cat! With me!'

* * *

'Oh dear God,' whispered Cat, zipping up her protective suit. 'I had no idea there were so many men in Greenborough with blond thatches and blue eyes.'

The dead man looked like a wicked parody of Chris Forbes, although this man's life blood soaked into plush cream carpet, not weeds and filthy rubble. His hands were tied carefully behind him and the wide gaping wound across his throat was beginning to look horribly familiar. Nikki looked across at Professor Rory Wilkinson. 'Don't have to ask if it's the same MO, do I?'

'It seems that way, although this one must have put up a fight. His face is badly bruised, and . . .' Rory's expression was uncharacteristically serious. 'I don't know, I've only been here a few minutes, but . . .'

'You have reservations?' She looked at the dead man's corn-blond hair. 'Why?'

He stood up and stared down at the body. 'Not reservations exactly.' He gave her a tired smile. 'I've learnt never to assume anything until my investigations are complete.'

Nikki nodded slowly. That was fair comment, but she had the distinct feeling that the professor was not comfortable. 'One of my men says we have ID this time.'

'You do. And maybe that's what is odd.' He nodded towards an expensive-looking solid wood table. 'Over there, credit cards and a valid security pass card, although I have no idea to what it gives access. Your man says there is a pocket diary too. Something I'm sure you will be happy to ferret through.'

'Makes a change, that's for certain,' said Nikki. 'Which makes me wonder if he was disturbed and left in a hurry. The others had been carefully stripped of all ID.'

'That or he actually wants us to know who this victim is,' added Cat thoughtfully.

'Maybe.' She looked around. 'Or perhaps he's losing his touch. His last attack was thwarted, now this victim has been left with clear identification with him. Seems as if he's either getting careless or distracted.' She looked back to the pathologist. 'No other obvious evidence?'

'One thing. This man is clean and his clothes are well cared for, but your officers found a pile of filthy, and I mean absolutely rancid, clothes in the bathroom.' He rolled his eyes at her. 'But other than that, nothing yet, and probably won't be. Our poor SOCOs are tearing their hair out at lack of physical or biological evidence. They are sure it's the same professional clean-up job.' He looked around, 'And this flat was no slum to begin with, was it?' He pointed towards a painting that hung over a modern futuristic-looking stainless steel fireplace. 'I keep looking at that landscape and trying to tell myself it's a print, that it can't in a million years be a genuine Milton Avery.' His eyes widened. 'No way would an Avery be hanging, unprotected, in a classy little flat in Greenborough. But hell, I still keep looking at it.'

'Milton Avery?' asked Cat staring suspiciously at the strange painting.

'My dear girl, he was called the American Matisse, and one passed through Christie's in New York not so long ago for the princely sum of over nine hundred thousand dollars.'

'Then it's a print,' said Nikki flatly. 'This guy was clearly no Rockefeller.'

'Well, naturally they don't all fetch that kind of money. Maybe it's a family heirloom, or an investment.'

'And maybe it came from eBay for 99p with free postage, but this is not exactly helping our enquiry.' Being careful not to touch anything, Nikki walked over to the table and looked down at the security badge. 'Kurt Michael Carson. You really are a dead ringer for William Sweet, deceased, aren't you?' she whispered. From the inch square photo, there was no doubt that it belonged to the murdered man. 'I'll bag the diary and take it, then we'll let you get on doing your usual admirable job, Rory.'

'Be my guest. And I'll get my preliminary report to you in my normal speedy and efficient manner.'

'I'd expect nothing less.' Nikki threw him an almost affectionate smile as she turned to leave. 'And if I find that weird picture hanging on the mortuary wall next week, remember, I know where it came from.'

* * *

Cat yawned and stretched. 'I think I've just about exhausted all avenues, ma'am.'

'So recap for me.' Nikki also stretched her aching back.

'Kurt Michael Carson. British born, Dutch mother, English father. Age thirty-seven. Single. Works abroad and his company owns the property in which he was killed, the flat in Granary Close. Seems to have a healthy bank balance and no outstanding debts. He worked for an exporter called Carel Flora Bloemenexport. They export exotic flowers and plants from Holland. I rang them and spoke to his boss. The man was obviously shocked but asked if he could be kept informed as he would travel over to represent the firm at the funeral.'

'I hope you told him that could be some time yet?'

'I did. Oh, and Carson's worked for that company for four years. He's some kind of top rep, I think.'

'And how long has he been at that flat?' asked Nikki.

'I haven't been able to confirm that yet. The owners of the upstairs apartment said they have rarely seen him. He goes away for long periods and they've never been in conversation other than a casual greeting.' Cat yawned again. 'Looks like his only problem in life was that he closely resembled Billy Sweet.'

'Okay, well, tomorrow we will need to get out there and find someone who knew him. What's the betting that he magically developed a new best friend in the last few weeks?' She looked at Cat and saw dark lines under her eyes. 'And now, home. Get some sleep.'

'But what about Bryony Barton, guv? We still don't know where the devil she is.'

'Look, there's still a chance I'm overreacting. She may have another man in tow. She's a stunning-looking woman, and she could be shacked up somewhere drinking champagne and being drooled over by some handsome stud, while we run round like headless chickens searching for her.'

'You believe that?'

Nikki shrugged. 'No. But I'm not sure what I believe any more. None of us know much about her, do we?' She took a deep breath. 'Although strangely I do think she cares for Joseph. I'm going to get someone to check out the local CCTV footage. See where she went when she left here yesterday, then I'm going to check on Linda Kowalski, and *you*, detective, are going to do as I say and throw in the towel for today. You look knackered, and I need you daisy-fresh, okay?'

Cat raised her hands in surrender. 'Thanks, boss. But I'll be back in early, I promise.'

Nikki watched the woman leave, then picked up the phone and rang Joseph. She had no intention of telling him about her concerns for Bryony, and she wasn't too sure about letting on about the latest killing either. Maybe she'd just give him her ETA, then tell him everything over a glass of wine when she got home later.

CHAPTER TWENTY-FIVE

'I've got her.'

Joseph froze, as the pale, expressionless eyes of Billy Sweet swam into his head.

'And before you say anything, Bunny dear, I want you to listen *very* carefully. The gorgeous Miss Barton's life depends on your silence and your full attention.'

Joseph struggled not to scream obscenities down the phone, but the thought of Bryony being held by that animal kept his mouth obediently shut.

'Naturally you will want proof that she's still alive . . .' there was a small giggle in his voice, 'knowing my past record. And in a moment, I'll let her speak, but right now, soldier, just listen and follow orders. You will be at the rendezvous in exactly half an hour. You will tell no one, especially your piggy friends. If I suspect anything at all, pretty Bryony will be executed. Assuming you still have a modicum of sense, you will arrive alone at Knot Cottage in thirty minutes. Now, listen to this . . .'

There were some scraping sounds, a muffled groan, then Joseph heard her voice. It crackled with fear, but he had no doubt it was Bryony. 'Joseph! Help me! Please!' There was a tiny break in her voice, then she whispered, 'He's insane. He *will* kill me.'

'Hold on, Bryony, I'll do anything he wants. I promise. Just hold on.'

There was a muffled cry, then he heard, 'Thirty minutes, Bunny-boy, and alone.' A hissing noise replaced the ugly voice, and then there was silence.

Joseph stared at the receiver, his face set in an expression of revulsion and fear.

Very slowly he put the phone down and took a long ragged breath. His first thought was to call Nikki. He was a police officer for God's sake, and not one to be intimidated by threats. Then he saw Bryony's face, and heard again the words, "He's insane. He will kill me." He of all people knew that she was right on both counts, and thoughts of talking to Nikki faded. He had to go to Knot Cottage, and he had to go alone.

* * *

Nikki sat alone in her office. Nothing was making sense any more, and the terrible feeling of wrongness was blocking cohesive thought and cramping her stomach. Bits of conversation filtered slowly into the word soup that used to be her brain, and she dropped forward, elbows on her desk and head in hands. What *was* it that was really tearing her up?

The thought came to her as clearly as a Fenland church bell ringing over the fields on a cloudless day. It was Bryony.

She pushed back her chair and almost ran out into the murder room. 'Dave! Yvonne! I need you! Now!'

As she turned back into her office, Dave was right with her and Yvonne only a step behind.

'Bryony Barton. I want to know everything you can dig up on her, and I mean everything.' She looked at them urgently. 'This is all I know to date, take it from there, and grab all the help you can.'

She rattled off the few facts that she knew about the woman and sat back.

'Why is this so important?' asked Dave anxiously.

Nikki frowned. 'I don't know, but trust me, it is. All I keep thinking is that Bryony arrived out of nowhere and has been Joseph's shadow ever since, and so has someone else, someone very dangerous.'

'Someone who kills people,' added Yvonne darkly.

'Exactly. There is something about Bryony that doesn't ring true, and now she's missing.' Her brow knit even tighter. 'Maybe she's not after Joseph at all. Maybe she's after the man we are calling Billy Sweet.'

'The killer?' asked Yvonne incredulously 'To stop him, or to help him?'

'I don't like the sound of either of those options,' muttered Dave. 'And there's another scenario, isn't there? What if the killer has snatched Bryony? We agreed that he is probably trying to get at Joseph, so who better to abduct than someone he really cares about?' Dave ran a hand through his hair and swallowed hard. 'We'd better get to work. Come on, Vonnie. You make a start; I'll grab a few more bodies and let's see what we can find.'

'I'll ring Joseph back,' said Nikki grabbing the phone. 'I'm really not happy with him being stuck out on the marsh alone.'

Joseph picked up almost immediately, and listened carefully to everything she said. After a moment or two he said, 'I'm okay, Nikki. I can take care of myself.'

'And I think you should come here directly, Joseph. Get off the fen.' She hadn't wanted to tell him, but hell, he'd hear soon enough. 'There's been another execution. Another Billy Sweet lookalike. You are not safe alone, Joseph. I want you where I can see you, so get yourself here, and fast. That's an order!'

'Okay. But there's something I must do before . . .' His words came out slowly and were edged with concern.

'Believe me, there is nothing more important than getting off Cloud Fen! And if you don't, I'll send a squad car to pick you up. Do you understand, Sergeant?'

'Don't do that, Nikki. I'll get there as soon as I can. I promise.'

'Be careful, Joseph. If anything happens out there, you are miles from help.' She lowered the phone back into its cradle but felt far from relieved by the call. Joseph had sounded strained and what on earth did he have to do that was so damned important? Nikki bit her lip. She had no idea what it was, but she was damned sure that for once it wasn't chopping bloody chilli peppers.

It took only fifteen minutes to get a basic profile of Bryony Barton.

'You're sure she has no siblings?' Nikki demanded of Yvonne.

'Absolutely. Only child of Dr Aaron James Barton, deceased, and Denise Clover Barton, née Bridgewater, of Kendal. Went to school in Carnforth, university at Lancaster, Bio-science degrees, honours, etc.'

'She said that she had a brother who was in the same ward in Greenborough Hospital as Joseph. And she told Joseph the same thing, said it was where she first saw him.'

'Well, that may be correct, but she wasn't visiting a brother, that's for certain. Mm . . .' said Yvonne thoughtfully, '. . . but she may have been visiting *someone* on that ward! I'll see if the hospital can open up Medical Records for me and get a list of patients treated over the same time as the sarge.'

As Yvonne disappeared, Dave placed a sheet of paper in front of her. 'Her whereabouts since she left Lancaster, according to the CV that she gave to her present employer.' He stabbed a finger onto the page. 'These were all verified by the PA lab manager. Some pretty technical posts, all with impressive titles that are Greek to me. Then six years ago she went to Germany for an interview, and from that point, things get fuzzy. She seems to have spent four and a half years chasing in and out of the country. One of our lads has identified her as a frequent flier with several major airlines, and all business class. Then bang, she takes a poorly paid job with the Public Analyst, buys a bijou property, and becomes Miss Perfectly Ordinary. Weird, or what?'

'Has anyone accessed her finances yet?' asked Nikki.

'Someone is onto that right now, guv. I'll go chase it up.'

Dave left and Nikki tried to calm the turmoil that was churning her guts into a tight knot. She played out an old conversation that Joseph had had with her about Bryony. Bit of a home-lover, he'd said. Didn't travel much except for the occasional winter sunshine top-up and her older brother was something of a tearaway. All lies. But why?

She rubbed at her sore eyes, then saw Yvonne approaching the door.

'We're in luck, guv! Just listen to this! One of the patients on Curlew Ward, who overlapped the sarge by one day, was Kurt Michael Carson. Bryony had to have been visiting the man who has just become the latest victim of Billy Sweet!'

'So they are all connected in some way!' Nikki banged her fist up and down on her desk. 'But hell's teeth, how?' She closed her eyes and tried to think. 'What was Carson in hospital for?'

'RTC with a drunk driver apparently, fractured cheek bone and some other minor injuries. The reason he was on the sarge's ward was they suspected abdominal bleeding. They did an exploratory op, sorted him out and he was discharged.'

'I think it's time to double-check that our dead guy is the same man.' Nikki picked up her phone and punched in the number for Professor Wilkinson.

Rory sounded exhausted. 'Yes, dear lady. I can confirm that our fresh cadaver has all those attributes, recently healed fracture of the zygomatic arch and a small surgical scar in the upper abdo, amongst numerous old injuries. He's one and the same, Nikki.'

'Thanks, Rory. Sorry to hold you up, I know how busy you are.'

'Mm, I'd be quite grateful if you could catch this public executioner. I've always loved variety, and I'm getting rather bored with identical methods of dispatch, not to mention the crow's feet that are multiplying around my eyes as we speak!'

'I'm working on it, believe me! Oh, Rory, by the way, what are pharmokinetics?'

'Ah, planning a change of career, are we? Well, it's the study of how drugs are absorbed into, distributed, then broken down and eliminated by the human body. Your scientist would work closely with each individual patient to make sure that they got the very best from a prescribed drug regime. It's a very personal, patient-focussed thing.' He paused. 'I assume you are referring to your friend Martin Durham? It's the sort of thing that he would have benefited from.'

'No, it's nothing to do with Martin,' said Nikki slowly. 'We have a missing person, and that is her apparent occupation.'

'Complex stuff, Nikki. She must be a bright woman.'

'I'm sure she is,' mused Nikki. 'Thank you, Rory.'

* * *

Joseph slipped the key from the lock of Cloud Cottage Farm and walked soundlessly down the path. There was little to show of the recent storm. A few puddles in sheltered spots, but the lane had dried out, and the air was still and warm. It would have been a beautiful evening, had his mind not been full.

He had a knife with him. It was carefully concealed in a small cash pocket in the waistband of his chinos. But even so, he felt naked, unprotected.

Knot Cottage seemed deserted, but it would. Sweet was a pro. There would be nothing on view to attract unwanted visitors. Vaguely Joseph wondered why Billy should even know about Martin Durham's home, but then Sweet would have been watching Joseph's every move, and the lonely little cottage was the perfect place for their reunion.

He wished with all his heart that he could be meeting Billy Sweet alone. To know that Bryony was close by was a distraction. She would be his Achilles' heel, his weak point. And Sweet would know that. In a military operation Joseph knew that he would have been steely cool, in total command of his responses, his actions and his reactions, but with a woman that you cared about in mortal danger, he had no idea how he would cope. Nothing like this had ever happened before. He slowed down. Except once. With Nikki.

Joseph gazed upwards into the dark sky, and murmured a small prayer. 'Keep us safe, keep us from harm, keep us from evil.'

The lane gave way to the track down to the cottage. Joseph braced himself. He had kept his side of the bargain. He had come alone. Now would Billy Sweet show some sort of respect for his action and spare Bryony?

He swallowed and involuntarily gave a soft humourless laugh. Who was he kidding? Sweet was a psycho, he wouldn't recognise morality if he tripped over it. No, if Bryony was to survive, it meant that he must dispatch Billy first, before he killed again.

Joseph shivered and reached out for the door handle. He wouldn't be entering in military style. No throwing back the door and charging in all guns blazing. He had nothing in his favour. He could do no more than walk into the spider's web and keep praying.

The door swung back silently. He took a step inside, half expecting a trip-wire and a flash of explosive, then when that didn't happen, he stood in the quiet and listened.

He knew he was not alone. His senses, still highly tuned to his surroundings told him that. The sound of a breath? The hint of a stirring of the air? A tiny movement in your peripheral vision?

Somewhere there was a light source. It was very dim, like a candle or a night-light. And in the shadows, Joseph knew that a figure was sitting in a high wing-backed armchair. It was angled away from him, but he saw the legs from the knees down, and the feet casually stretched out in front. He saw desert boots and the cuffs of army fatigues.

He wanted to leap on Sweet. Take him from behind and crush his windpipe. But he knew that he would never get close enough to even touch him.

'I came alone.' His voice sounded odd, even to his own ears.

The figure moved slightly, and Joseph saw the dull glint of metal in Sweet's lap. The muzzle of a gun was pointing to the only other chair in the sitting room. 'I knew you would. Sit down, Joseph.'

Whatever he had imagined, it was not this.

The light came from a tiny battery-powered storm lantern that stood in the hearth, and in its feeble glow, Joseph saw Bryony.

'Bry? My God! You're safe!' There was elation in his voice, and he wanted to rush forward, to grab her, hold her . . . but something stopped him. A trap? He steeled himself, then scanned the dark corners of the room. 'Where is he? Where's Sweet?'

Her voice was little more than a whisper. 'He's not here, Joseph.'

Confusion flooded his brain, and in the absence of a better idea, he moved numbly towards the other chair and sank slowly into it. 'Bry? The phone call? I don't understand.'

'My poor sweet Joseph, of course you don't understand, and why should you?' There was something like compassion in her voice. 'This is all such a mess, such a terrible mess.'

He stared at her, trying to make out the woman he cared so much about, but she was little more than a wraith in the darkness of the armchair. And he had been wrong about the camouflage trousers and boots. Maybe that was what he had expected to see. Actually she was wearing a dark long-sleeved T-shirt, khaki cargo pants and casual suede short boots. It was the gun that he really couldn't get his head around.

'Do you love me, Joseph?'

He swallowed. It was not what he had expected her to ask him. And not at gunpoint. His mind twisted itself into knots. What was expected of him? What should he say? He took a few deep breaths and calmed himself. The truth had always worked in the past 'I was beginning to think that way, yes.'

She eased forward in the chair and the light from the tiny lantern caught her eyes. For a minute he thought he saw hope in them, along with the traces of recent tears.

'Then we need to talk, Joseph. Because a lot depends on it.'

CHAPTER TWENTY-SIX

Dave placed a sheaf of papers on her desk and stepped back. 'I don't get it. Bryony is loaded! Accounts everywhere, both here and abroad, and they are just the ones we've managed to identify. Heaven knows what other offshore ones she has.'

Nikki jutted her jaw forward. 'God! We need to know more about her. Especially what she was doing from Germany onwards.'

'Sorry, but I'm stuck there, ma'am,' said Dave. 'She had no regular wage, but very large amounts of money were being paid in, and all untraceable.' Dave gave an exasperated sigh. 'I reckon she's one of those spooks. A spy.'

Nikki stared at him and a picture of Bryony swam into her mind. Strong, athletic, by her own admission a very strong swimmer, and highly intelligent, even if she made out otherwise. A highly qualified scientist.

Dave raised his eyebrows. 'I *was* joking, guv.'

'Maybe you're not so wrong,' breathed Nikki. 'I think I need the super to make some delicate enquiries to see if any other departments or agencies have interests in her.'

Five minutes later the superintendent appeared in her office doorway. 'There have been some very hot secure lines active on your behalf, Nikki, but I'm sorry to say that she is not one of ours, and as far I can ascertain, not military or government either.' He looked anxiously at her. 'And as I wasn't warned off by anyone, I'm pretty confident that she's not in deep cover either.'

Nikki felt a rush of foreboding.

'Be careful, Nikki,' the super turned to leave. 'There are other agencies out there. Powerful ones that we have no connections to, so tread warily, okay?'

She nodded and watched him go. As the door closed, she lifted the receiver and dialled her own number. 'Come on, come on!' The phone rang on until the answerphone cut in. She banged it down and rang Joseph's mobile, praying he was on the road to the nick. 'Damn you! Why switch your bloody phone off at a time like this?'

She threw the phone down, then grabbed it back up as it rang again.

'Joseph?'

'Sorry, dear heart, it's me, Rory. Just something I thought I needed to mention regarding the late Mr Kurt Carson. I said he had old injuries, and although this may mean nothing, at least two of them were gunshot wounds.'

'What?'

'Doesn't quite tie in with pretty Dutch flowers and plants, does it? I'm sure it's a cut-throat business, but one does not generally shoot the competition, does one?'

Nikki replaced the receiver, and stood up. Something told her that Kurt Carson was the odd man out regarding the killer's executed victims. If he'd been shot sometime in the past, maybe he had also been a soldier or a mercenary. She needed to get Joseph to look at the body. There was a chance he would recognise him and fathom out what the hell was going on. She pulled on her jacket. It was an outside chance, but if nothing else, it was a damned good excuse to go find Joseph and drag him back to Greenborough.

'Dave! Keep me posted on any developments. I'll keep the radio open.'

* * *

Joseph's eyes were becoming accustomed to the gloom in the tiny cottage, but he wanted to see Bryony's face as she spoke to him.

'Can we have some more light in here? I don't like talking to a shadow. I want to look at you.'

'No. It's better as it is. The things I'm going to tell you belong in the darkness.' There was a shaky sigh. 'I just don't know where to start.'

Joseph could think of a hundred places, but all he could do was stare at her helplessly. 'What's going on, Bryony?'

'Your boss told me you hated lies, and I'm afraid I've had to tell you some, but that was before I realised how I felt about you. I don't want to lie anymore. But you may not like the truth, Joseph.'

'Try me.'

'I am in trouble, Joseph. Big trouble.'

His shoulders stiffened almost to the point of spasm. 'Please, Bryony, don't tell me this concerns Billy Sweet?'

Bryony laid the gun on the hearth, then reached across and took his hands in hers. 'I'm afraid it does. And I'm out of my depth and I'm scared.'

Her fingers were cold despite the warm evening, and he felt them tremble in his grip. 'How could *you* know that freak, that animal . . . that . . . ?' Words failed him, then a feeling of unease crept up his spine. 'Where is he, Bryony?'

'I don't know,' she shivered. 'All I know is that I've been playing a dangerous game, and I don't think I'm winning anymore.'

'Then you'd better tell me everything, lies and all.' Joseph mustered a smile and looked into those deep brown eyes. Such sadness. 'Maybe I can help you.'

Still clasping his hands, she blinked a few times then said, 'You know that I work for the PA laboratory, well, that's not my only job. I'm a doctor, Joseph. A scientist. I'm employed by a medical foundation. I used to work with a large team, now there are just two of us. We look after, well *looked* after, the welfare of a group of very special patients.'

Suddenly Joseph heard Linda Kowalski's voice. *They even have highly qualified liaison managers to help with problems.* Awareness flooded through him in a great wave. 'My God! *You* were looking *after* the clinical trials' victims?'

'Yes, and very well, until Billy Sweet arrived here.' She almost spat the name out, and Joseph recognised the venom as almost equalling his own. Bryony let go of his hands and flopped back in the chair. 'The foundation was closing down, relocating abroad. There were so few patients left from those old trials, that we offered them the chance of relocating with us and having continued care, or taking a very substantial final settlement. The choice was theirs.'

Joseph thought about Martin and his friends, now all dead, bar one that he knew of. 'How many were there, Bryony?'

'Forty years ago there were over two hundred. Now just a handful.'

Joseph frowned. He had had no idea there had been that many. Then he remembered Nikki saying that Martin had a bit of interesting news to tell her. Had that been it? 'And Martin Durham? Did he take your final settlement by any chance?'

'No, Joseph, he was one of the few who decided to go with us to Germany.'

Joseph screwed his eyes up tight and massaged the bridge of his nose. 'So . . . what happened to him?'

'Billy Sweet happened,' muttered Bryony tightly.

'What the hell has that psycho got to do with a medical foundation? Or with you for that matter?' His voice was little more than a growl. 'And who is it you work with?'

'I knew this wasn't going to be easy.' Bryony shook her head miserably. 'Well, my colleague is a lovely man called Kurt Carson. He is an ex-army medic, although his cover job is working for a flower wholesaler.' She bit her lip. 'And he was due to meet me here earlier but he hasn't turned up. I'm worried about him, Joseph. His phone is turned off, and we never do that.'

Pictures of Billy swam across Joseph's mind. He didn't know this Carson guy, but he certainly hoped that he hadn't run into Billy on his trip to the marsh. 'And Sweet's somehow connected to your organisation?'

'He had nothing at all to do with us. He was employed abroad mainly, as a troubleshooter. We needed to speed up the closure process and he was sent to help Kurt and I tie up loose ends, only his methods were not what we were expecting.' She moved in her seat. 'And then things got even worse. His past caught up with him. He saw you, Joseph, and he flipped.'

'But why?' whispered Joseph.

'He was scared of you. He said you were the only one who ever saw through him. Most people distrusted or feared him, but Joseph Easter understood him.'

'I could *never* understand that monster!' Joseph felt bile rising in his throat. 'But why kill those poor men who resembled him? Why not just kill me?'

'You are wonderfully naïve, Joseph.' Bryony sighed. 'Killing you was his endgame. But before that, he wanted to see on the other side of the fence for once. To be suspected and accused of murder. You must have realised that he engineered it so that only you ever saw him.'

The individual notes were suddenly playing a tune in Joseph's head. That was where it was all heading. He had already been suspended. He was clearly suffering from stress and was always conveniently in the vicinity of the killings, the military-style killings. And who was the sick copper blaming? An imaginary soldier from his past. Very clever! Let's hear it for Billy Sweet! Joseph tensed as a thought crossed his mind. 'So what's this dangerous game you said you were playing?'

Silence spread through the cottage, then the harsh call of a night bird over the marsh broke the quiet and Bryony softly said, 'I pretended to help him. He asked me to watch you, get to know you.'

'That's why you came out with me?' croaked Joseph.

'Initially, yes. I needed to know what we were dealing with. I went along with him for a while in order to keep a close eye on him.' She looked at him unblinkingly. 'When I realised the danger you were in, and what a madman he was, Kurt and I decided to pull the plug on him. We made a phone call. Billy Sweet should have been removed by now, but . . . ?' She gave another little shrug of her shoulders, then moved closer to him. 'The thing is, everything has gone wrong. The foundation is spiriting me away. I will be out of the country by tonight, Joseph.' She slipped from the chair, knelt in front of him, and placed her head in his lap. 'Please, come with me.'

* * *

Nikki was about a mile from the town when she heard Dave's voice.

'Ma'am, I've just had some news from the pathologist. He says to tell you that Kurt Carson was not killed by the same person. There are subtle differences in the angle that the throat was cut, something that tells him Carson's killer was at least four inches shorter than the original murderer.'

'Oh shit.' Nikki put pressure on the accelerator. 'Anything else?'

'Plenty, guv. But I have to tell you that our enquiries about both Kurt Carson and Bryony Barton are going to rat-shit, if you'll pardon the expression. Everything seems to be shutting down on us.'

'How exactly?'

'Like when Yvonne rang Carson's company back, the number is unobtainable. Then she checked them out with the registry of Dutch exporters. They don't exist.'

'And Bryony?'

'Her accounts are closing down, ma'am. Funds are being electronically moved out and transferred, but we can't find the path they are taking. IT says an automated fail-safe system has been set in motion. One click on a computer or a single phone call could have activated it.'

She's closing up shop, thought Nikki . . . Whoever she is, she's on the move.

'And that's not all, ma'am. I've saved the best till last.' Dave spoke animatedly for a few minutes, then hung up. Nikki took a moment to assimilate the information, then floored the accelerator pedal and headed for the marsh. The farmhouse was in darkness when she arrived, and the door was locked.

Joseph's car was still around the back, and Nikki felt a frisson of fear snake across her shoulder blades. She pulled out her own keys and slipped in through the backdoor.

She stood still and listened. She knew the house was empty, but she checked anyway, running from room to room calling Joseph's name out loud. A few moments later she was back in the kitchen. Either he had been taken by force, and there was no evidence to support that, or he went off with someone he knew, or . . . Nikki paused . . . or he went out on foot.

Nikki ran back outside and stared over the oily black waters of the marsh. There really was only one place that you could walk to, unless you were in training for a marathon, and that was Martin's place. As soon as she thought it, she knew she was right. Joseph had said he had something to do, and that something, or someone, was waiting at Knot Cottage. Quickly checking that she had her phone safely in her pocket, she began to run down the lane towards the marsh edge and Martin's old home.

* * *

Joseph ran his hand gently through her hair, then lifted the beautiful face up, and kissed her. For a moment he remembered his dream of cooking for her, of getting a little place where they could be together, of getting to know each other better. But now he knew that would never happen.

'I'm good at my job, Joseph. My organisation will look after us, and I have money, a lot of money. And contacts. We could start again, Joseph. Another life in another country, somewhere far away from the shadows of the past. Be honest, what is there here for you in this crummy backwater town?'

Joseph methodically listed them in his head:

Friends that I care about. A job I love. Colleagues that would walk on hot coals for me. And I have a beautiful daughter that I want to get to know one day. A daughter who has high ideals and believes that good will always triumph over evil. One that would turn her back on a fugitive father for ever. Oh yes, for all the good it has done me this time, at least I now know that I have the capability to love again.

'Say something,' whispered Bryony.

Joseph wished he could. He wished he could have said, "Yes. Let's go!", but the alarm bells in his head were drowning out everything. He wanted to believe her. He could have easily convinced himself to do just that. It wouldn't have taken much, but instead he heard himself say, 'The telephone call from Sweet. The one that got me here. How did that work?'

'I got him to record it the other day. I told him we could use it as a lure, to get you to walk into a trap. I would play it at a given time, and he would be waiting for you.'

'So why use it tonight?' Joseph asked quietly. 'I would have come simply because you asked me, without the theatricals. You know that.'

'Because I had to be sure you'd come alone, Joseph. I couldn't risk you telling anyone that you were meeting me, not if we are to get away together. No, the tape ensured that you'd say nothing.' She looked up at him pleadingly, 'We need to go soon. It's all set up. My people . . .'

'And who are your people, Bry?'

'Just believe that they are taking medical science forward for the greater good. Every single person who works for them, no matter what their role, is deeply committed. But we really don't have time for this, Joseph. I'll explain everything later I promise you.' She sank back on her haunches and looked up at him imploringly. 'Come with me, please! First, because I love you, and second, because the alternatives are not good.'

He looked at her, pain etched all over his face, and knew that she realised he was going to refuse her.

At that point, the dynamics in the room suddenly changed. For the first time since he entered the cottage, he felt threatened. He straightened and felt a rush of adrenalin course through him. He knew what was wrong.

Bryony's hand was moving imperceptibly towards the hearth, and the gun.

Joseph acted instinctively, lunging forward, grabbing the gun, then rolling away. In a fraction of a second he had pulled her to her feet and was behind her, with the muzzle pressed to her temple. 'Tell me about those alternatives?' he enquired coldly.

'Oh, Joseph, you've made a terrible mistake.' Her voice had changed, lost the softness. 'And don't fool yourself. You couldn't do it.' Bryony slowly and deliberately turned her head to look him in the eyes. 'Sorry, but it's just not in you to hurt me, let alone kill me.'

'Don't underestimate me, Bryony.' Joseph stepped back, gripping the gun with both hands and keeping it trained on her head. 'I was a soldier too, remember? Killing people is on the curriculum.'

She smiled at him. 'But not like this.'

He knew that she was right. He had been a good soldier, not a homicidal lunatic like Billy. But then he was also a good copper, and his instincts were screaming at him to recognise Bryony, not as the woman he had fallen for, but as a treacherous liar.

'Bryony, I'm sorry, really I am. But there are questions that need to be answered.' He stared at her down the barrel of the gun, and fought back tears of his own. Why did it have to be like this? 'You've lied to me, haven't you? All along the line.'

'Oh, I've lied, Joseph, about practically everything.' A brief look of pain passed across the beautiful face. 'Although not about my feelings.' She took a deep breath. 'But you've made your choice. Now I'm walking out of here, and you, my love, are going to let me.'

'Oh, I don't think so.'

The voice made both Joseph and Bryony spin round in surprise.

Nikki moved away from the doorway, and Joseph vaguely saw a set of bar cuffs in her hand. 'It's all over, Bryony. Time to go.' She began to step towards the woman.

'No, guv! Keep back. Switch on the lights.'

Nikki stopped mid-stride, then eased back to the door and flipped down the switch.

Nothing happened.

'Just stay away from her, ma'am. I believe she's dangerous.'

'Oh I know she is, Joseph . . . I've recently met Mr Kurt Carson, or should I say Billy Sweet, posthumously, that is. I've seen Bryony's work first-hand.'

Joseph felt a horrible coldness seep through him, but he never let his eyes, or the muzzle of the gun, leave Bryony. 'What are you saying, Nikki?'

'She killed your nemesis, Joseph. Amongst others.'

'Well done, Detective Inspector.' Bryony slowly and deliberately clapped her hands together. 'Excellent work.'

'We need support, ma'am.' Joseph tried to keep his voice steady, but inside he was boiling with rage and hurt.

'Already on their way. Let's just keep everything calm,' said Nikki.

'I couldn't be calmer, Inspector,' said Bryony sardonically. 'It's you who looks a trifle agitated. But then I suppose you must be *so* relieved that your little puppy dog here is still breathing.' Her eyes glittered in the pale light of the lantern. 'I know it's happened to you before, but it must be terrible to see him bleed!'

Before Joseph knew what had happened, a burning pain seared through his left hand. The nerves and muscles went into spasm, his finger involuntarily jerked on the hair trigger and the gun exploded upwards and away from his grasp.

'Keep totally still!'

Joseph's ears still rang with the report from the gun, and he realised that he had made a potentially fatal mistake. In the poor light he had not seen the wicked looking blade that

Bryony had strapped to the inside of her wrist. With a groan of pain, he grasped his injured hand, pressed it to his body and tried to staunch the bleeding.

Nikki remained by the door, her mouth slightly open in shock, and hatred burning in her eyes.

And once again, Bryony held the gun. 'Make no mistake. I am leaving now, and I will kill you if you try to stop me.'

'No, you're not.' Nikki's voice was husky, but the words were slow and determined. 'You are a cold-blooded killer and you've assaulted my colleague. I can't let you.'

'Do as she says,' gasped Joseph. 'Please, Nikki.'

'Ooh, please Nikki!' Bryony imitated Joseph's appeal. 'How touching. But also practical, Inspector. I'd listen to Joseph, if you value your life.'

'Ah, but there's the problem,' returned Nikki, her voice as cold as an Arctic night. 'I don't.' And without hesitation Nikki threw herself forward.

Joseph's scream mingled with the roar of the second shot, and the two figures crashed to the floor in front of him. Before he could even move, something hit his foot. He swung down, pain like acid flaring through his hand, but somehow he managed to grab the gun.

By the time he had straightened up, one of the two women was on her feet and running towards the door.

'Stop, or I fire,' he yelled.

Bryony halted and turned around. The knife was still in her hand. 'Oh Joseph, I told you before, you're a lovely man, but you're no killer.'

When the blast from the third shot had died away, he whispered, 'And I told you not to underestimate me, my love.'

EPILOGUE

Joseph pushed open the door to her room with his shoulder. One hand was strapped firmly across his chest and held there by a padded sling, and the other hand grasped a large bunch of candy pink roses and silver-grey eucalyptus. 'I've just seen Linda Kowalski. Her brother is out of ITU and doing well. Now, how goes it with you?'

'I'm glad to hear about David, and I'm easier today.' Nikki eased herself up the bed and grimaced. 'Well, a bit easier. For a flesh wound, it damn well hurts! And you?'

'Extremely inconvenient, especially getting dressed and anything else that requires pulling up your trousers.' He grinned at her. 'Other than that, pretty good. The surgeon reckons I should get most of the movement back, as long as I keep up the physio.'

'I bet you and the therapists are on first name terms by now?'

'Yes, there is a certain amount of déjà vu to my visits.' He smiled and laid the flowers on the bottom of the bed. 'For you.'

'They're lovely, Joseph. Are you going to arrange them for me?'

'Probably not. It was difficult enough just carrying them into the lift and pressing the button. I'll leave it to the nurses.'

He sat in the chair next to her bed and looked at her searchingly. 'How are you really?'

Nikki dropped the smile. 'If you must know, I'm still pretty shaky.'

'Me too.' He stared down at the floor. 'I can't get my head around the fact that she was so *ruthless*. You know, I really thought . . .' his voice trailed off into silence.

'That she cared? Well, for what it's worth, I think she did, until you rejected her, then the *woman-scorned* bit came into play. Don't beat yourself up, Joseph, she had me fooled, and I was actively looking for things to distrust. You, sunshine, had no hope.' She picked up a thin folder from her locker and passed it to him. 'The super gave me this. It's for our eyes only. He thought it may help.'

'A dossier on Bryony?'

'Just a précis of what they've already compiled.'

'I don't think I want to see it right now,' said Joseph, placing it unopened on the locker.

'I've read it,' Nikki shrugged. 'You should too, when you're up to it. The main thing to know is that she alone was designated to bring 'closure' to the Gordon Peace guinea pigs, and that included Martin. She was no carer, Joseph. She killed the carer, she was the fixer.'

'I thought as much,' said Joseph with a sigh. 'When Dave told me about her expertise with drugs and their effects, it all fell into place. It was her organisation that provided the white boxes of medication, wasn't it?'

'In the guise of caring and generous healthcare professionals, they provided everything for their precious guinea pigs. The big financial payouts, the close follow-up treatment and ongoing medical care, which included their medication.' Nikki moved uncomfortably. 'The super reckons that eighteen months ago there must have been a leak, forcing them to wrap up their British operations, but they decided to do it slowly and insidiously so it wouldn't lead back to the old trials.'

'And who would notice the odd suicide or accidental death, when they were months apart?'

'Exactly. Bryony was sent in to doctor their drugs and send them to their death. And she was doing fine until the organisation wanted everything speeded up and Billy Sweet was seconded to help out.' She looked at him painfully. 'You did hear that Sweet was headhunted for his dubious talents by Bryony's organisation? That they 'killed him off' in South America, then gave him a new identity, as Kurt Carson?'

Joseph nodded, then asked, 'Did you know immediately that the last killing was Sweet himself?'

'No, I only found out as I drove out to find you. His face was pretty battered, intentionally of course, Bryony didn't want us to recognise him too quickly. And we didn't, but Dave had given a photo of Billy to Rory. In it he was holding a weapon of some kind and it showed a badly deformed finger, and Kurt Carson had an identical injury. Rory then used the picture and a computer-generated version of Kurt's skull, and hey presto. One and the same.'

'If you believe in Karma, one would consider that a fitting end for such an evil man.' Joseph gave a little shiver. 'Bryony's organisation may be powerful but they made a mistake recruiting Billy Sweet. Although I'm sure he was very effective until he finished up in hospital, saw me, and went on that killing spree. One thing though, I'm surprised that Bryony managed to get the better of him so easily.'

'Simple. She did what she did best. She drugged him. That was something else Dave informed me of on my trip to Cloud Fen. Rory picked up on tell-tale signs and later found that Sweet had been immobilized before his throat was cut.'

'Dear Lord, and to think that I . . .' Joseph shook his head, then swiftly changed the subject. 'And Bryony's organisation? Do we have any leads?'

'We're out of our depth there. With the Kowalskis' statements the super knew that we were on to something, but guess what? He's been ordered not to pursue it.'

Joseph gritted his teeth, 'And the shadows close ranks and block us out.'

Nikki nodded, and for a moment they sat in silence with their own thoughts. 'So when did it dawn on you that you were being spun a yarn?' she finally asked.

Joseph gently massaged his injured hand. 'Several things didn't ring true, but the main one was when she told me that Martin was going abroad. It took a second or two, but I remembered all you'd told me about him, about his love for the marsh, how fond he was of his sister, and his precious Knot Cottage. He wouldn't have upped and buggered off, just for the sake of some medical care.'

'You're right. Linda Kowalski told me that they were all promised a big final settlement, then their care would be down to their respective GPs, but in truth, the organisation could never have risked it. Their death sentences had already been signed.'

'And the executioner dispatched,' Joseph added painfully. 'But let's forget all that for a moment.' He turned to her and she allowed those dark, earnest eyes to bore into hers. 'There is still one question I have to ask.'

Nikki had known this moment would come, but said nothing.

'Did you really mean that you didn't value your life? I've played those last few moments over and over, and I'm still not sure why you did what you did.'

Nikki stared down at the pale green counterpane. What could she tell him? The truth was that there was no way she could have risked his life again. Not for a second time. She had to stop Bryony somehow, and her method may have been a tad gung-ho, but that was Nikki Galena for you. 'I guess I saw the red mist, that's all. I thought if I could distract her, you might finally get your finger out and actually do something!'

'Right. I see,' Joseph pulled a face. 'Okay, so you're not going to tell me.'

'Not yet. Maybe I'm not sure of the answer myself.' She smiled at him, 'Now my turn for a question. When you shot Bryony . . . ?'

'Did I mean to kill her?' He shook his head. 'No, she was right about that. I couldn't have done it. That would have made me no better than Billy Sweet.'

'I'm glad, Joseph. Because for Martin's sake, I want her to stand trial.'

Joseph drew in a breath. 'Don't get your hopes up. If her dark and shadowy employers are as powerful as I believe, she'll never get near a courtroom.'

Before Nikki could answer, the door opened and two women stood beaming at them.

'Elizabeth! Janna! Come in.' Nikki patted her bed for Janna to sit, and Joseph stood up and gave Elizabeth his chair.

'To cheer you up,' said Elizabeth brightly, and placed a large, colourful plant on her locker.

Nikki stared at it. It had a mass of dark green heart-shaped leaves and huge waxy red flowers, each with a thick, fleshy cream spike rising from them. 'My! That's, uh, exotic! Thank you.'

'Latin name, Anthurium Andreanum,' said Elizabeth knowledgably.

'Common name, Willy Lily!' laughed Janna.

It was agony to laugh, but suddenly Nikki felt great. She could afford to laugh again. The nightmare was over.

'And this is to cheer *you* up, Sergeant.' Janna handed Joseph a fob with two keys hanging from it. 'We have no problem at all with your suggestion, and Martin would most certainly have approved.'

Nikki threw an enquiring glance at Joseph.

'I'm renting Knot Cottage.' He looked at her earnestly.

'Really?' Nikki's mouth dropped.

'Are you quite sure that you won't be haunted by everything that happened there? Janna asked.

'I'm absolutely certain,' Joseph nodded determinedly. 'I know what happened was terrible, but in a funny kind of way it finally gave me closure from Billy Sweet.' He turned to Nikki, 'From the moment I set foot in Martin's home I knew it was a very special and well-loved place. And of course I'd be closer to you, if you don't mind having a new neighbour?'

Nikki felt a warmth suffuse through her. So there would be smoke rising from the chimney, and the lights would burn in the evening again, and like before, they would have been lit by someone she cared for. 'No objections at all. When are you planning on moving in?'

'As soon as my new landlords here have replaced the sitting-room carpet. It's in a shocking state!'

Nikki placed a hand tentatively over the large dressing around her waist. 'Eh, sorry about that.'

'Oh, don't feel too bad,' said Joseph. 'Professor Wilkinson took great delight in telling me that there are actually three different blood groups splattered between the hearth and the front door. Something of a record in his book.'

Janna groaned theatrically. 'I was warned about police humour.' She stood up and smiled across at Elizabeth. 'And we should go. Let Nikki rest.'

'Yes, we only came to say thank you. Without you both; Martin's murder would never have come to light. His death would have always been thought of as a callous drug-fuelled act of madness. His memory would have been tainted for ever.' Her voice caught, and Janna continued for her.

'But now we can grieve properly. And so can the friends and families of Paul Cousins, Amelia Reed and the other poor souls who died.'

Joseph nodded, then smiled to lighten the mood. 'Yes, it's lucky that there are still a few tenacious old bulldogs left on the force.' He tilted his head towards Nikki, 'Or should I have said, stubborn, fool-hardy, pig-headed, persistent, obstinate . . .'

'Let's stick with tenacious, shall we, Sergeant? Or do you actually have a hankering to go back to traffic for the next ten years or so?'

* * *

After the two women had left, Joseph sat back down and grinned wickedly at Nikki.

'So, there is just one thing left. One mystery that has yet to be solved.'

Nikki looked at him suspiciously. 'And that is?'

Joseph leaned closer. 'Dr Helen Latimer. Martin's GP at Cloud Fen? You said that when the case was over you'd dish the dirt regarding your mysterious feud.'

A knowing smile spread over Nikki's face. 'I'm sorry, Joseph, you must be mistaken. I have absolutely no idea what you're talking about.'

Section of article in *The Times*, 14 August

GREENBOROUGH POISONER DIES

The body of Bryony Barton, the woman accused of engineering the 'suicide' deaths of more than ten people in the last eighteen months, was found yesterday. The manner of her death remains a mystery, as she was in the process of being transported to court. On arrival she was found dead on the floor of the police transportation vehicle. The Fenland Constabulary are asking for information regarding one of the escorting officers who has since disappeared.

Full story on pages 4 and 5

THE END

THE JOFFE BOOKS STORY

We began in 2014 when Jasper agreed to publish his mum's much-rejected romance novel and it became a bestseller.

Since then we've grown into the largest independent publisher in the UK. We're extremely proud to publish some of the very best writers in the world, including Joy Ellis, Faith Martin, Caro Ramsay, Helen Forrester, Simon Brett and Robert Goddard. Everyone at Joffe Books loves reading and we never forget that it all begins with the magic of an author telling a story.

We are proud to publish talented first-time authors, as well as established writers whose books we love introducing to a new generation of readers.

We won Trade Publisher of the Year at the Independent Publishing Awards in 2023. We have been shortlisted for Independent Publisher of the Year at the British Book Awards for the last four years, and were shortlisted for the Diversity and Inclusivity Award at the 2022 Independent Publishing Awards. In 2023 we were shortlisted for Publisher of the Year at the RNA Industry Awards.

We built this company with your help, and we love to hear from you, so please email us about absolutely anything bookish at feedback@joffebooks.com

If you want to receive free books every Friday and hear about all our new releases, join our mailing list: www.joffebooks.com/contact

And when you tell your friends about us, just remember: it's pronounced Joffe as in coffee or toffee!

Milton Keynes UK
Ingram Content Group UK Ltd.
UKHW041820210924
448622UK00004B/180